**Joe Castaneda lowered his hands. Tears
traced down his cheeks. "Where . . ."**

"Your son is in our morgue, Mister Castaneda,"
Horatio explained. "He's being well taken care of
there while we determine exactly what happened
and who killed him. We'll release him to you as
soon as we can, so if you'd like to make arrangements—"

"My wife, she—"

"Faustina told us that your wife was also shot,
and I'm very sorry. We try to do our best for every
crime victim, but some cases aren't solved immediately. Some take years, and I can't lie to you,
some are never solved."

"Because the cops don't care about our people,"
Faustina said. "That's why our people have to join
gangs, so we'll have someone who will look out
for us. Everybody knows the po-po don't give a
damn."

"That, young lady, is not true. We care about
every victim." Horatio paused. "*I* care. And I guarantee you, I will do everything in my power to get at
the truth. I will find out who killed your brother."

Faustin_____ _____ ____ ____. Not with
words, a_____ _____ _yes locked
on his, d_____rything.

She di_____

He wo_____ong.

Other **CSI: Miami** books

Cult Following
Riptide
Harm for the Holidays—Misgivings
Harm for the Holidays—Heart Attack
Cut & Run

Also available from Pocket Books

CSI: Crime Scene Investigation

Double Dealer
Sin City
Cold Burn
Body of Evidence
Grave Matters
Binding Ties
Killing Game
Snake Eyes
In Extremis
Nevada Rose

CSI: NY

Dead of Winter
Blood on the Sun
Deluge
Four Walls

CSI: MIAMI™

RIGHT TO DIE

JEFF MARIOTTE

CSI: MIAMI produced by CBS Productions, a business unit of CBS Broadcasting Inc.
and Alliance Atlantis Productions Inc.
Executive Producers: Jerry Bruckheimer, Ann Donahue, Carol Mendelsohn, Anthony E. Zuiker, Jonathan Littman
Series created by Anthony E. Zuiker, Ann Donahue, and Carol Mendelsohn

POCKET **STAR** BOOKS
New York   London   Toronto   Sydney

Pocket Star Books
A Division of Simon & Schuster, Inc.
1230 Avenue of the Americas
New York, NY 10020

This book is a work of fiction. Names, characters, places, and incidents either are products of the author's imagination or are used fictitiously. Any resemblance to actual events or locales or persons, living or dead, is entirely coincidental.

First Pocket Star Books paperback edition September 2008

POCKET STAR BOOKS and colophon are registered trademarks of Simon & Schuster, Inc.

For information about special discounts for bulk purchases, please contact Simon & Schuster Special Sales at 1-800-456-6798 or business@simonandschuster.com.

Cover design by Richard Yoo

Manufactured in the United States of America

10 9 8 7 6 5 4 3 2 1

ISBN-13: 978-0-7434-9954-5
ISBN-10:   0-7434-9954-9

Acknowledgments

Many experts helped with the science in this book. Anything I got right can likely be credited to them; mistakes are solely my own. Among others, I'd like to thank Janeen Crockett and Lisa Reed of Cochise College, and Dr. D. P. Lyle, MD.

Great thanks also to Anthony Zuiker, CSI mastermind, the producers and writers of *CSI: Miami*, and David Caruso and the incredible actors who bring it all to life.

1

Emilio Durazo turned away from the glare spiking at him off the water of Biscayne Bay and adjusted his plastic safety goggles. He could feel them pressing into his skin; they would leave red marks, rings around his eyes, for hours after he was done here. His wife would call him "raccoon" when he got home at dinnertime.

For safety reasons his employer, a landscaping contractor working for Miami's Department of Parks and Recreation, liked him to wear the glasses, a face mask, bulky ear protectors, and long sleeves—in spite of the April morning's warmth—when he used a weed whacker. He also wore a straw cowboy hat and long canvas work pants. It was true that one never knew what kind of debris the spinning lines might kick up. At home, outside dry, dusty Hermosillo, Mexico, he had never encountered the sort of thick vegetation that grew in south Florida, and the few times he had used weed eaters there, they hurled small stones and sharp sticks every which way. He had been a skilled electrician, and had hired a gardener to look after his small yard, but when the weak economy had destroyed his business he headed north, like so many others, in search of whatever work he could find.

Today he would need the power cutter, because he'd be tackling a patch of tall growth that he had been putting off for a couple of weeks. Since arriving in Florida he had been amazed by the speed with which the plants grew, as different as could be from his arid home.

But then, everything in Miami was different. The humidity, the amber sunsets and pastel buildings, the beautiful, wealthy people he saw everywhere. Miami had an undeniable Latin beat but filtered through a coastal atmosphere, beach culture, and buzzing nightlife. He suspected no place on Earth was quite like it. Certainly not the deserts of Sonora.

Properly suited up, Emilio tugged on the motor's starter cord. The machine roared to life and he headed for the thick stretch of out-of-control grass he had to tame before lunch. Twin black lines whirled, and when he brought the machine's cutting head to the grass, barely skirting the ground, the whirling plastic lines sliced easily through the vegetation.

Within minutes he had chopped the first section, about a meter square. The cut grass, formerly half a meter high in spots, was scattered around him, bits of it plastered to his pants and work boots. Emilio raised the weed eater's head and balanced the machine in his right hand, peeling off his hat with his left and using that forearm to wipe sweat off his forehead. Then he stuck the hat back in place, ready to tackle the next section. He figured he could complete the whole task in about an hour, then take a break for his bag lunch and a bottle of water. After that he could rake up the grass and move on to his next project.

He lowered the weed eater's head to the grass again. In the deepest grass, beside a stretch of concrete block wall on which graffiti needed to be painted over, an indentation caught his eye. He waded through the thickest of it, rubbing flecks of vegetation off his goggles, until he could see what had crushed the grass down.

Madre de Dios! he thought, instinctively crossing himself.

Maybe he wouldn't be home in time for dinner after all . . .

Lieutenant Horatio Caine stood on the manicured lawn of Bicentennial Park, hands on his hips, watching a cabin cruiser slice the surface of the bay. Around him was a beehive's worth of activity. Uniformed officers had strung yellow CRIME SCENE

DO NOT CROSS tape from trees, establishing the perimeter within which Horatio's team of CSIs would work. Tourists, joggers, businesspeople, park employees, and others had gathered outside the tape but were kept from crossing it by the presence of the uniforms. Inside the perimeter, Medical Examiner Alexx Woods knelt by the corpse of a young male, which a gardener had found in the grass near a wall that delineated a particular section of the park. Criminalist Ryan Wolfe crouched beside her with a camera in his hands. Detective Frank Tripp talked to the gardener, while criminalist Eric Delko searched the area for shell casings or any other evidence left behind.

Horatio liked to stand back when he could, to view a body *in situ*, as the early Roman crime scene investigators would have said—and there had been, he knew, crime scene investigators in ancient times—although they would have had much more primitive technologies available to them, and the causes of crime were more often attributed to things like demonic possession or an imbalance in a person's "humours," according to Hippocrates. Taking the long view of a crime scene before getting into the close-up work of looking for hairs and fibers, transfer from a killer, bullets, and the like, enabled Horatio to gain needed perspective on a crime. He liked to see where the participants had entered and exited the scene, liked to know what they saw around them, how sheltered they were from public view (if at all), what natural or man-made obstacles they might have encountered.

To solve a murder, one had to be able to answer all these questions and more. The close-up stuff was crucial, but the long view helped too. Hands on his hips, his blazer flared out behind him, his sunglasses safely tucked around his neck inside his open collar, he turned, taking in the three-hundred-and-sixty-degree view of park and bay (Watson Island and then Miami Beach gleaming on the far side, like a mirage made of money and opportunity), of trees and grass and pathways, a maintenance shed, streets and businesses in the background.

Frank Tripp approached Horatio, his balding, blunt, pale head gleaming in the sunshine. The Texas transplant tucked two fingers under his collar and turned his head. His striped tie was knotted tightly, as always, and he wore a light green suit over a white shirt. "Gonna be a hot summer, if this keeps up," he said.

"It could well be, Frank. Did you get anything from the gardener?"

"Not much," Frank said. "Guy's uncomfortable talking to cops. I'm pretty sure he's an illegal."

"I don't have the slightest interest in his immigration status," Horatio said. "I just want to know what he saw."

"Short answer? Nothin'. He was cuttin' the grass, found the body. No one around when he got here at eight, so the guy got killed sometime during the night or early morning."

"If you think you've got everything he knows, Frank, I don't have a problem with cutting him loose. He's not likely to get any more work done around here today."

"I'll let him know," Frank said. Horatio watched the detective walk away, his solid bulk like a physical manifestation of his commitment to the job. As with Horatio and his entire crew at the Miami-Dade Police Department Crime Lab, concern for the victims of crime drove Frank. In his long law enforcement career, first in New York, then Miami, Horatio didn't think he had known many better cops.

"Horatio!" He looked over at the sound of his name and saw Alexx Woods beckoning him toward the patch of tall grass, partially shaded by the wall, that obscured the body. An open-necked magenta blouse set off her brown skin beautifully, and she wore it with a black suit—all business, but with a sense of style undeniably her own. She squatted in the grass. Horatio knew she'd have preferred to keep the suit clean, but the needs of the deceased overruled any sartorial preferences on her part. "You're going to want to see this."

He started toward her and Ryan. "What is it, Alexx? You have a cause of death?"

"No COD until we're back in the lab." She threw him a smile that silently added, *But you knew that.* "But I think we have some good candidates."

Some? Alexx didn't choose her words imprecisely. "Do tell."

She and Ryan waited until he was close enough to see the body: a Hispanic male, probably in his early twenties or late teens. He wore baggy blue nylon pants and a jacket over a red T-shirt, with expensive sneakers. His skin was dark olive, hair black, cropped short. With his square jaw and high cheekbones, he had been a handsome kid.

As Horatio approached, Ryan pointed out a neat hole in the young man's chest, through the shirt. "Here's one entry wound," he said. "Upper torso."

"One?" Horatio repeated. The shot looked like a heart wound, and would probably have been sufficient to kill the man. He scanned the body but didn't see any more injuries.

"Help me turn him," Alexx said. Ryan lifted the man's shoulder and pushed. Together they raised his back off the ground, and Alexx drew aside the jacket. On his back was an exit wound—raw and ragged, the shirt matted to his back with blood—a few inches above what could only be another entry wound.

"And here's the other," Ryan said, pointing to the smaller, neater of the holes.

"Along with a single exit wound," Horatio noted.

"That's right," Alexx said. "One bullet was a through-and-through, and the other must still be inside him."

"So he was shot twice," Horatio said. "Maybe he

turned after the first shot struck him? Shot in the back first?"

"There's no indication of that from the way the grass is flattened," Ryan said. He was a young officer, a relatively recent transfer from patrol. Horatio had taken a chance on him, and he had proven his worth many times over. He looked up at Horatio, heavy brown eyebrows arched, still holding most of the weight of the dead man. "It looks like he was standing here—maybe with someone else—and then he got shot, twice, and fell down. He might have swiveled, but he didn't move his feet."

"I'll leave it to Calleigh to make the final determination," Alexx added, "but to me it looks like he was shot with two different caliber bullets. From two different directions." She nodded toward the bay, then back toward the city streets. "Over there and over there."

"I see," Horatio said. He nodded and Alexx and Ryan lowered the body carefully back to its original position, faceup in the grass. "What makes you think he had a companion, Mister Wolfe?"

"Not a companion," Ryan said. "And not the shooter—both wounds are distance wounds, not close-up. But the grass was trampled about eighteen inches in front of him, and there are two trails where they walked through the highest part. The other person used the same path to leave."

"Careful," Horatio said. "Or maybe concerned about leaving clues."

"That's right. So I'm thinking maybe the second person was more of a customer than a companion. I don't see any signs of panic, so I think their transaction was completed before the shooting started."

"A customer?"

Ryan held up a small glassine envelope that contained a white powder. "The victim's jacket pockets were full of cocaine," he said. "No weapons, no cash, but plenty of coke, both powder and rock."

"Someone robbed him after he was shot," Horatio mused, "but didn't take the drugs? What kind of a criminal does that?"

"You got me," Ryan said.

"We'll have to find out," Horatio said. "Someone caught our victim in a cross fire, then kept a cool enough head to use an existing path through the grass, take the weapon and cash that we have to assume a drug dealer would be carrying, and leave the dope behind."

"That's the way it looks," Alexx said. "I'll know more when I get this young man on my table."

"We'll all know more soon, Alexx. Drug dealer or no, our victim is counting on us to find his killer, isn't he?" Horatio said. "And that, my friends, is what we are going to do."

2

"YOU WEREN'T READY for this, were you?" Alexx Woods looked at the face of the deceased. At the outer corner of his right eye, someone had tattooed a single black teardrop, as if he mourned for a death he had known would come to him too early.

Even people who suspected that were never quite prepared for *how* early, she had found.

Sometimes, in the gang world, teardrops signified a murder committed or the death of a loved one. She hoped it was the latter, in this case, as the victim looked too youthful—and, in peaceful repose on her stainless steel autopsy table, too innocent—to already be a killer as well as a dealer. Hard experience had taught Alexx that there was no minimum age for that, but if she couldn't hang on to her optimism about people, she couldn't come to work every day in the morgue.

The young man had been brought from the park in a clean body bag, after she and Ryan had secured paper bags over his hands and given the okay to move him. At the morgue, he was removed from the body bag and placed on Alexx's autopsy table. After taking the paper bags from his hands—placed there to make sure no evidence, such as epithelials, or skin cells, he might have scratched from an attacker, was lost or contaminated—she weighed and measured him, determining that he was five feet, six inches tall and weighed one hundred and seventy pounds. She noted those facts, along with her initial identification of him as a Hispanic male, on a digital record of her autopsy. She speculated that he was still in his late teens, but she could narrow that down further as she went. No identification had been located on the body. She inked his fingertips and rolled those onto a ten-card, then sent the card over to a fingerprint tech at the crime lab to run against local and national databases.

"I need you to tell me some things, honey," she said as she walked his length, her practiced eye examining his clothing and what skin she could see. He smelled of heavy tobacco use; the stink of smoke had wafted from the body bag as soon as it had been unzipped. "I need you to tell me who you are. I need you to tell me the cause, manner, and mechanism of your death. And if you can, I need you to tell me who killed you. Can you do that for me?"

The dead man didn't answer her. They never did—not verbally, at any rate. Alexx spoke *to* the dead so she could speak *for* them, so she could take what their bodies told her and put it into words in a report. The dead needed her voice because their own voices had been stilled. She had put herself through an ordeal of schooling that ground down and spat out many people—college, medical school, a one-year medical internship, a four-year pathology residency, and a yearlong forensic pathology fellowship—to be able to provide that service.

During that time, she had worked with people who referred to the deceased as "the body, the corpse," or worst of all, "it." No matter how brilliant those people were otherwise, she found her respect for them minimized by that. The dead people she encountered were still people, not empty vessels or husks, and she had no patience for those who felt otherwise.

His body had already begun to answer some of those questions. The *manner of death*, for instance, was almost certainly homicide. One couldn't shoot oneself from a distance, in two different directions. The multiple gunshot wounds also contraindicated accidental death. Natural causes could still win out, but the amount of blood soaking the man's clothing and on the ground beneath him made her think he had been alive until he was shot. Once the heart stopped pumping, the blood stopped flowing.

The blood answered another of her questions.

The *mechanism of death* was almost certainly ex-sanguination, bleeding out because of the bullet wounds.

When she got inside him and ruled out heart attack, poison, drug overdose, and so on, then her suspicion—that the *cause of death* was the gunshot wounds (one or both)—would be confirmed, or, far less likely, denied.

She approached any body with her own hunches and suspicions, but she didn't let those presumptions dictate her actions or conclusions. She stuck to the process she had learned, and the conclusions would be drawn only when the process was finished, all the evidence considered. The dead told their own stories, but you didn't know how the story ended until the last page was turned.

Cameras, still and video, photographed every inch of the man's clothed body. Once she had checked to make sure that removing his clothing wouldn't destroy any evidence, she would undress him and photograph him again.

The nylon jacket and pants were from a budget store tracksuit, white with blue ornamentation and piping. The red T-shirt was cotton, with no logo or message, a common brand that could have come from almost anywhere. The white sneakers had probably cost him several times what the rest of the outfit had. He wore them untied, and Alexx always wondered why gangsters, who might have to run at any moment, would leave their shoes untied, or worse, wear those baggy pants that could fall down at the slightest provocation.

At the park, she and Ryan had found the bullet holes in the shirt, front and back, and the corresponding holes in the back of the blood-soaked jacket. Other than normal wear and tear, she couldn't see any additional damage to the clothing. It had vegetation all over it, grass from where the young man had fallen, and patches of moisture from the morning's dew, but she couldn't find anything else she could specifically point to as evidence. She carefully removed the clothing and set it aside, to be sent over to the crime lab for further processing.

"I know this is a terrible imposition," she said as she tugged off his shoes. "I wouldn't do it if I didn't have to, believe me."

His athletic socks were white, worn at the heels, washed many times. She pulled them off and put them on a stainless steel counter, revealing feet with thick calluses and blunt, uneven toenails that had probably been cut with a knife instead of clippers or scissors. The familiar—common but by no means universal—odor of sweaty feet drifted up. "You've spent some time walking around barefoot, haven't you?" she asked him. "By choice? Or because your family couldn't always afford shoes that fit?"

Dialogue with the dead—they didn't put that in the job description, but for Alexx, it was the most important part. They had so much to say, if only people knew how to listen.

"Well, Alexx?"

She didn't hear him at first. She was bent over the John Doe's head, working with a rotary bone saw. Bits of blood and shards of skull flew everywhere, spattering Alexx's scrubs, safety glasses, and mask. A burning smell filled the autopsy theater, competing with the odors of disinfectant and death; between the grinding sound and the stink, every one of Horatio's childhood dentist's office fears might have been coming true.

Alexx had pinned her hair up and wore dark blue scrubs instead of the stylish suit she'd had on at the park. She was a beautiful woman in any setting, but here in her morgue she dressed for function, not fashion.

She would have started by making an incision from ear to ear, across the top of the head—taking the polar route, he sometimes thought—and peeled the victim's scalp forward to reveal his skull. Now she used the bone saw to cut through the skull itself, exposing the brain. She would examine that in place, then remove it for a more thorough inspection and to take tissue samples.

The fact that the man had been shot twice would never leave her thoughts, but she wouldn't let that dictate her procedure. Every ME had come across bodies that seemed to have died one way, only to find out that something else entirely had really killed them. Alexx was thorough and precise, and she would give this victim the same consideration she gave them all.

After a few moments she noticed Horatio, who stood well away from her autopsy table, and shut off her saw.

"Anything yet, Alexx?" he asked when the blade stopped spinning.

"I'm still working on him," she said, stating the obvious. "But so far I'm betting on those gunshot wounds. The through-and-through severed his aortic semilunar valve."

"Which carries blood from the heart's left ventricle into the aorta," he said softly.

"That's right, Horatio. After that, with every succeeding pump of the left ventricle, the blood was carried away from his heart and out the exit wound in his back."

She beckoned him closer and showed him the torso wound, a small hole with a dark bruise haloing it. "It's an abrasion collar," she said. She had made a Y-shaped incision in the victim, from the shoulders to the sternum and then down the abdomen to the pubis, and removed his intestines, stomach, heart, lungs, and other organs to be weighed and examined separately. Reaching down through the opening, she had cut away his spinal cord and pulled it free. "The shooter was several feet away from him, at least. I've already pulled out the second bullet, which entered through his back and lodged in his costal cartilage, but that one hadn't done what I'd consider to be significant damage."

"So the round that killed Mister Doe is the forty-five that we found at the scene," Horatio said. "The through-and-through."

She offered him a wide smile. "That's for you to prove, Horatio, not me. The one I gave Calleigh looked like a nine-mil."

Alexx undoubtedly knew that it was a nine-millimeter, but bullets were not her area of expertise so she would leave that determination to Calleigh.

"Time of death?" Horatio asked her. He brushed a lock of light red hair—what his mother had called "strawberry blond"—off his forehead. It promptly fell back where it had been, and he left it alone.

"I put TOD between two and four this morning," she replied.

"Thank you, Alexx." He started to turn away.

"One more thing, Horatio," she said, touching a remote control button. An image flickered to life on one of the big monitors by her table. "Take a look at these tattoos. Do you think they might help you identify this boy?"

At the park, Horatio had noticed the teardrop beside the man's eye, but he hadn't seen the flesh of his back. It was covered in ink. The stylized letters LDB dominated the display, running from one shoulder blade to the other, about eight inches high, as ornate as a newspaper's logo. Above the letters, centered between the shoulderblades, was a sun with daggerlike flames leaping from it. Below the letters, his back was filled with incredibly detailed images—men and women, several knives, various snakes and dragons, and other things that Horatio couldn't identify in all the clutter, especially with the bullet wounds deforming some.

"They just might, Alexx. His back is his canvas."

"And his ID badge," Alexx said.

"Print me out a copy of those tattoos, please, Alexx. I'll see if our friends at the gang unit recognize our victim."

"That's a good idea," Alexx said. "Maybe you'll get a hit from his ten-card, too. Otherwise I think you can probably do it from dental records—the vic's had a bit of dental work done."

"That's good, Alexx. The more avenues, the better—we need to know who this boy is in order to find out who killed him,"

"I don't know him by sight." Sergeant Gabe Ramos handed the photos back to Horatio. "But he's with Los Danger Boys, for sure. That's what the big LDB on his back means."

"And you think he's currently a member?" Horatio asked. He had worked with Gabe on several cases, including his investigation into the deadly Mala Noche gang, and trusted the man completely.

Gabe scratched his left eyebrow, which was thick and black. He kept his hair cut short and his face shaved clean, but even by noon his five o'clock shadow was beginning to show. "Pretty sure, yeah. For one thing, he's still young. Usually guys don't try to get out of gangs until they're older, a little more mature. In their thirties, maybe forties. Unless something happens."

"Something like . . . ?"

"Usually, the surest way out is to be killed," Gabe said. "Otherwise, some who are arrested try to go straight after they serve their time, and will try to keep far away from their former gang members. Those will often get their tats removed, because wearing a gang tat when you're not in the gang anymore can be a death sentence. This guy hasn't tried to remove the LDB, and given his apparent age, I'd have to guess that he's still with them. Or was, until just before you found him."

"Was," Horatio agreed. "He took the most common exit route. What can you tell me about Los Danger Boys?"

"They're one hundred percent Hispanic," Gabe said. "Mostly Puerto Rican, but they've let in a few Mexican-Americans and even some Cubans."

"That's rare, isn't it?"

"Most gangs are more discriminating," Gabe answered. He was in uniform, leaning against a filing cabinet in the gang unit's suite of offices. Other officers worked around them, some typing on

20

keyboards or talking quietly on telephones, others gathered around a map of Miami, plotting out the afternoon's patrol routes. "But Los Danger Boys feel that all Hispanics have something in common, even if it's just a mutual hatred of other gangs, so they've opened the doors. Besides, Miami's been getting a lot more Mexican-Americans lately, so part of it might just be a pragmatic consideration."

"How many members are there, Gabe?"

"Statewide, I'd say in the neighborhood of two hundred, maybe two-twenty. Of those, probably forty or fifty are in the system. In Miami, about sixty or seventy, mostly in the Overtown neighborhood."

"Some mean streets there," Horatio said.

Gabe tapped the filing cabinet behind him. "We shake them down pretty regularly," he said. "Try to get ten-cards and photos, known aliases, that kind of thing, for our files. But I don't know them all, and your boy there is one I haven't had the pleasure of meeting."

"And you won't," Horatio reminded him. "I may have to have a talk with some of his fellow Danger Boys, though, to find out who he is."

"You need any help, let me know, Horatio."

"I appreciate it, Gabe. Thanks."

Horatio left the gang unit, heading back to the crime lab, but Frank Tripp stopped him en route. "We were just on our way to see you, Horatio," he said. "You saved us a trip."

"Glad to help," Horatio said. He eyed the man behind Frank. Brown hair cut and combed neatly, crisp dark suit, silk tie, sunglasses tucked into his breast pocket—*a Fed*, he thought.

"Lieutenant Horatio Caine," Frank said quickly, like a party host remembering his manners, "this is Special Agent Wendell Asher. He's with the Bureau."

Horatio gave Asher a quick handshake. Asher was a few inches taller than he was, and from his build and carriage, Horatio was willing to bet he'd played college football. "It's a pleasure," he said. "You're not in the Miami field office."

"Denver," Asher said. His teeth were white and even, his voice smooth as silk. "Here on special assignment."

"Dennis Sackheim vouched for him," Frank said. "Apparently these two are old pals."

"Acquaintances, really," Asher corrected. "We went through the Academy together. I could tell you some stories—"

"What brings you to Miami?" Horatio interrupted. He really didn't want to hear stories about Dennis's Academy days.

"A serial bomber," Asher answered.

"But we haven't had any bombings lately."

"Not yet." Asher held up his right hand, with his index and middle fingers crossed for luck. "I think I'm ahead of him, for a change."

"Guy targets, what'd you say? Abortion clinics, that sort of thing," Frank added.

"That's right. Clinics where abortions are performed. Even the homes of some of the doctors who perform them. He's killed nine people so far, and injured scores more."

Horatio kept up with law enforcement journals. "I've heard about him," he said. "The one they call the Baby Boomer?"

"That's the name a newspaper stuck on him," Asher said, suddenly pinching the bridge of his nose. "I guess that's what passes for ironic cleverness in the media. He bombs birth control clinics, so he's the Baby Boomer."

"What makes you think he's here in Miami?"

Asher let out a loud sneeze. "Excuse me."

"Gesundheit," Horatio said.

"Thanks. Think I caught a cold on the flight out here. Damn airplanes."

"More and more common," Frank said. "I drink that fizzy yellow stuff when I have to fly. Nasty, but it seems to help."

"Anyway," Asher went on, "I've been on his trail for a couple of years, all over the Western states. The last place he hit was in Albuquerque, and I got closer than ever to him there. I found his motel room, but he had already checked out. I did a garbage pull, and in the motel's Dumpster I found a bookstore receipt in his room trash. He had paid cash for Florida and Miami maps and a guidebook. It's not much, but if I'm right, it'll be the first time

I've been able to get ahead of him, instead of having to wait for his next bombing."

Horatio tried to picture Wendell Asher climbing into a Dumpster in his nice Italian suit. Hard to envision, but he admired the dedicated police work it showed. "Is he associated with any radical groups or organizations?"

"Not that I've been able to pin down," Asher replied. "Most of them publicly decry his methods, even though privately many of their members, and some of their leaders, are glad he's out there. He's brutal but effective—clinics have closed, and doctors have stopped providing abortions in areas where he's struck. So while the groups can't come out and announce that he's their hero, when you talk to a lot of their people one-on-one you get the sense that he's kind of a Robin Hood figure to them."

"I see," Horatio said. "I hope you catch him before he pulls anything. My people will be ready to process any crime scenes that might come up."

"We'll be keeping all the city's abortion providers under heavy guard until he's in custody," Frank assured them. "But just in case, I wanted you two to meet. I know your people are pros, Horatio, but this is a highly charged issue, emotionally, and I wanted your guarantee that none of your CSIs will let their personal beliefs interfere with the investigation."

Horatio tensed up at the suggestion. There had been some problems in the past between the crime lab and other parts of the police department, Horatio knew. He and his people remained under the microscope. But they didn't have a bigger booster in the department than Frank Tripp, so he guessed that the question was for the FBI agent's benefit and not his own. "My people have their own opinions," he said. "As do I. But when we put on our badges and come to work, we leave those opinions at home. We believe in letting the evidence speak, not our prejudices. We couldn't be effective criminalists otherwise."

"I appreciate that," Asher said. "I look forward to working with you, Lieutenant Caine."

Frank walked Horatio part of the way to the door, leaning close and speaking in low tones. "I don't trust Sackheim any farther'n I could toss him," he said. "So just in case, I called the Denver field office."

"And?"

"They confirmed Asher's identity and his assignment. Guy is who he says he is. Got some demolition experience in the first Gulf War, so they assigned him the case, and he's run with it ever since."

"All right," Horatio said, satisfied by Frank's due diligence. "I just hope he can catch his man. Ideally, before he sets off any explosives here in Miami."

3

CALLEIGH DUQUESNE HELD up a deformed slug, using forceps so as not to contaminate it with her own fingerprints or body oils—this precaution in spite of the fact that she wore latex surgical gloves. "This one," she said, "was the fatal bullet."

"That's the forty-five?" Horatio asked. They were in Calleigh's gun lab, where she had removed the bullet from a small paper envelope. Behind her was her gun cage, where she kept an array of firearms that would have delighted any gun enthusiast.

"That's right." Calleigh's long blond hair was tied back out of her face, and her blue eyes sparkled in the fluorescent light, showing faint green highlights. She spoke with a lilting Southern accent. "The through-and-through, recovered from the wall beside the victim. The concrete didn't do it any favors. The other bullet's a nine-millimeter, the one

Alexx removed from the body, but she determined that it didn't do any real damage."

"At least, not fatal damage."

"Right."

"Has she definitely determined that the gunshot was the cause of death?"

"She's at least leaning that way," Calleigh said. "And one more thing came up while you were at the PD."

"What's that, Calleigh?"

"The victim had P-GSR on his right hand."

"Is that so?" Primer gunshot residue was left behind by soot residues from a pistol. Since the victim had been shot from a distance, he wouldn't have had any from the guns that shot him—especially on his hand. "So he fired a weapon, too."

"But we didn't find any spent casings around him, or anywhere else at the scene for that matter."

"Which means," Horatio said, "that at least one of our shooters is the careful sort, and picked up after him or herself."

"We also didn't see any blood spatter other than the victim's, Horatio."

"So the victim's shot or shots probably missed their targets."

"That's how I read it."

"In that case, we'll have to take another look around that park. There may be bullets there that we didn't know we were looking for."

"I've still got some work to do here," Calleigh

said. "I want to get these scanned and into the FBI ballistics database."

To see if the striation marks matched those on any bullets known to have been used in other crimes, Horatio knew. "I'll send Eric and Ryan," he said. "Thank you, Calleigh."

Eric Delko loved to be outdoors. He didn't mind working in the lab, with its artificial light and canned air, but he preferred the real thing—sunlight, fresh air, green grass, the calls of birds, and the smells of life—when possible.

Besides, some of the beautiful babes for whom Miami was justifiably famous might be in the park, and Eric liked being in the presence of babes.

So being sent back to Bicentennial Park was no hardship for him.

He had driven the crime lab's Hummer, with Ryan Wolfe riding shotgun. Wolfe was, as he put it, "a little OCD," and Eric suspected his fellow CSI was actually happier in the controlled conditions of the lab. But he went where he was needed, and he didn't complain, even if he wasn't as enthusiastic about this particular assignment as Eric was.

"It's weird that someone went to all the trouble to pick up shell casings—even from a gun they didn't fire," Ryan said. "And still left all of that cocaine behind."

"I guess our killer doesn't use or deal," Eric said. "Not everybody does."

"I tend to think of murderers as being among the less discriminating citizens out there. But you're right—not every killer is a user."

They stood at the edge of the tall grass. Eric was glad the gardener hadn't come back to cut it yet. The removal crew had trampled some of it down when they took the victim's body out, but the area where he had fallen, beside the wall, was still fairly distinct. Eric had photos and diagrams in his hand showing precisely where the body had been and in what position. Blood spatter on the wall and the mark the bullet had made chipping the concrete would confirm where they needed to be.

The first time out, they had brought a male bendy dummy with them, a life-size figure they could manipulate into any position a man could get into, and trajectory rods with built-in laser pointers. By working backward from the John Doe's position on the ground, they were able to approximate how and where he must have been standing when he was shot. Inserting the trajectory rods where the victim's wounds were, they used the lasers to show them where the two shooters would have been. One of the shooters had been standing upright, they had determined, the other crouching or exceptionally short.

In both spots they had found pressed-down grasses, and in one, beneath a flowering tree, a couple of fibers had been removed from the knife-edge of a blade of saw grass. Those fibers were back at the lab waiting to be identified. Their task now was to find whatever bullets their victim might have fired, which meant following the imaginary lines from the victim toward and past the shooters' locations. Of course, his shots might have been wild, especially if he had fired after being hit, which meant the stray bullets could be just about anywhere.

"Which way do you want to start?" Eric asked.

Ryan shrugged. In his melon-colored shirt with the tail hanging out, a periwinkle suit, and spiked hair, he could have been one of the models so common in Miami, instead of a cop. "I can go toward the road," he said. "You go toward the water?"

"Okay, but I'm not going in unless I have to. I've got a wet suit in the vehicle, just in case." Eric was the team's diver, and as much as he liked being outside, he cherished time spent underwater, in that special environment like nothing else on Earth. Getting in and out of the gear was a hassle, though, that he hoped to avoid for now. Finding a single bullet out there could be an all-day task.

"Works for me," Ryan said. "Let's get started." He didn't wait for Eric's answer but headed out to walk a slow, steady line following the probable path of any bullet the victim might have shot at the shooter with the nine-millimeter weapon. The .45, the shot presumed to have been fatal, had come from the direction of the bay.

Eric didn't see anything between the body's

location and the trampled-on spot they believed the shooter had used, but he hadn't expected to. Assuming the gun had operated correctly, the bullet would have kept going until it ran into something, and there was no evidence to indicate that it had hit the shooter.

At the tree, however, a willow with long, narrow leaves and tiny, pale yellow flowers, Eric found something he had missed before. He'd made the mistake of looking for what he expected to find, not looking for what was there. And what was there was a bullet, sunken into the dark wood of the trunk. At a glance it looked like a fold in the wood, or maybe an insect hole, but by shining a mini Maglite into the opening, he caught the telltale glint of metal.

He took some photographs of the bullet's position in the tree, then tried to get it out with forceps. It was lodged in too tightly. He glanced back toward Ryan, who was still searching among the trees and shrubs in the other direction.

No way to tell from the GSR how many shots the vic had fired, of course. And if he was caught in a cross fire he might have squeezed one off in both directions. But Eric smiled, knowing that he had won this race, however insignificant that victory was. Certainty, not speed, was their goal.

He took a pocketknife from his crime scene kit and set to work boring around the bullet, wanting to get some tree with it to make sure his blade didn't accidentally knick the round and obscure any striation marks, or add any tool marks that might confuse a jury. As he worked, Ryan joined him.

"You got something?"

"Bullet," Eric said. "It's really buried in this trunk. At first it barely looked like a hole, but there's definitely a bullet in there. And you can tell by the exposed wood inside the hole that it's fresh."

"Good eye," Ryan said. "I haven't found anything over there. Well, not *nothing*. Cigarette butts, candy wrappers, the usual junk people leave behind. I don't understand why people bother visiting parks if they're just going to use them as trash cans. Why not stay home, admire their own trash, and leave the parks clean for others?"

Eric kept digging. "If I could explain people, I probably wouldn't be a CSI. Whole point of this job is to let the evidence do the explaining."

"You're right," Ryan said. "Working patrol, you really see the worst of people sometimes. You don't get a call unless something's gone wrong— someone's home has been broken into, someone's been assaulted, someone's drunk and disorderly, that kind of thing. It kind of colors your opinion of people, and not for the better."

"You're still glad you made the switch, right?"

"Definitely." There was no hesitation in Ryan's response, no dissembling. Everyone on the team

had been a little uncertain about Ryan, at first—H
had brought him on board not long after Tim Speedle had been killed on the job, and it was rare for
a uniformed patrol officer to have the educational
background required of a criminalist. But Ryan
Wolfe had the qualifications, and he'd proven to be
damn good at the job. Eric was glad they had him,
and glad Ryan had made his way into the job he
was best suited for.

The cylinder of tree trunk he had been boring
out came loose, and he inched it free with the tip of
the knife blade. "Got it," he said. "Can you grab me
an evidence bag?"

Ryan went to Eric's open kit and removed a
paper envelope. He opened it up, and Eric dropped
the wooden plug containing the bullet in. "Thanks,
man."

"No problem." Ryan flashed a wicked grin. "I'm
a little sorry I won't get to watch you dive—but
that's just my evil nature wanting to see you have
to suit up."

"Could be more bullets in the water, I guess,"
Eric said. "But this one will give Calleigh something
to work with, and there's almost no doubt that it
came from our John Doe." He pointed back along
the line. "Must have been some fireworks going
on here last night, huh? Guns blazing all over the
place."

"Officers canvassed the area for witnesses," Ryan
pointed out. "They came up blank."

"It's pretty deserted around here at night. That's what makes it a good place for drug deals."

"And apparently," Ryan added, "a good place for murder."

Miami was a city of stark contrasts. The very wealthy ran smack up against the very poor on a regular basis. Sun-splashed daytime pursuits—sports, family time at the beach, and tourism—were followed by the nighttime pleasures of fine dining, a raging club scene, and other, more adult-oriented activities. Luxurious beachfront hotels stood just blocks away from neighborhoods of stupefying poverty. The beautiful people . . . well, they mostly chose to hang with others of their breed. To Horatio, his adopted city was a complex stew, and while he loved every part of it, there were days that he wished its extremes were a little less so.

The Overtown district, he knew, had survived more than its fair share of difficult days. It had been a predominantly African-American area for a long time, and although the ethnic mix was changing these days, it was because more poor whites and Hispanics were moving in, not because the neighborhood had suddenly become more upscale. The city had tried to do something about it by building the Miami Arena there, but Miamians tended to keep away from the arena, which mostly hosted second-tier events. Major concert acts and the Miami Heat played at the AmericanAirlines

Arena instead. So the city's biggest attempt to drive wealth into Overtown had failed disastrously, and the district continued to be dominated by poverty, crime, and street gangs.

Including Los Danger Boys.

Horatio drove up Northwest Second Avenue with Eric Delko beside him, past scraggly palm trees with spray paint on their trunks and trash blown up against their bases, shops with bars on their windows and graffiti on their walls, homes with low fences and patchy lawns. A tiny terrier chained in one of the yards yapped at the Hummer as it drove past, as if it were a tiny cat and he a huge, ferocious hound.

"Maybe they should put him on the force," Eric said, nodding toward the dog. "Pooch looks like he means business."

"That might not be a bad idea," Horatio said with a smile. "Small but scrappy. He could put some of those K-9 officers on notice."

He made a couple of turns, relying on his intimate familiarity with the city's streets, and drew to a stop outside a bungalow surrounded by a four-foot-high chain-link fence. The house had been painted pastel green, but at least a decade before; Miami's harsh sunlight had faded it to a faint lime wash. Bars fronted the windows on the house, but no graffiti showed anywhere on the walls or the surrounding fence. The lawn was recently mowed, but not trimmed at the base of the house or around the spindly palm that leaned toward the street like a flower chasing the sun.

"That's the place," Horatio said. "According to Gabe Ramos of the gang unit, that's where Felix Granado lives."

"He's the big *jefe* of Los Danger Boys?" Eric asked. "I'd expect him to have a nicer place. Guy must rake in the dough, right?"

"For all I know, he also has a mansion in the Gables," Horatio said. "But it's a Danger Boys neighborhood, and he has to have a local presence too."

"I don't see any muscle around," Eric pointed out.

"Maybe he doesn't need it. Anyone who hit him here wouldn't make it three blocks."

"Good point." Eric waited until Horatio opened his car door, then followed suit. Together, they walked through the gate and up to the front door, which appeared to be solid steel, mounted behind a steel security screen. Horatio remained alert, sure that eyes were on them even though he couldn't see anyone at the curtained windows. Above the door, he found the reason—a pinhole camera pointed out at the walk, and inside someone certainly watched them on a monitor.

Instead of knocking, he held his badge in front of the camera for a moment, then moved it aside. "Horatio Caine, Miami-Dade Police. I want to talk to Felix." He couldn't tell if the camera had a microphone, but figured the watcher would get the idea.

He put his badge back on his belt, on his left hip. On his right were his ID card and his gun. He placed his hands on his hips, holding his blazer open so all were visible to the camera while he waited. Eric wore an open-collared, short-sleeved blue shirt and white pants, and stood with his arms folded over his chest. They looked like they meant business, but not harm. Standing in front of a gang leader's house without guns in their hands might have been dangerous, but Horatio wanted to send the right signal. They hadn't come for a confrontation.

The guy who opened the inner door might not have received that message.

He held a P90 submachine gun in his hands. Even if Horatio reached for his SIG Sauer P229 nine-millimeter now, he would be vastly out-gunned.

The weapon was the first thing Horatio noticed. He caught the distinctive tang of gun oil, which always reminded him of Calleigh. With a trained eye, he sized the man up in a fraction of a second. Prison-buff, he had arms as big around as most people's thighs and a chest like a bull's. His black hair was cut close to the scalp. Tattoos ran up his neck, onto his head, and down his arms from underneath a strained black tank top.

"You're not Granado," Horatio said. He kept his voice casual, conversational. Every muscle had been tensed, ready for action, even before the door opened, but he projected a cool, relaxed stance. He kept his shoulders lowered—most people raised their shoulders when they were stressed, but that kinked circulation to the brain. Lowering them enabled better blood flow and therefore quicker, calmer decision making. Eric, not quite as practiced, had lowered his hands when the man appeared with the big gun, and his right hand hovered near his own service weapon. "I asked for Felix. Tell him it's Lieutenant Caine of the crime lab, and I have some questions about one of his people."

The big man studied him through the screen for almost a full minute, eyes narrowed, head inclined back slightly as if looking down his stub of a nose at Horatio. Finally satisfied, he gave a slight nod and closed the door again.

Eric blew out a breath. "Big guy."

"Yes, and that P90 makes him bigger. But they aren't any more interested in trouble than we are."

"That's a good thing."

"Yes it is."

The door opened again, and this time Horatio knew he was looking at Felix Granado. This man was a few years older than the big guy, in his early thirties. He was slender and handsome, with light olive skin and fashionably long hair in that style that made it look as if he didn't own a comb but cost hundreds of dollars to maintain through cutting and styling products. His long-sleeved shirt, unbuttoned at the cuffs and collar, was silk, brown with diagonal gold stripes. Horatio wouldn't have been surprised to learn that there were real gold fibers woven into those stripes. Designer jeans fit snugly beneath the shirt. He wore no socks, and his shoes were Bruno Magli loafers. *O. J. shoes*, Horatio noted. What did that say about the man?

All in all, the guy looked as out of place in this little house as an undertaker at a wedding, confirming Horatio's supposition that it was a headquarters but not a home.

"Lieutenant Caine," he said, reaching forward and opening the security door. "I've heard of you."

"Then it's mutual, Felix."

Instead of inviting them in, Granado stepped outside and offered his hand. Horatio shook it, then Eric. "This is Eric Delko, one of my CSIs."

"Welcome to Overtown. You like it?"

"Like anyplace else, it has its good points."

"I caught a great Buena Vista Social Club show at the arena a couple of years ago," Eric said. "Some good restaurants around, too."

Granado eyed Eric, who was tall and dark, with short black hair and a heavy five o'clock shadow already showing on his cheeks. "Cubaño, eh?"

"You bet." Eric's parents had fled Cuba for Miami while his mother was pregnant with him—a precarious journey under any circumstances, and even more so under those.

"You know Orishas?" Granado asked.

"*El Kilo*'s a good CD, but I still like *Emigrante* best."

Granado nodded, Eric apparently having passed some sort of test. "There some special reason for this visit, Officers, or did you just want to get acquainted? I have kind of a busy schedule today."

"I'll bet you do, Felix," Horatio said. He drew a photograph of the victim from the park out of his inside jacket pocket and handed it to the gangster. "Tattoos indicate that this young man was one of yours. He met an unfortunate end this morning, and I'd like to be able to notify his family. But so far we haven't been able to identify him, and I was hoping you could help."

Granado looked at the picture, then shook his head. "Sorry," he said, handing it back. "I'm always happy to cooperate with the police, but I don't know the guy."

"He has 'Los Danger Boys' tattooed on his back," Horatio said.

"Lots of people do. I don't know them all, and I already said I don't know him."

Granado looked and sounded absolutely sincere. Horatio didn't believe him for a second. "If you should hear about anyone who might know him," he said, "get in touch with me right away. I'd hate for his family to hear about this on the news or some other way."

"I'll do that, Lieutenant."

"Thank you."

"Will there be anything else?"

"Not for today, Felix." Horatio caught Eric's gaze

and tilted his head slightly toward the street. "Not for today. You stay out of trouble."

"Always," Felix said. He stepped back inside, locking the security screen and then closing the heavy front door.

"You believe him?" Eric asked on the way back to the SUV.

"Not at all, Eric. But I believe he told us as much as he was going to, which was nothing."

"Funny how some guys can give you nothing and make you feel like they're doing you a big favor."

"That's probably what took him to the top." Horatio started to open his car door, paused, looked at his companion. "And, Mister Delko . . . Orishas?"

"Cuban hip-hop band. They're good. I can loan you some CDs if you want."

"Thanks, Eric. That probably won't be necessary. But I appreciate the offer."

4

INSTEAD OF HEADING directly back to the crime lab, Horatio drove around the neighborhood awhile longer. The streets looked more or less alike, except that as they got farther away from Granado's place there had been more turf struggles, indicated by gang graffiti painted atop other gang graffiti. *Warfare by spray can.*

He didn't know why Felix Granado would refuse to identify the victim, but he had some ideas. In spite of the gang leader's comment, being seen helping the police in any way couldn't be good for his standing. He would rather obstruct an investigation than aid it, just out of general principle. Then there was the strong possibility that the shooting was gang-related. If the victim had been shot by other Los Danger Boys members, maybe for breaking a gang rule of some kind, Granado wouldn't want to identify him because he would want to stifle the investigation. If the shooter had been a member of a rival gang, then Los Danger Boys would want to avenge it themselves, without police interference.

Horatio had hoped to appeal to the human being that Felix Granado was, but the gangster inside had won out.

A few blocks away from Granado's little house, they spotted two young men standing on a street corner outside a little *bodega*. Hand-lettered signs in the windows advertised *cerveza*, *loteria*, ice-cold Dr. Pepper, and *menudo*. The boys were teenagers, one holding a can of Coke and a lit cigarette in the same hand, with his other tucked into a pocket of his baggy black denim pants. The second boy leaned out over the curb and spat into the street as they drove past. Horatio was sure it was an expression of opinion.

"H, I know that kid," Eric said.

"The spitter?"

"The other one, with the smoke. He's Los Danger Boys, I'm pretty sure. Let's talk to him."

Horatio turned into the mouth of an alley, backed out, and reversed direction. The two boys had started walking away from the *bodega*, but he passed them and then pulled onto the sidewalk, blocking their way with the big SUV. When Eric shoved his door open, he was right in front of them.

"Hold up a second," he said. Horatio stayed

where he was, his hands on the steering wheel, as Eric stepped down to the sidewalk and addressed the kid he had mentioned. "You work at Graciana, right, in Little Havana? Busboy?"

The kid's face clouded over, as if he was embarrassed at being revealed as a working stiff in front of his friend. "Yeah. So?"

"I've seen you there. I'm Eric."

"Maybe I've seen you there, too. What about it?"

"I'm not looking to jam anybody up, man, but I need some information. You're Los Danger Boys, right?"

The kid flicked the cigarette butt to the pavement and stamped it out, transferring the Coke to his left hand. Now his right dove into the deep pocket. "No."

"I've seen the tattoos on your knuckles," Eric said. "It's okay, we're not with the gang unit or anything. We're with the crime lab, and we're trying to identify a body."

"Just don't say nothing, dude," the other teen said. He refused to meet Eric's gaze, but kept glancing into the vehicle at Horatio.

"If you want to help your friend, keep your mouth shut," Eric warned. Horatio was proud of the way Eric had managed the conversation so far. He released the wheel long enough to hand over the victim's photograph when Eric reached for it.

"This is the guy," Eric said. "You know him?"

"Dude . . ."

Eric kept his gaze locked on the first kid. "Do you know him or not?"

"Maybe I've seen him around," the kid said.

"I need a name. His address too, if you know it."

The kid was nervous now. He took a long swig from the can, emptying it, then crushed it in his fist. He looked like he wanted to throw it to the ground but had suddenly realized that littering in front of two cops wouldn't be the wisest course of action. Instead, he held the can awkwardly in his hand and stared at the picture. "Your mom owns Graciana, right?" Eric asked. He sounded like he was just making conversation, but it was really a thinly veiled threat. *If you don't help me, I'll go to your mother.*

The threat worked. "His name's Silvio."

"Last name."

"Castaneda. Silvio Castaneda. That's him. He get whacked or what?"

"Something like that."

"That's weird, dog." Now that he had spilled the name, he seemed to have gotten past his anxiety about talking to the police. His friend stared at him, as if astonished at his behavior.

"Why is it weird?" Eric asked.

"He's just . . . he's nothing, you know? Not an important guy. Not really a player. He hasn't been LDB for long, never got very far up in the organization."

"Has he ever been arrested?"

"No way. He never done nothing to get arrested for."

If you don't count the possession and sale of cocaine, Horatio thought.

"We need to inform his family of his death," Eric said. "You know where he lived?"

The kid shuffled his feet, switched hands on the crushed soft drink can again, shot a glance at his friend, and gave Eric an address. "I think that's right," he said. "Anyway, it's a gray house there, one down from the corner."

"We'll find it," Eric said. "Thanks."

"No problem."

"See you at the restaurant." Eric climbed back up into the Hummer and closed his door.

"That's close by," Horatio said.

"Yeah, couple blocks."

"Good work, Eric." Horatio started the Hummer again and watched the kids saunter up the block, not hurrying, like they didn't have a care in the world.

Joe Castaneda's eyes filled with tears, and he backed out of the doorway, his legs wobbling. Horatio was afraid he might faint or fall down and braced himself to catch the man if it came to that. "May we come in for a minute?"

"S-sure," Castaneda stammered. "Y-yeah."

Horatio entered the modest home, with Eric

close behind. They had driven over straight from the *bodega* and found Joe Castaneda at home. The man was heavyset, his gut straining a thin white undershirt. He hadn't shaved today, and his eyes were puffy with sleep. On his legs were a pair of cotton pajama pants in a red plaid pattern, and his feet were bare. Horatio thought that perhaps he worked nights, and they had interrupted his sleep. A faint smell of tortillas hung in the air, possibly his morning meal.

Castaneda dropped into a well-worn easy chair. At a sound from an interior doorway, Horatio swiveled, reaching for his weapon.

"What is it, Papa?" a young girl asked. She looked to be in her midteens, petite, not even five feet tall. She wore a black T-shirt with a heavy metal band's logo on the front, tight jeans, and yellow sneakers with black checks. The makeup around her eyes was thick and dark, as if she had applied it with a trowel, and her lips were painted fashionably black. "Who the hell are these dudes?"

"Are you Silvio's sister?" Horatio asked her. When talking with young people, Horatio liked to get on their level, but this girl was an awkward height—crouching would lower him too much, but standing fully upright made her have to look up at him. He settled for tilting his head to one side, lowering his face a little.

"Yeah, I'm Faustina."

"I'm very sorry, Faustina, but your brother was

killed last night. We just now found out who he was so that we could tell you."

Joe Castaneda sat in the chair, his face buried in his hands, utterly still. He could have been sleeping for all the noise he made. "My son . . ." he said quietly, then went silent again.

"Is your mother at home?" Horatio asked the girl.

"My mama's dead," Faustina said. There was an angry, brittle edge to her voice. "Three years ago. Someone shot her where she worked, at a gas station. No one did jack about it."

"I'm very sorry about that, Faustina. I guarantee you, something will be done about Silvio's death."

"How did it happen?"

"He was shot, Faustina. One of the bullets hit his heart."

"Just like my mama."

"I wish it wasn't."

Joe Castaneda lowered his hands. Tears traced down his cheeks. "Where . . ." he began. He didn't seem to know how to ask his question. "Where is he?"

"Your son is in our morgue, Mister Castaneda," Horatio explained. "He's being well taken care of there while we determine exactly what happened and who killed him. We'll release him to you as soon as we can, so if you'd like to make arrangements—"

"My wife, she . . ."

"Faustina told us that your wife was also shot, and I'm very sorry. We try to do our best for every crime victim, but some cases aren't solved immediately. Some take years, and I can't lie to you, some are never solved."

"Because the cops don't care about our people," Faustina said. "That's why our people have to join gangs, so we'll have someone who will look out for us. Everybody knows the po-po don't give a damn."

"That, young lady, is not true. We care about every victim." Horatio paused. "*I* care. And I guarantee you, I will do everything in my power to get at the truth. I will find out who killed your brother."

Faustina Castaneda didn't answer him. Not with words, anyway. But her deep brown eyes locked on his, dry and bitter, and told him everything.

She didn't believe him.

He would just have to prove her wrong.

5

"YEAH, HORATIO."

"You're driving, Horatio?" Calleigh asked.

"I am. Heading back to the lab. We've identified the victim from this morning and notified his family."

"I'm glad to hear it, and I won't keep you," she said. She was riding, with Ryan Wolfe behind the wheel, and she knew that talking on a cell phone distracted a driver just as much as a few drinks did. "Two things I wanted to tell you. One, the fibers Ryan and Eric found at Bicentennial Park are dyed hundred-percent cotton denim. The dye matches a proprietary color used in Wrangler jeans."

"So there are only tens of thousands of pair sold worldwide every year," Horatio said, grasping her point. She liked the fact that her boss rarely required much in the way of elucidation. "If not hundreds of thousands."

"It's safe to say that the fibers don't help us much, unless we find someone with a pair of jeans we can try to compare. The other thing is that I wanted you to know that Ryan and I are rolling to a new crime scene."

"Tell me more."

"It's a homicide," she said. "Out on Leonard Highway."

"That's off the Tamiami Trail, right?"

"On the way out to the 'Glades, yes. Here's the worst part, Horatio. The first patrol officer on the scene identified the victim."

"And?"

"She's Wendy Greenfield."

"As in the wife of Sidney Greenfield?"

"The pro golfer, right." You didn't have to follow golf to recognize his name. She had known it right away, and she didn't follow golf. But she knew the names of Tiger Woods and Jack Nicklaus and Arnold Palmer. During the past couple of years, Sidney Greenfield's performance had demonstrated that he would soon be breaking into that exalted company. And he was a local, too, who had started out golfing on Miami's public courses and gradu-ated from Miami University.

"We'll change course and see you there, Calleigh."

She ended the call and put away her phone. "He and Eric are on their way over."

"We'll get there first," Ryan said. "But with a high-profile victim like Wendy Greenfield, I'm glad the LT will be on hand to deal with the media."

Calleigh had to agree. Ryan had experienced some rough times at the hands of the press—specifically, being used by WFOR-TV reporter Erica Sikes, of the local CBS affiliate, who he had also dated for a time—and had been instructed not to comment publicly on police matters. This case would have a much higher profile than the young gangbanger they had found in Bicentennial Park this morning, and she sure didn't want to be the lab's public face on it.

Ryan didn't pay undue attention to speed limit signs, and they made good time. When they reached the Leonard Highway turnoff from the Tamiami Trail, Ryan made a left turn, taking them south. While the road had the name "highway" attached to it, in truth it was more of a byway with very little traffic. Tall trees and thick brush hemmed it in on both sides, masking farm fields beyond that. After a couple of miles, they spotted the flashing lights of the patrol cars and ambulance already on the scene, and Ryan pulled in behind them. The closest car to the scene, so probably the first responder, was a Highway Patrol Camaro, mostly black but with a white roof and trunk. Those were *fast*, Calleigh knew, and looked like sharks as they cruised the state's roadways.

Ryan would no doubt prefer one of those to the lab's H3.

"Ryan, how many speeding tickets have you paid since you got your license?" she asked. Needling him had proven to be an amusing pastime. Calleigh was a good Southern girl raised with three brothers in a traditional Southern lawyer's home (so traditional that the old joke describing a Southern breakfast as a bottle of Jack Daniel's, a steak, and a hound dog—give the steak to the hound dog—unfortunately applied to her father, Kenwall Duquesne), so the streak of dark humor that provided defense against the stresses of the job came naturally to her. Emerging from beneath the veneer of good manners and her fierce intelligence, it often took people by surprise, even after they thought they knew her.

"All of them." He took his kit from the backseat. "Any more questions?"

"Not just now, thanks." She got her own kit and joined him, Ryan walking—almost as fast as he had driven—toward the scene.

Inside the yellow tape perimeter, sitting on the narrow shoulder just off the road, was a white Mitsubishi Eclipse convertible. In the convertible, Calleigh could see platinum blond hair, even lighter than her own, on a still form occupying the passenger seat. That had to be Wendy Greenfield.

A Florida Highway Patrol officer she never had met kept an eye on the perimeter. He studied their badges as they approached, and she scanned the name tag on his muscular chest. *Briscoe.* "Thank you, Officer Briscoe."

"Glad to see you guys," Briscoe said, handing over the security log. A handful of officers and EMTs had already signed it. "The scene's all yours."

"Who was first on the scene?" Calleigh asked as she signed her name. She handed the log to Ryan. Everyone who entered the scene had to document their presence.

"My partner and I."

"Was there a suspect at the scene?"

"It was just like you see it now. We were patrolling the road and saw her parked there. Thought maybe she'd had a mechanical problem. We pulled over behind her, approached the vehicle, and"—he paused, staring hard at the grassy shoulder of the road—"well, you'll see what we found. I called in a 187, and we didn't touch the car, just set up the perimeter. The EMTs took a look, but backed off when they saw her."

"How did you identify the victim?" Ryan asked.

"I follow the pro tour," Briscoe replied. "Wendy Greenfield is always at the eighteenth when Sidney finishes a round, and she's a beautiful woman, so the cameras always kind of linger on her. Plus I've attended the PGA Ford Championship at Doral and seen her in person. I didn't check her purse or anything, but I'm sure it's her."

"Okay," Ryan said. "The ME's on the way, and we'll go ahead and get started processing the scene."

Calleigh and Ryan both set their kits down outside the tape and gloved up. Briscoe held the tape for them, and when they were ready they passed beneath it.

Ryan started by photographing the scene, getting wide shots that encompassed the car and the area around it. After capturing the overall scene, he began moving in for closer shots. While he did that, Calleigh took a sketchbook and pencil from her kit and made a quick sketch of the scene, showing the relative position of the car, the road, and the trees and brush beside it.

"I've got footprints and tire tracks," Ryan said as he drew closer to the convertible. He took more photos of the tracks he had found. "The tire tracks are not from this car, and the prints aren't from Wendy Greenfield. Definitely male, maybe size ten or eleven. They look like they head from the convertible to where the other car was waiting."

"Easier to get away from here in another vehicle than on foot," Calleigh observed. "We're a long way from anything."

Her curiosity burned to look inside the car, especially because of the way Briscoe had talked about it. She was a professional, though, and knew that taking things in the right order led to criminals being convicted.

After this overview, she would get a look at the dead body. Then they would work backward in even more orderly fashion, spiraling away from the car and inspecting every square inch of the ground in case the killer or killers had left evidence behind. They would make castings of the impressions the tires and shoes had made in the soft earth. They would view the area without the blinders of prejudice or initial opinions, and they would find whatever was there to be found.

After about twenty minutes of studying the scene, she and Ryan converged at the Mitsubishi.

The woman Briscoe had identified as Wendy Greenfield had, in fact, been a beautiful woman.

That beauty was marred somewhat now by the fact that her throat had been sliced open. Her head tilted back against the seat at an angle it couldn't have in life. Her white blouse and pants had been drenched in blood, which had also soaked the windshield and dashboard. Almost as if she had known what would happen to her and wanted to remain color coordinated, she wore a crimson leather belt and matching pumps, and the convertible was white with a red interior.

"That's definitely Wendy Greenfield," Ryan said.

"You recognize her?"

"I catch the occasional golf game on TV."

"Apparently she had an enemy," Calleigh said. "Or maybe a friend who turned into an enemy. This looks personal to me." She bent forward, still not touching the car, for a closer look. "Wound is short and angled, dropping toward the right."

"So her assailant wasn't sitting behind her,"

Ryan observed. "Which would have been more of a sweep, up on both ends."

"The second smile. Not this time. I'm guessing that the killer was in the driver's seat. No question that she was sitting right there when it happened." She pointed to the blood drops on the inside of the windshield, which had impacted and made satellite spatters where smaller, secondary droplets had hit the glass after splashing from the bigger initial drops. The blood was still wet, trickling slowly down, streaking as it went. "Projection spatters," she said. "From her arterial pulse."

"Be hard to use those," Ryan said, "because of the streaking and running."

"Fortunately we don't have to rely on them. We have the arterial spatter on the dash that's easier to read. And the lower-velocity spatter on her clothing and seat, as her heart weakened. It's all here, like an open book." Even as Calleigh talked and studied the dash, she noticed something else.

"And look here," she added, pointing to a spot on the dashboard where there wasn't as much blood spatter as there was around it. The space was just to the left of where Wendy Greenfield sat. "It's hard to make out because there's a little spatter, but there's a void pattern here. The droplets of blood that did impact this area came after the first, heaviest gush."

"Which means blood ended up on some other surface."

"Probably the killer's arm. Assuming he was right-handed, which I think we can based on the angle of the cut, it would have been an awkward reach for him to slice her throat from the driver's seat. He would have had to turn and face her. She probably turned as well, toward him, which would have made his task a little easier. Maybe she thought he wanted a kiss. Then he cut her, with little or no warning, and the first spray hit the windshield, dashboard, and his arm. She fell back into the seat, and that's when the blood sprayed the area in front of her, gradually slowing and soaking her clothing."

Calleigh knew Ryan could figure out the same scenario by looking at the spatter patterns, but talking it through as she studied it helped her keep things straight in her own head. She might eventually have to explain her thought processes to a jury. If she made sense to herself from the start, it would be easier to make sense to them.

"If he was driving, then you're right, chances are good that he knew her," Ryan said. "And I don't see any other signs of struggle."

"No," Calleigh said. "But there is one strange thing."

"What's that?"

"There's a woman's purse in the driver's-side foot well. Red leather, matching Wendy's shoes and belt. It has to be hers, but if she wasn't driving, why didn't she have it on the passenger side with her?"

"That, Calleigh, is an excellent question."

She walked around to the driver's side of the car. Before touching anything, she put on two more pairs of latex gloves. This was going to be a bloody scene, and if she had to write anything down or answer a phone or just hope not to contaminate other parts of the car with blood she had already touched, she would need clean gloves. It would be easier and quicker to remove or cut away additional pairs rather than stop and switch.

Ryan did the same, she noticed, but if he held true to form he would avoid touching the DB if at all possible. His OCD didn't keep him from doing his job—and he was good at his job—but he didn't like getting down and dirty when he could avoid it.

Triple-gloved, she reached into the car (supporting herself with one hand on the edge of the door, the steel burning hot even through the triple layers of latex) and took out the purse. Kate Spade. Pricey, but Sidney Greenfield had finished in the money several times last year and could afford to buy nice things for his wife. As far as Calleigh knew, Wendy's only job was being a PGA Tour wife.

She opened it and found a leather wallet inside. A Florida driver's license confirmed what they already knew: the victim was Wendy Greenfield, who lived on Hibiscus Island. Also pricey. The wallet contained seven hundred dollars and change, and all her credit cards seemed to be there, judging by the way they fit into the leather grooves. "It doesn't appear that she was robbed," Calleigh said.

"Which points back to the idea that there was a personal element to the attack."

"That's what I was thinking."

"The backseat is empty. Pop the trunk, Calleigh, and let's see if there's anything interesting in there."

Calleigh, still standing by the driver's door, reached in again and pulled the trunk release. The rear hatch opened and Ryan pushed it up. "More than interesting, I'd say."

"What is it, Ryan?" Calleigh walked to the rear of the car and looked inside.

Ryan had found two shotguns, a Mossberg and an Ithaca, both 12-gauge. Tucked in with them were several boxes of buckshot shells. Ryan opened a plastic bag that one of the guns rested on. "Men's clothes," he said. "New. Size XL Hanes T-shirt, Levi's jeans with a thirty-six-inch waist and thirty-four-inch inseam. No shoes, socks, or underwear."

"You're right, Ryan. This is more than just interesting. This looks like someone's planning to go to war."

6

RYAN AND CALLEIGH were about to start their methodical, inch-by-inch search of the crime scene when a Miami-Dade Police Department cruiser pulled up with a civilian in the passenger seat and two others, teenagers, it appeared, in the rear. A uniformed officer got out from behind the wheel, followed by the adult civilian, and had a brief conversation with Briscoe of the Highway Patrol. Briscoe pointed toward the CSIs.

"It looks like we have company," Ryan said.

"So it appears."

Ryan let Calleigh take the lead, since she had seniority and had recently been promoted to lieutenant. She went to meet the newcomers at the taped perimeter line, Ryan following a couple of steps behind. Alexx Woods had recently arrived and was beginning to examine Wendy Greenfield's body.

"Is there something I can help you with, Officer?" Calleigh asked.

The uni was a few pounds overweight, his gut threatening to sag over his duty belt. His skin was deeply tanned and creased by the sun, his hair shaved almost to the scalp. "Thought maybe I could help you," he answered. "This man here thinks he saw your vehicle there involved in a crime."

"The Mitsubishi?"

"That's right," the civilian said. He had a pudgy physique, casually dressed in a striped Polo shirt, khakis, and moccasins. Black hair curled over his ears, and his face didn't look like one that smiled often.

"Tell me about it."

The guy looked at the uniform cop, as if he needed permission to talk to the criminalists. The cop gave him a subtle nod. "I was at the Quick Spree, this convenience store a couple miles from here. Right at the intersection with the Tamiami Trail. Buying a couple of twelve-packs, right?"

"It is a warm day," Calleigh replied.

"Yeah. So anyway, I saw this hot blonde sitting in a convertible out in the parking lot, like she was waiting for someone maybe."

"And you believe it was this car?"

"Pretty sure, yeah. I wasn't really looking at the car so much, on account of the girl inside it being such a babe."

"I get the picture," Calleigh said. "What happened?"

"Well, I saw this guy come around the corner, toward the car. She noticed him, like, and I thought maybe it was who she was waiting for. But then he stopped in front of her—his body was blocking my view, so I couldn't see what he showed her, maybe like a gun or something. I could see her face, though, and she looked scared. Then she moved over to the passenger side and he got in behind the wheel and drove away."

"So it looked like a carjacking to you?"

"Pretty much, yeah."

"Did you report it from the store?"

The man looked away, his jaw tight. "Not so much."

"Why not?"

"I . . ." He glanced back toward the patrol car. Ryan read the meaning of that glance, the hesitation.

So, it seemed, did Calleigh. "You were buying beer for those boys, who are underage."

Ryan's first case with the crime lab had involved Calleigh's father, who struggled with alcoholism. He knew the subject was a tender one for her.

"That's my nephew and a friend of his," the man said. "It wasn't like I was trying to get them drunk or anything. They were coming over to do yard work at my place, and I promised them some brews when they were done."

"But they are underage, and you knew that it was a crime," Calleigh said. Her tone was a little cooler than it had been before, but Ryan thought one would have to know her to recognize the difference.

"That's right." The man, having admitted his offense, caught her gaze and held it, as if daring her to do something about it now that he had finally come forward. "But when I thought about what I'd seen for a while, I realized that it might have been something important. Like maybe she was in some real trouble."

"She was," Calleigh said. "She was murdered. It doesn't get more real than that."

"I know that now. I'm so sorry."

"By the time we got his call, the vehicle had already been reported," the officer said. "I swung around to his place and picked them up so he could talk to you."

"Thank you, Officer," Calleigh said. To the witness she said, "Can you describe the man who got into her car?"

"He was a big guy. Tall, you know, and muscular. Like an athlete or something. Pretty good-looking, not like a model, but for an average guy."

"Hair color? Any tattoos or other marks you could see?"

"Brown hair. A little longer than mine." He touched his neck, just beneath the collar of his shirt. "Maybe about to there. And a mustache."

"Do you remember anything about his clothes?" Ryan asked.

The man looked at Ryan, eyes widening, as if he hadn't noticed anyone except Calleigh. Since he seemed to have a thing for attractive blondes, maybe he hadn't. "Blue jeans. A regular short-sleeved sport shirt. I think maybe it was blue or, like, slate gray or something."

"And he just walked up to the convertible? You're sure he didn't arrive in a vehicle?"

"That's what I saw. I couldn't tell where he came from because I was inside the store. I just saw him when he came around the corner and headed for her. If he had parked something around the corner, I wouldn't have known it."

"Where were the boys at the time?" Calleigh asked.

"They were at the magazine rack in the store, looking at car magazines."

"And the clerk?"

"Behind the counter."

"We stopped by the Quick Spree on the way over," the uni said. "The way the counter is set up, the clerk can't see out into that part of the parking lot. But he does have a video surveillance system, so if he'd been looking at the monitor he might have seen something. Says he wasn't, though."

"You probably should have let a detective handle that," Calleigh pointed out.

"Sorry," the uni said, not looking the least bit apologetic. Ryan wondered if he had any idea how many cases were blown every year by cops trying to help out in areas where they didn't have specialized training. It was one of the reasons he had been so anxious to get off patrol, into a field where people were more careful.

That, and the patrol locker room was a stew of germs.

"Where is that store again?" Ryan asked, fishing his mobile phone from his pocket.

The officer gave him an address, and Ryan opened the phone, punching the speed-dial button for Horatio Caine. He stepped away from the others so the civilian wouldn't listen in.

A moment later, Horatio's voice responded. "Mister Wolfe," he said. "We're almost to you now."

"Don't come here, H," Ryan said. The words were out of his mouth before he realized they sounded more like an order than a suggestion. "It turns out there's another crime scene." He described the carjacking and gave Horatio the address of the Quick Spree. "We've still got some work to do here, so I thought maybe you and Delko could—"

"That's fine, Ryan. We're close to there, so we'll just stop off instead of coming out to your location."

"Okay," Ryan said. "By the way, we have identified the DB as Wendy Greenfield, so somebody's going to have to notify her husband. There's no press here yet, but I'm sure it won't be long now."

"I'll take care of the notification after Eric gets started at the Quick Spree. Can you swing by there after you're finished with your scene and pick Eric up?"

"No problem, H. We'll bring him back to the lab with us."

"All right, then. Anything you can tell me about Mrs. Greenfield that might help her husband?"

"I wish there was. She probably didn't suffer much. Killer sliced her carotid artery, it looks like, and she bled out fast. Alexx is here checking her out. It's a mess here."

"It would be. Thank you, Mister Wolfe. I'll see you later."

Horatio ended the call, and Ryan folded his phone and tucked it away.

The uni was leading the civilian back to his squad car, and Calleigh had turned toward him. "H and Eric are headed to the Quick Spree," he reported. "They were almost here."

"I'm sure there'll be plenty to keep them occupied," Calleigh said. "It's turning into a busy day."

"Do we ever get any other kind?"

"Very seldom," she agreed.

"So a carjacking explains some things," Ryan said as they walked back toward the car. Coming toward them on Leonard Highway he could see the first TV van. It looked like the one from WFOR/ CBS-4 News, although he hoped he was wrong because he really didn't want to see Erica Sikes today.

"The purse on the driver's side, for instance," he continued. "She shoved over but was too scared to remember to grab her purse."

"Maybe." Calleigh stared at the convertible as if it could be persuaded to speak. "But it doesn't explain everything. If the only weapon he had was a knife, why didn't she try to drive away instead of just giving in? Since it's an open convertible, why didn't she jump out and run into the store? And why carjack a vehicle just to go a few miles, where there's a getaway car waiting? Why couldn't the other car have picked the killer up at the Quick Spree? It just doesn't add up."

"The math gets even more complicated when you factor in the shotguns. And the clothes. They're not for Sidney Greenfield, and from the description that guy gave us, they wouldn't fit the carjacker either. Thirty-six waist and thirty-four inseam is not a body I'd call tall and athletic."

"Neither would I," Calleigh said. "There's a lot more to this case than we've seen so far. Let's finish up here so we can get that car back to the lab and examine it more closely."

7

AN ACCIDENT ON the Dolphin Expressway and traffic on the surface streets had impeded Eric and Horatio's progress toward the crime scene. That had worked out for the best, Eric decided, because they had been diverted to the Quick Spree shortly before reaching it. Without the traffic they would have had to backtrack, and Eric hated backtracking.

As it was, H had wanted to get to the golfer's house, so he dropped Eric and his kit at the Quick Spree and told him that Calleigh and Ryan would pick him up on their way back to the lab. He had filled Eric in on his conversation with Ryan, so Eric knew what he was looking for.

The first thing he noticed when Horatio drove away was that the convenience store's parking lot was busy. Eric stood outside the store for a few minutes, on a shaded concrete island that had once held gas pumps. During that time, eleven vehicles drove in, out, or both. People parked and dashed into the store for smokes or soft drinks or beer. Some stayed longer, microwaving burgers or dogs or burritos, preparing fountain drinks, buying lottery tickets, but still, five minutes seemed like the absolute longest anyone spent inside.

All the in-and-out traffic would likely mean that the lot would be close to useless, in terms of trace evidence. He didn't have to worry about tire tracks—the vehicle they knew had been parked here was the one they already had—but footprints or other trace would have been nice.

The parking lot was a combination ashtray, garbage can, and oil pan. Cigarette butts, gum, gum wrappers, candy wrappers, food wrappers of every sort and more had been strewn about as if there hadn't been both an ashtray and a trash can flanking the store's doorway. Vehicles had leaked every kind of fluid imaginable on the pavement, and human beings had added more fluids of their own.

Eric wouldn't get anywhere standing around here. He walked into the store, a one-story stand-alone building with a fluorescent sign box above the door and various neon and paper signs in the windows advertising beer and other goods. The air inside smelled sour, as if something had spilled and spoiled behind a display case. When he entered, he passed through an electric eye and caused a bell to chime. A couple of girls were choosing drinks from refrigerated, glass-fronted cases. A skinny man with greasy dark hair framing a gaunt face glanced up from his stool behind the counter, eyes flitting in every direction. *Looks like a meth-head,* Eric thought, *but at least he's holding down a job.* He showed the clerk his badge.

"Lot of you guys around today."

"I'm with the Miami-Dade Crime Lab," Eric said. "You talked to another officer about a carjacking that took place in the parking lot today?"

"I didn't see shit," the guy said. "Which is what I told the cop."

"I understand that. But there's a video surveillance camera over the doors, facing the parking lot, in addition to the"—Eric scoped the open store, spotting one behind the counter recording anyone who approached it, and another facing toward the door from above what must have been the entrance to a storage space—"the two in here."

"Yeah, we got cameras. What about it?"

"I'm going to need those tapes."

The clerk pinched his upper lip, then released it and rubbed it as if he had hurt himself. "Got a warrant?"

"I can get one, if you want to play hardball."

"I don't care one way or the other, but my boss'll want to know I asked. He's a bastard for rules."

"Tell him you asked. If he has a problem, tell him that if I had to come back with a warrant I'd be angry because my time was wasted, and I'd make him come into the lab to be questioned. You're saving him a lot of time and effort."

The guy cracked a gap-toothed grin. "I'll be sure to let him know." He stepped off the stool and crouched down behind the counter. Eric leaned over to make sure he was reaching for tapes and not a weapon. There was a single black-and-white monitor parked on a low shelf beside three stacked VCRs. "Might as well give me all three tapes that cover the time the carjacking happened."

"They hold six hours each," the clerk said. "So they're all the ones that are still in there now."

"I'll take them."

The clerk muttered a curse and ejected the tapes. Eric could see their slipcases from where he stood, but the clerk didn't bother putting them in, just rose and set the tapes on the counter.

"Do you know where the car was parked?" Eric said. "Mitsubishi Eclipse convertible?"

"Like I said, I didn't see shit. Cop was here before said it was parked in the last slot before the corner, in front." He pointed to the western side of the building, behind his position at the counter. It made sense to Eric—from where he stood he could see that parking space, but the clerk would have to lean far forward and peer past a rack of maps and a window poster to get a view of it. "Far as I know, that's where it was."

"You don't know if the woman whose car it was bought anything?" Eric asked. He had a pretty good idea what the answer would be but had to ask.

"I don't know who she was or what she looked like, so how would I know?"

"I figured." The tapes would tell him, anyway. The quality would be terrible, no doubt, but Dan Cooper, the A/V tech at the lab, could coax something from them if anything was there to be found.

He carried the tapes outside and set them on the sidewalk with his kit, in front of the parking space the clerk had indicated. The space was empty at the moment. When he had arrived with Horatio, there had been an old VW bus parked there. Nothing like a crime scene that had been wide open and heavily trafficked for what could have been hours since the crime. This would be a game of exclusion—checking every cigarette butt and wad of gum and Snickers wrapper and determining that whoever had left them there had not been connected to the carjacking and murder, in the nearly futile hope that one of them might be connected after all. It would be tedious, grueling work.

With any luck, evidence from the murder scene would pan out quickly, so he wouldn't have to put himself through the entire process.

Putting off starting wouldn't help it go any faster, though.

And there was always the possibility that H

would want all of it anyway . . . dotting the I's, crossing the T's.

Eric blew out a long sigh and got started.

A few facts were essential to any close understanding of Horatio Caine. Although he was not a man who dwelled on his own life's history, who spent much time examining himself, in the wake of the murder of his wife Marisol—Eric Delko's sister—and his killing of those responsible, Horatio had spent many long, sleepless nights trying to grasp how he had reached that stage of his life, and where it could go from there.

The facts were these: His mother had been a fan of Horatio Alger, the nineteenth-century American author whose novels included many well-known "rags-to-riches" stories. Alger's persistent theme was that anyone could succeed at any task through hard work and determination, and by that success would become a useful and productive citizen. She had named her son after the author and had instilled in him, as a boy, those same basic tenets.

Another fact was that Horatio Caine's father had been an abusive man who had beaten his sons and finally murdered Horatio's mother. Horatio had, in turn, killed his father. Oedipal, perhaps, but to Horatio it was not about wanting to possess a woman who had already died, but about simple, tragic justice.

His mother's murder had twisted the rags-to-riches part of Horatio's own story toward a different goal. Where he had once intended to become financially successful, as his mother had hoped, instead he chose a path virtually guaranteed not to provide an abundance of material wealth. He would become a cop, and he would devote his life to bringing to justice those who preyed on the innocent. His brother Ray made the same decision, for some of the same reasons.

As supervisor of the Miami-Dade Police Department's Crime Lab, Horatio did fine financially, although the job would never make him rich. But through the years, first in New York as a beat cop and then a detective, then in Miami, where he began in homicide, switched to the bomb squad, and finally moved to the crime lab, he had put away plenty of bad guys. He suspected that his mother would have been pleased with his midstream course correction.

These things crossed his mind as he drove the MacArthur Causeway to Hibiscus Island. One of three small, exclusive islands north of the Causeway in Biscayne Bay, which had provided homes over the years to a variety of celebrities including Gloria Estefan, Damon Runyon, and Al Capone, Hibiscus was where golfer Sidney Greenfield had chosen to spend his real estate dollars, and where Horatio had to go to tell Sidney that his wife had been killed.

The only more difficult task was when he had

to inform someone of a child's death. People who killed or abused children were the lowest of the low, and sometimes Horatio could barely stand to look at them.

He had never fathered a child, so he didn't have the same terrible, personal experience with it that he did the murder of a wife. That, he had felt, and not so long ago. He had suffered intensely and he had mourned. He was trying to get past it, to move on, but he still felt her loss every day.

The best he'd be able to tell Sidney Greenfield was that he had survived it, and Sidney would too.

But survival would not be easy. It never was.

This would be Horatio's second notification of the day—first a son, now a wife—and thinking about that made Horatio feel very weary indeed.

Weary, but determined.

Sidney Greenfield's home was a sprawling Tuscan villa-style mansion that backed up against the bay. The front yard, if that term could be applied to such a vast tract of land, was green and rolling, and a couple of short practice holes had been carved from one section. Tall palms swayed and the leaves of spreading oaks rustled in a welcome breeze that snapped the flags of the golf greens' pins. The house itself was ocher with red tile roofs; contrasted with the green grass and the blue sky and water, it was a picture that might have made a home-and-garden magazine editor weep with joy.

Maybe it had been a pleasant place earlier in the

day, but it didn't look that way to Horatio now. Now it was just one more dead victim's former home.

He parked the Hummer on a sweeping paved driveway, removed his sunglasses, and tucked them into his shirt. Before he made it to the massive carved front door, a man came around from the side of the house with a big pair of garden shears in his hands. *A gardener,* Horatio thought for a moment, but then he recognized the seemingly casual saunter that nonetheless quickly ate up the yards of a golf course, the trim physique, the way a ball cap fit snugly onto a head that seemed just a little too big for its body. Sidney Greenfield in the flesh, and doing his own yard work.

Horatio waited at the foot of the front steps, hands on his hips, as Sidney approached. When he came nearer Horatio was able to make out short, straw-colored hair, deeply tanned skin, and a winning smile that had graced magazine covers and sports reports for years.

"Mister Greenfield," he said as the golfer approached. "I'm Lieutenant Horatio Caine of the Miami-Dade Crime Lab."

Those words stopped Sidney in his tracks as surely as if Horatio had smacked him with a mallet. The smile faded. "Yes . . . ?"

"I'm very sorry to inform you that your wife has been killed, Mister Greenfield."

The shears fell from the golfer's gloved hands, clattering onto the driveway. His face seemed to lose all structural integrity; lips quivering, jaw going slack, eyes filling with tears. His shoulders slumped, and in the space of seconds he seemed to have aged twenty years. "Wendy?" he asked. "But she . . . I just saw her . . ."

"When did you see her last, Mister Greenfield? It might help us."

"Around ten, I guess. Ten-thirty. She was going shopping."

With two shotguns in the trunk, Horatio thought. *Interesting shopping trip.*

"Do you know who she planned to go shopping with?"

Sidney shook his head. "She has plenty of friends who like to go out with her. I think she buys things for them, you know. She's very generous with her money, and—"

"Her money?"

"Our money, whatever. I don't mind. She grew up with nothing, and if she wants to share with friends who haven't been as fortunate as we have, that's not a problem at all."

"That's very admirable," Horatio said. "It would be helpful if I could get a list of those friends."

Sidney looked away from Horatio, blinking back his sorrow, then turned his head back. He seemed to have become a different person, angry and defensive, scowling at Horatio. "How do you know it's her? Are you sure? If you've made some kind of mistake, I'll have your badge, buddy."

"I'd like you to identify her, Mister Greenfield, if you can. But she's a fairly public figure, and we know what she looks like. We've got her purse and her identification, and she was found in a Mitsubishi Eclipse that is registered to her. We're certain that your wife is the victim."

"I just don't see how it's possible."

"Like I said, if you'd like to come in and see her, that would help us too."

"I . . . I'll try to fit it into my schedule."

Horatio couldn't think of many activities more important than making a positive identification of a dead wife's remains, but he understood that Sidney was still processing the news, in shock and off balance. "Just let me know," he said. "About her friends?"

"I . . . I can probably put something together." Sidney sniffed, ran the back of his leather glove across his nose. He might have been two different people, one shocked and saddened, the other furious at the messenger who had brought him the news.

"Do you know of anyone who might want to hurt her, Mister Greenfield? Or to hurt you, through her?"

"I play golf," Sidney said. "It's a good living, but it's not the kind of thing that attracts mortal enemies. Rivals, sure, but they want to slaughter me on the course, not for real."

"The gentleman's game."

"It used to be. I think it still is in a lot of ways. I mean, you don't see professional golfers going into the crowd and beating up on fans, or arrested for carrying guns at nightclubs, beating up spouses, all of that. Maybe we're too middle class, or too bland, or something, but we just don't tend to be a violent bunch."

There didn't seem to be anything middle class about the way Sidney Greenfield lived, but Horatio decided not to press him on that point. The man's eyes were filling up again, tears running down his cheeks, and he kept balling his hands into fists, then relaxing them, like he wanted to hit something but didn't know what or even why.

"What happened to Wendy?" he asked after a minute. "Did she suffer much?"

"I'm told that it was very quick," Horatio said. "She probably didn't feel anything at all." A white lie, but a justifiable one. She no doubt felt outright terror from the time the carjacker first entered her vehicle, and even more when he moved to cut her throat. The actual moment of her death, though, was probably painless—shock would have dulled the physical sensation of the knife's blade, and she would have died before it wore off.

"Do you have her killer?"

"Not yet, sir. But we will."

"I guess not, or you wouldn't be asking me about enemies." Sidney's voice quavered as he spoke, despite his efforts to hold himself together.

Horatio wanted to get away, to let the man begin to grieve in peace.

He took his business card from his pocket and stepped forward, offering it. "Mister Greenfield, I'm very sorry for your loss. Believe me when I tell you that I know exactly how you feel. I've been through it myself. If you need anything from me, or if you just need to talk, you can reach me at the numbers on this card."

Sidney took the card and pocketed it without looking at it. Horatio could have handed him a 1962 Roger Maris baseball card, for all the attention he paid it.

That's okay, Horatio thought. *When he needs it, he'll have it.*

He had a feeling Sidney would be needing it soon. His grief seemed absolutely genuine, as did his surprise.

Horatio filed that away in his mental evidence locker. You always had to look at the spouse when a married person was murdered. However solid a marriage seemed from the outside, there were interior stresses that could fracture it with little warning and few visible signs.

In this case—unless Sidney Greenfield was a hell of an actor in addition to being a tremendous golfer—the husband was taken completely off guard. Horatio believed that he had not killed his wife, or arranged for her death, and he had truly expected her to come home from her expedition with an armload of shopping bags.

As he drove away, Horatio knew that Sidney would keep expecting her to show up any time, and that it would be a long while before he truly accepted the fact that she would never pass through their front door again. He knew that from hard experience, and the memory of that sensation made his gut churn.

He also knew that the only thing he could do to quiet his gut was to find whoever had killed Wendy Greenfield—and Silvio Castaneda, the day's other victim—and bring the law's full wrath down on them.

Marisol would have wanted nothing less.

8

WHOEVER HAD FIRST established how much paperwork police departments had to generate had been
a bureaucrat or possibly a lawyer, Horatio speculated, but not a cop.

He understood the reasoning behind it. To get
convictions meant keeping precise, accurate records of every aspect of an investigation. Defense
attorneys would—rightfully—attack any gaps or
shortcomings in those records. And as supervisor
of the lab, Horatio had to read everybody else's
reports in addition to generating his own, to make
sure he had all the bits and pieces of every case
straight. The CSI team was like his family, and as
head of the household he had the ultimate responsibility for everyone else's work.

But handling all those records meant spending
hours in his office that might otherwise have been

spent out on the street, actually solving crimes instead of merely documenting them. Tonight he sat at his desk working through what seemed like hundreds of sheets of paper. He was lost in them when a knock on his door brought him back into the world.

"Horatio?"

He looked up and saw Alexx standing in his doorway, tentative, her fingers clutching the jamb. They'd known each other for a long time and she was comfortable with him, but she didn't like to interrupt when he was involved in a task. "Yes, Alexx?" He smiled and waved her toward a guest chair. "You're working late."

"So are you," she replied, remaining standing. "I just wanted to let you know that I'm finished with the post on Wendy Greenfield."

"Any surprises? The COD looked pretty straightforward on that one."

"Her cause of death was the slit throat, no question about that. But there was still a surprise, at least to me."

"What's that?"

"Well, her tox screen came back clear. She's a clean-living woman. She hasn't always been—her liver was not in the best shape, for one thing. But there were no signs of *recent* drug abuse or excessive alcohol use. The big surprise was in her hCG beta test."

Horatio knew she meant human chorionic gonadotropin, or hCG, a peptide hormone produced in pregnancy to maintain progesterone production. It was the hormone that home pregnancy tests checked for. "She was pregnant?"

"That's right. Somewhere just over twelve or thirteen weeks, I'd say. Her husband didn't tell you that?" He caught a faint accusatory tone in her voice, as if she thought he'd been holding out on her.

"No, Alexx, he didn't. Which means," he said, "that Sidney Greenfield was not as forthcoming as I thought. He definitely seemed surprised, but not too surprised to remember something that significant."

"Pregnancy doesn't seem like something that would slip your mind," Alexx said.

"No, it doesn't. It's not impossible, of course. People in shock can forget their own names."

"You're going to have another talk with him, I take it?"

"Yes, I am. I think I'll let it wait until tomorrow, though. If he did keep her pregnancy a secret on purpose, then he's guilty of something, and I want to let him stew in it overnight. If he didn't, if he just forgot to say anything because of the shock, then I don't want to bother him a second time today. I don't think he's much of a flight risk."

"Celebrities seldom are," Alexx agreed. "They have the money, but they're too easily recognized."

"That's what I was thinking. Thank you, Alexx,

for the report. That definitely puts a different light on things. That's good work."

"I'm going home to my kids, Horatio," she said. "You should get out of here too."

Alexx had two children, a husband, and a nice house in Coral Gables. Horatio didn't have kids or a wife. But he understood the necessity of having a life away from the lab, even though he sometimes wished he didn't. "I will, Alexx. Thanks."

She left his office and he returned to his paperwork, his mind turning over the news she had brought him. A couple of minutes later, he heard the distinct *click click* of a woman walking in the hall and thought it was Alexx returning for something else.

But it wasn't. Instead, Calleigh Duquesne poked her head in. "Horatio, you're burning the midnight oil?"

"No rest for the wicked," he said with a grin. "You have anything going on tonight, Calleigh?"

"As a matter of fact, I do. Do you remember Nina Cullen?"

"I do indeed." When Calleigh spoke the name, Horatio pictured a slender thirteen-year-old girl with long brown braids and a shy smile that, when it reached full radiance, could illuminate the darkest Florida night. Nina Cullen had been targeted for death because she had witnessed a double homicide, and when it turned out that one of the people after her was her own estranged father, the case had turned even more personal for Horatio. Calleigh had taken a deep interest in the girl too, and Nina had spent a few nights in protective custody at Calleigh's condo. Calleigh had eventually been able to identify bolt cutters Nina's father had used to cut a padlock on the gate to Nina's backyard, in a final attempt against her life. Horatio had found the bolt cutters locked inside the man's residence, where no one else had access to them. With her father's fingerprints all over them, and Calleigh's definitive tool-mark evidence, they had been able to force a confession from the man. Nina and her mother had moved to the Midwest, but Calleigh and Horatio still heard from her now and again.

"She's coming into town tonight for a couple of days," Calleigh said. "I'm going to pick her up at the airport."

"Just her?" Horatio asked. "Her mother's not coming with her?"

"Horatio, she's nineteen now. She's going to Northwestern. And majoring in forensic science, I'm happy to say."

"What's the occasion for this trip?"

Calleigh's expression softened, the smile fading. "Actually, Nina's pregnant. Her mom asked if I would spend some time with her, try to impress upon her how difficult it is to be a single working-woman, even without a child. I told her that I'd be at work most of the time—workingwoman, right?—but that Nina could stay with me and we could be together whenever I wasn't on duty. Her mom thought that would be fine, that the more I was gone the more it would drive home her point."

"She doesn't want Nina to carry the child to term?" Horatio asked.

"Either that, or to put it up for adoption right away. She kind of has a point—nineteen is very young, and Nina's got years of school ahead of her if she wants to be a criminalist."

Horatio had long wanted children of his own, most recently with Marisol Delko. Although Marisol's cancer had been in remission when they married, the disease would have made childbirth difficult and risky. They were both willing to try, but her murder had made it impossible. "That's true, Calleigh. On the other hand, she might never have another chance. Life is unpredictable, isn't it?"

"I suppose it is. I don't know that I'm comfortable making her mom's case for her, but I'm happy to have Nina visit anyway. I just wish she could stay longer."

"I hope she'll come around the lab."

"I'm sure she'll want to do that first thing. Maybe not first thing tonight—you should go home, after all, and I don't think she knows anyone on the night shift. But at her first opportunity."

"I'll look forward to seeing her," Horatio said. He meant it—he bonded easily with children, appreciating their unshielded forthrightness and often little-noticed courage. And those bonds, he had found, tended to hold up remarkably well over the years.

Calleigh left, and he returned once again to his paperwork, wanting to get through one more stack before he went home to a late dinner and bed.

Calleigh loved her work, but there were times when it began to feel all-consuming and she had to back away from it. It was too easy to dwell on the job constantly, to wake up thinking about a case from the day before and to drift off to sleep running through the day's events in her mind. She knew that wasn't healthy. A person needed other interests, something to occupy her attention besides weapons and blood spatter and tox reports.

In her case, family offered only so much relief. Her parents had divorced more than a decade ago, and she had to make an effort not to be drawn into taking sides, but to provide both her mother and her father with a neutral listener. Her father's drinking problem exacerbated that situation, and while she loved him dearly, spending time with him was often more draining than satisfying. She could talk to her brothers, and sometimes went to a target range with one or another of them—but there again, she wound up with a firearm in her hands. She had been drawn to law enforcement, and specifically forensic science, because of her long interest in guns, but guns as a hobby had to be kept separate from her working life. She dated— usually men in law enforcement, as it happened— she went out, she read glossy *Ocean Drive* magazine in addition to professional journals and popular gun magazines, and she had a rarely discussed addiction to Southern writers, from Eudora Welty and Thomas Wolfe to Pat Conroy and Anne Rivers Siddons.

But anything that promised a more complete distraction from the job, like the imminent arrival of Nina Cullen (in spite of the fact that she had met Nina on a case, that had been long ago and years of letters, holiday cards, emails and phone calls had built enough of a bond separate from that first meeting that she didn't consider Nina a work-related friend), was more than welcome.

Calleigh reached Miami International a little after eight, about twenty-five minutes early for Nina's flight. She browsed one of the gift shops, bought a paperback novel by the always-delightful Fannie Flagg, then sat down on a bench to read and wait.

When the display board showed that Nina's flight had landed, she put the receipt into the book as a bookmark, tucked it into her purse, and stood up, waiting with a throng of others for the passengers to make their way from the gate toward baggage claim and ground transportation. She always got a kick out of watching people at airports, and did so now, enjoying a family with young children in pajamas, stifling yawns while they angled for the first glimpse of Grandma, a young man laden with flowers and balloons for an arriving girlfriend, and a pair of proud parents waiting anxiously for a son or daughter in uniform.

Halfway through the flood of passengers from the Chicago flight, Calleigh spotted Nina. She wore a coat far too heavy for Miami weather, but it had been cold in the Midwest for the last several days, the advance of spring notwithstanding. Taller than Calleigh since her fifteenth year, Nina wore jeans, a snug sweater, and sneakers, and she strode down the ramp with a confident spring in her step. Her slender face was framed by brown hair in a pixie cut, and it went from solemn and a little sleepy to vibrant and joyful when she saw Calleigh wave.

Nina broke into a jog, shouldering past other passengers, and threw her arms around Calleigh. Her canvas messenger bag swung from her shoulder and bumped into Calleigh's hip, with enough force that it might have been packed full of rocks. A light, vaguely aquatic perfume wafted from her. "Calleigh!" she shrieked. "It's so great to see you!"

"Welcome back to Miami," Calleigh said. "You look great, Nina."

"So do you! Look at you, girlfriend! You are so beautiful!"

Calleigh felt a blush wash over her cheeks. "I love your haircut," she said. The last time she had seen Nina, the girl's hair had fallen most of the way down her back, and she'd still been a gangly, awkward high school student. She had, in the interim, become a woman, and the changes in her, from posture to self-confidence, were remarkable. "How was the flight? Are you hungry?"

"I could eat something," Nina admitted. "Unless Miami rolls up its sidewalks early these days."

"If that ever happens, it'll be a sure sign of the apocalypse," Calleigh said. "Come on. I bet you haven't had any decent Southern food since the last time you were here."

"Not unless you count pizza from south Chicago."

"I don't. Let's get your luggage and go." She hadn't counted on dinner, but she realized she should have; airplane food was nothing to rave about these days. It would make for a later night than she had anticipated, but she had plenty of late nights. At least this one wouldn't involve any dead bodies.

There would, she was sure, be plenty of those to deal with tomorrow.

9

THE DAY WAS FINE, the sun a huge golden ball in a blue sky that warmed the earth to perfect picnic temperature, and Horatio and Marisol took advantage of the opportunity to get out of town. They ate on a blanket spread out on a grassy, gentle slope that angled down toward a swiftly flowing river. On the river's far side, sunlight spiked down through the branches of a dense orange grove, the trees arranged in careful rows.

Their food was Cuban, spicy and rich, and they ate their fill of it before turning their attentions to each other. Marisol tucked plates and utensils and serving containers back into the big picnic basket she had brought, because an unexpected breeze was blowing up out of the east, off the unseen ocean. When everything was put away and the breeze tugged at the edges of the blanket and at their clothing, they undressed and made love where they had so recently eaten, their bodies fitting together perfectly, puzzle pieces that were always meant to be joined as one.

Afterward they lingered, enjoying the sun on their flesh, until Marisol announced that she had to be going. Horatio tried to protest, but she insisted, dressing quickly. She was starting to put on a hat Horatio didn't remember having seen before, straw with a wide brim and a patterned sash around the crown, when the wind snatched it from her hands and sailed it out over the water.

Horatio was tugging on his own clothes, although they seemed to fight him, his feet catching in his pants, shirt buttons refusing to cooperate, when Marisol waded into the river after the hat. She said something to him that he couldn't hear, her words snatched away by the increasingly furious wind, and he started toward her, wrestling with the last of his buttons. He was almost to the riverbank when the water suddenly became a whirlpool, raging around her, drawing her down, down . . .

The ringing of his bedside phone was a relief. Horatio sat upright in his bed, sweat running off him in sheets, and grabbed the receiver. "Horatio Caine," he said. The digital clock by his bed read 4:11.

"Horatio, it's Frank." Frank Tripp. Horatio would have known that accent anywhere. "There's been an explosion. A doctor's house in the Grove."

Horatio was instantly alert, his bad dream fading under the weight of someone else's real-life tragedy. "Victims?"

"At least a couple, but it's still hot and we haven't really been able to get inside yet for any extended searches. Doctor Greggs lives there with his wife and seven-year-old daughter."

Horatio remembered the FBI agent who Frank had introduced him to. "Frank, does this look like the work of that bomber Special Agent Asher is after? The Baby Boomer?"

"I don't see how. This doctor has never performed an abortion in his life, and he doesn't work at a clinic that performs them. He's a neurologist, with neurosurgical credentials at Dade Memorial. Or he was—I'm pretty sure he's one of the crispy corpses inside."

"A brain surgeon? Frank, preserve the scene. I'm on my way."

Doctor Marc Greggs and his family lived on Devon Road, just a couple of blocks inland from the mission-style, coral-rock Plymouth Congregational Church. Coconut Grove had been the first European settlement in south Florida, and the residents liked to try to preserve elements of that past. The church dated to 1917, which for Miami was ancient. Coconut Grove had tried to remain independent of Miami, but the growing metropolis had annexed it in 1925. Ever since, dwellers in the

Grove had subtly—and sometimes not so subtly—resented the big city and worked to maintain the ambiance of their small, historic neighborhood.

The Greggs place had been no different. It had been built of wood and stone and surrounded by a jungle's worth of native plants.

That was before a massive explosion, and the resulting fire, turned it into charred, twisted wreckage.

Horatio had called his team from the road, hesitant to wake them after a busy day but knowing he would need all hands on deck to process the scene. When he reached Devon Road, it was easy to see where the Greggs house was, marked by bomb squad vans, fire trucks, radio cars, ambulances, press, and other vehicles jamming the street. He parked two blocks from the house, almost in front of the old church, and hustled to the scene. Calleigh and Eric had arrived before him.

Calleigh saw him coming and met him as he approached. "Horatio, it's pretty bad here."

"I can see that, Calleigh. Who's in charge?" No CSIs were allowed onto a bombing scene until it had been cleared by the bomb squad. The officer who ran the scene for that squad was called the bomb-scene manager, a position Horatio had held many times during his years on the squad. Only when the scene manager had determined to his satisfaction that no more explosives were hidden inside would anyone else be let in.

"Jorge Ortiz."

"He's a good man." With a practiced eye, Horatio scanned the perimeter Ortiz had set. Ortiz would have determined where the probable seat of detonation was, measured how far debris was thrown from there, then set the perimeter line to enclose a space half again as large.

In the brilliant glow of floodlights set up on stanchions and powered by noisy generators, Horatio could get a sense of the damage. The front wall of the house was almost completely demolished, including what appeared, from the glass strewn everywhere, to be many large windows. It looked like the wall had been peeled away, as if someone had been making a doll's house with one wall missing so a child could reach inside. The second floor of the two-story house sagged precariously where a supporting pillar had been blown out from beneath it, and most of the upstairs furnishings, at least from the rooms Horatio could see, had tumbled down onto the ground floor. Timbers and stones had been hurled into the street, and the front yard, with its thick growth, looked like a madman's storage area for used building materials.

"This was quite a blast, wasn't it?" he asked, mostly of himself.

"It looks that way." Calleigh had pulled herself together well for the middle of the night, dressing in typical business attire—a blue suit with a striped, V-neck blouse and high-heeled shoes, but she still looked sleepy. She had probably stayed up late catching up with Nina, not expecting a call-out at four-thirty. "Not that I have anywhere near your experience with such things."

He ignored the comment. "How's Nina?"

"She seems good. A little anxious, maybe, but you know."

"That's to be expected." They kept walking, and in a moment reached the tape line, where a uniformed officer handed Horatio a clipboard with the sign-in sheet. He signed it and passed beneath the tape, joining Eric and Frank on the other side. The smells of burned wood and plastic and wire and flesh were everywhere, inescapable.

"Sorry to roust you," Frank said when he saw Horatio.

"Is there any news on Doctor Greggs and his family, Frank?"

"Not yet. Bomb squad guys say there are bodies inside, but no one's been able to ID 'em."

"How much longer?"

"Fire was controlled in a hurry, so that's not a concern. Last time I talked to Jorge he seemed to think they were almost done. Can't be too much longer now."

"All right," Horatio said. He looked down the street and saw a lone figure approaching the perimeter with a crime scene kit in his hand. "And here comes Mister Wolfe. The gang's all here."

By the time Ryan reached the others, Jorge Ortiz

had emerged from the wreckage of the house, walking awkwardly in his heavy protective suit. He took off his helmet, wiped sweat from his brow, and showed Horatio a grim smile. He wore a thick handlebar mustache, and his eyes were gray and clear. "Horatio," he said. "Place is clear."

"Thank you, Jorge. Anything we should know?"

"Just be careful. Fire didn't spread far, but it's hot. Stairs are about gone, and it's pretty dicey in there."

"Okay. What about the Greggs family?"

"No one came out of that house after the explosion," Ortiz said. "I saw some DBs, but I don't know who's who."

"That, Jorge," Horatio said, "is something that we'll find out."

Horatio went in first.

Even though Jorge Ortiz had given the all-clear, he didn't trust bomb scenes or bombers. His time on the bomb squad had taught him more than he had ever hoped to know about what explosions and fire could do to the human body—not to mention what he had learned about the powerful, twisted forces that drove those who set the bombs. One thing bombers liked to do was to set explosive devices in series, so that the people investigating the first blast would be threatened by another one. Charlie Berringer, a former bomb squad compatriot who had turned bomber and who killed Horatio's squad mentor Al Humphreys, had used that technique.

Horatio didn't have any special sixth sense that would let him smell a device that the squad had missed, and the equipment he could use was the same the squad had no doubt already employed. All he had was an unformed hope that if someone was watching the scene (and arsonists and bombers were among the most likely people to do so—they notoriously loved standing among the onlookers at their own crime scenes), he would detonate the second one while Horatio was alone in the house, sparing those who worked for him. He thought of his team as his family, and losing members, as he had lost Tim Speedle, was a loss that was too painful to even think about.

The floor creaked under his weight. Inside—despite the fact that the wall had been opened up like a sardine can lid—the bitter odor was worse, stronger, intensified by the water the fire department had used to quench the fire. He could taste wet burned wood, as if he'd taken a big bite of ash. Using water to put out the fire would make the collection of evidence even more difficult. He was walking through a thick soup of ash and debris, in which vital clues could be floating away from their points of origin at every second.

The power of the blast was even more evident in here than it had been outside. A copper pipe that had obviously run straight down from the second floor through an interior wall had been bent at an almost ninety-degree angle, and the end that had been sheared off had penetrated a dense wooden beam. Everything in the house that hadn't been thrown clear or splintered had been bent away from the seat of detonation by the explosion's shock wave: aluminum window frames, a light fixture suspended from the ceiling, even a brick fireplace.

Outside the house, Ryan had started taking pictures. Horatio took a deep breath, figured the place was as safe as it was likely to be, and waved his team inside.

"We do a full walk-through first," he said when they joined him. "We're looking for any obvious evidence. Fragments of the bomb casing, parts of the timer—I think we have to assume at this point that it was a timed device, or remotely detonated, and not set off from inside the house. Ryan, keep that camera handy."

Ryan hadn't stopped taking pictures; capturing every foot of the scene would be critical later. "You bet, H."

"Watch your step, everyone," Horatio added. "It's hard to see through the muck, and we don't want to break anything."

They lined up and walked slowly, not raising their feet up out of the layer of soup on the floor. Their shoes would never survive. They had to cover every inch of the ground floor, which was where the device had gone off—apparently against the wall that separated the living room from the kitchen. The living room faced toward the street, which was why the blast had mostly affected the front of the house. Every few steps, one of them would call a halt and would bag some bit of plastic or metal—in one case a spring, in another a piece of a circuit board—that might have been part of the bomb.

Or part of a home computer or a microwave oven. They couldn't know until they got it all back to the lab and studied it more closely.

They found the first body beside what remained of the wooden interior staircase. It was badly charred, its skin blackened, features vague, as if melted off, beneath the char, but it appeared to be an adult. Its hair was gone. Horatio guessed male but he couldn't be certain. The body was drawn into a tight fetal position, legs and arms flexed, fists up under the chin. "Classic pugilistic position," Calleigh said.

"That's right, Calleigh," Horatio agreed. "Indicating extreme heat. Fire dehydrated the muscles, causing them to contract and leaving the victim looking like he or she is curled up in pain."

"Or ready for a boxing match," Eric added.

Horatio looked at the staircase. Bodies could have fallen from upstairs through the hole blown in the bedroom floor over the living room, but not this one. This person had tried to get to the stairs, possibly to escape. Or maybe this person had heard something downstairs and was going to investigate when the blast went off, knocking him down the stairs, and he landed where the fire could sweep over him. "Definitely ready for a fight," Horatio said.

"Severe alligatoring of the wood, too," Ryan pointed out. He indicated the scaled, alligator-skin-like appearance of the burned staircase wood, where it had taken on a checkered aspect from the heat. "Do you think an accelerant was used in addition to the blast?"

"We'll have to find that out, won't we?" Horatio said. He kept moving, and the others joined him.

"This wasn't a homemade explosive, was it?" Ryan asked when they had completed the initial sweep.

"That depends on what kind of home you come from, I suppose," Horatio said. "But it wasn't a Molotov cocktail or gunpowder or a fertilizer and gasoline bomb, no. Not something that could be brewed up in your average kitchen. We'll have to do some tests, but it looks like high explosives to me."

He set the other members of the team to work scooping debris out of the muck and into small piles, to determine if any bits of evidence had been missed the first time through. He went to the seat of the blast, which was where any traces of the explosive were most likely to be found. Although the jagged bits of casing had already been picked up, he thought the explosive device had probably been put on the floor, hidden behind a piece of furniture, a chair or table. Something big enough to disguise its presence but not so big that it would interfere with the blast. Splintered wood backed up his theory, but there wasn't enough of it left to determine what the wood might have once been part of.

In a relatively clean spot, he opened his crime scene kit and took out his spot-test kit, a stainless steel box about the size of a small cosmetics case. He opened it to reveal three bottles of reagent, a UV lamp and charger, and the necessary supplies and utensils: test tubes, plastic bags, and the like.

Picking what seemed a likely section of the scorched, cratered floor close to where the blast had destroyed what the bomb had been sitting on, Horatio turned on the UV light. He swiped a sheet of filter paper against the floor, then blew off the excess dust. There were circles marked on the filter paper. Setting the filter paper down on a paper towel, he took out the first bottle of reagent. With a dropper, he put a drop of the first reagent in one of the circles and waited. The fluid spread throughout the circle and a little over its borders, but the paper didn't change color. That ruled out TNT as the explosive, which would have shown purple or black under the UV. A drop from the second bottle went into another circle. This one might not react as immediately, so he went ahead with the third bottle.

As a control, while those drops dried a little, he repeated the process on another sheet of filter paper, which had not been wiped on the floor.

When he finished that, he checked the first sheet again. The third circle remained blank, but the second one showed blue-black.

"Interesting," he said aloud, but mostly to himself.

"What'd you get, H?" Eric asked from across the room.

"Reagent B reacts."

"Which means RDX or HMX," a new voice said. "The Baby Boomer always uses C-4."

Horatio looked up to see Special Agent Wendell Asher walking toward him, taking care not to contaminate the scene. "And C-4 contains RDX, so we have a possible match," Horatio said. "We'll get some samples back to the lab and use gas chromatography/ mass spectrometry to find out for sure if it's C-4."

"Sounds good," Asher said. "What else have you got so far?"

Horatio described what they had found, which admittedly wasn't much. As he spoke, Asher nodded and interjected a few questions. When Horatio finished, Asher said, "Sure sounds like our guy. Using a timed device, using C-4, timing it to detonate in a home while the victims are asleep—those are all part of his signature."

"Excuse me, Horatio," Calleigh said. "We're going to take a look upstairs."

"Just be very careful, Calleigh. The staircase and floors are treacherous."

"Will do."

Horatio turned his attention back to the FBI agent. "I don't know much about your suspect, Special Agent Asher. But I know evidence, and we'll find whatever's here. You'll get our full report when it's ready. For now, I'd appreciate it if you stayed out of my crime scene, all right?"

Asher raised his hands defensively and showed an awkward grin. "Absolutely, Lieutenant Caine. No problem at all. I'm around if you need me, but otherwise I'm the invisible man. Okay?"

"That, sir, will be perfect. Are you working on the hotels and motels and car rental agencies? It would be good if we can find this guy before he strikes again."

"Working on it, Lieutenant. In fact, I've got some places to check out right now."

Horatio watched as the agent backed away, then turned and walked out along the same path he had taken in. Horatio didn't have much use for FBI agents in general, but at least this guy seemed to know what he was doing. He just didn't like anyone on his scenes except his own people, when possible, to reduce the possibility of anyone compromising evidence.

"H!" Eric called from the staircase. Horatio was sealing the filter papers into bags to preserve them, but he looked up at the sound of Eric's voice.

"We've got two bodies upstairs. One of them's a child. We've cleared all the rooms, so we're looking at three vics total."

"Thanks, Eric." The victims were probably Marc Greggs, his wife, and their daughter, but their identities would have to be confirmed at the lab.

Horatio called over the EMTs and told them where the bodies could be found. "Take care with them," he said. "And be sure they're all thoroughly fluoroscoped. There might be bomb fragments inside them, and we'll need those."

As the EMTs went to work, a wave of sadness washed over Horatio, especially for the child. Whatever her parents may or may not have done to attract the attention of a murderer, certainly she had been uninvolved.

That was the trouble with bombers and arsonists, though. Of every breed of killer, they were the least concerned about collateral damage. They didn't care who was murdered in their attempts to sow destruction and fear.

Horatio cared, though. He was more determined than ever to get this guy, and to get him soon.

10

AT MIDMORNING, while the rest of the crew finished at the Greggs house or hauled evidence back to the lab for closer examination, Horatio and Calleigh drove out to Hibiscus Island to visit Sidney Greenfield again. The day had turned warm, although not as hot as yesterday, the humidity moderate. A few puffy white clouds added interest to the azure sky. It was the kind of day that made tourists start poring through real estate ads and reminded locals of why they had never left.

The Greenfield estate hadn't changed overnight. Horatio thought that maybe it should have, that there should be some physical manifestation of grief that would display itself at the houses of the dead.

The only difference was that this time, Sidney wasn't working in the yard. When Horatio rang the doorbell, they had to wait a long time before the golfer answered the door. He was dressed in jeans and a blue T-shirt, his sandy hair uncombed, face unshaven. He had clearly not slept well, if at all. Horatio thought he might have been drinking, too, but his breath smelled like mouthwash, not booze.

"Caine, isn't it?"

"That's right, Mister Greenfield. And this is Calleigh Duquesne from the crime lab. May we come in for a minute?"

Sidney gave a desultory nod and beckoned them into a grand foyer, floored in Italian marble, with a few pieces of fine antique furniture. A tiny painting on the wall, in an ornate gold frame, looked like an original Rembrandt. Golf had done very well for Sidney Greenfield. "You find out anything more about Wendy?" he asked. "I still can't really get my mind around the fact that she's gone. I'd like to think all those taxes I pay are being put to some useful purpose."

"There is one thing, Mister Greenfield," Horatio said, ignoring the jibe. "You didn't mention to me yesterday that your wife was pregnant, did you?"

"Of course, I—" He froze, staring wide-eyed at Horatio. "What are you talking about?"

"Wendy was pregnant, Mister Greenfield," Calleigh said gently. "Our medical examiner confirmed it. I'm very sorry."

"But she never . . . I would have . . . " Sidney stammered. He couldn't find his way through a sentence, apparently unsure of where he wanted to end up.

"Maybe she was waiting for a special occasion to tell you," Horatio suggested. "According to the ME's findings, she was less than fifteen weeks along."

Sidney nodded, but all the life seemed to have been sucked out of him by the news. He appeared to have visibly shrunk, deflated, in the space of two minutes. "Maybe that's it. She wanted to make sure there wouldn't be any complications. I think I told you before, Caine, she's had a pretty tough life. Happiness never came easily to Wendy. Neither did trust. She was probably waiting until she was absolutely sure nothing would go wrong before she said anything."

"You did mention that, Mister Greenfield. Once again, we're very sorry for your loss."

"Thank you," Sidney said. "By the way, the Masters is coming up in Augusta soon, and—"

"You may not be wearing that green blazer this year, sir," Horatio interrupted. "I don't want you leaving Miami just now."

"But—"

"That's not a request, Mister Greenfield."

He and Calleigh left the man alone. When they were in the Hummer, Calleigh turned to Horatio. "He seemed genuinely surprised by the news."

"Yes, he did, Calleigh," Horatio said. "Which is a little bit of a surprise itself, isn't it?"

*   *   *

"I have some video to show you, H," Ryan Wolfe said when Horatio and Calleigh made it back to the lab. "Cooper was able to enhance that lousy convenience store video pretty well."

"Dan's a genius at that sort of thing," Calleigh said.

"Whatever he did, it sure worked this time."

"I'm going to get to work on the bombing scene materials," Calleigh said. "You men have a good time watching your movies."

"We'll try not to let the smell of popcorn bother you," Ryan teased.

Horatio followed Ryan into the A/V lab. The lights were dim, so that whatever Dan put on the monitors would show up better. It didn't smell at all like popcorn, but like most of the crime lab—with the notable exception of the gun lab—the air had a bland, odorless quality because of the high-tech air filtration system running at full power all the time.

"Time for some show-and-tell?" Cooper asked.

"That's what Mister Wolfe says. What do you have for me?"

"I don't know if you saw the tape originally," Cooper said. "But it was pretty weak. Grainy, bad focus, and I think they reuse the same VHS tapes until they literally fall apart. The whole system was probably made in the seventies—I'm just glad it's not Betamax. I was able to digitize the footage and enhance it, though, and this is what I came up with."

He pushed a button on a remote control, and an image flickered to life on one of the monitors. It showed the inside of the Quick Spree, as seen from behind the sales counter. A clerk sat on a stool in the foreground, doing Sudoku puzzles on the counter.

"He's using a pencil," Ryan said with a chuckle.

"You don't?"

"Of course not. That's cheating. Anyway, the graphite gets all over your hands."

"Yes, it does." Horatio kept watching. The front door opened, and a pretty, voluptuous blond woman entered wearing a tight white top and pants. She paused for a second just inside the door, as if letting an imagined audience get a good view of her physique, then sauntered over to the candy section. She stayed there for a minute or so, bending over to peruse the racks, pressing her finger to her chin, finally settling on a pack of gum. When she paid for it she smiled at the clerk as if he were a Hollywood producer and she a desperate starlet. Then she walked back outside.

"That's Wendy Greenfield," Horatio said. "Interesting performance."

"Right," Ryan agreed. "Like she knows she's being observed."

"Body like that, she's probably used to being gawked at," Cooper pointed out.

"That's true. But this is Miami, too. Beautiful women are hardly a rarity here."

"Doesn't mean they aren't appreciated. And that market's a long way from South Beach."

"Also true." There were more models per capita in South Beach than anyplace else in the United States. Sometimes they ventured into other parts of the city, but running into one at a rural Quick Spree was hardly an everyday occurrence.

"Now we pick her up outside," Cooper said. There was a momentary flicker and then the scene changed. A camera over the store's doorway showed the parking lot. Wendy Greenfield went to a white Mitsubishi convertible, opened the driver's-side door, and sat down behind the wheel. She didn't seem in a hurry to go anywhere. She took great pains opening her package of gum, then removing a piece, unwrapping it, and placing it in her mouth. As she chewed, she tossed the wrapper out of the car onto the pavement, where it presumably joined its fellow gum wrappers. The camera was off to her right, though, so it was possible—not at all likely, but possible in the same way that world peace and the Easter Bunny were possible—that an open trash container had moved up right beside her car door after she had closed it.

She kept chewing her gum—mouth open, Horatio could almost hear the smacking despite the lack of audio—for a while, then reached into the car's glove compartment. From there she withdrew a nail file. Still sitting in the driver's seat, she continued chewing while also filing her nails.

"Does this go on for long, Mister Cooper?" Horatio asked.

"About fifteen minutes."

"Fast-forward."

"You don't want to watch the part where she checks her teeth in the rearview? It's Oscar-worthy."

"I'll take your word for it."

Cooper fast-forwarded. He wasn't joking, except about the Oscar. At one point she opened her mouth in front of the mirror, poking and prodding like a dentist doing a self-exam. Eventually she got tired of that and returned to just chewing and staring. Horatio could tell why Sidney had initially been attracted to her—she was a genuinely stunning woman. But on the tape, she came across as vacuous, and he couldn't quite see how she had retained Sidney's interest.

Cooper slowed the footage down to regular speed again. "Here's where it all goes down," Ryan said.

A man walked around the corner and into the frame, his face turned away from the camera. As the witness had told Ryan and Calleigh, he was tall and athletically built, with brown hair curling over his collar. He wore faded jeans and a short-sleeved shirt, darkened down the sides with streaks of sweat, and he walked with a confident swagger that didn't match the downcast angle of his head.

Unless, Horatio thought, *he's just trying to hide his face. Does he already know the camera's there?*

The man walked past the car without seeming to look at it. Then he stopped and turned toward Wendy Greenfield. By now his back was to the camera, and he stood with his bulk blocking its view of her face as well. "That's strange, isn't it?" Horatio asked.

"It's like he had it all paced off ahead of time," Ryan said. "Like he knew exactly what the camera's angle of view was and how to get in front of it."

"Exactly what I was thinking, Ryan."

The man raised his shirt and pulled out something, but there was no way to know if it was a gun, a knife, or something else. He held it in front of him, out of camera range. Wendy's hands remained on the steering wheel. "Mister Cooper," Horatio said. "Could you zoom in on her hands?"

"Her hands? No problem." He froze the action and moved in tight on the hands, which barely showed around the man's body. Zooming in blurred the image, so he punched a few keys and sharpened it. "How's that?"

"That's perfect. Look at those hands, gentlemen. If she was frightened by whatever it is he's showing her, wouldn't she be gripping the wheel more tightly, her knuckles going white?"

"That's what I'd expect to see," Ryan said.

"But they're not, are they?" In fact, she held on to the wheel loosely, hands dangling, as casual as when she had just been chewing gum and staring into space.

"Not at all," Ryan agreed. "We can't see her face, but her body language hasn't changed a bit."

"As if the whole scene were staged," Horatio said. "As if this weren't a real carjacking at all. Let's keep watching, Daniel."

Cooper tapped at the keyboard again and the video reverted to its earlier angle. The guy moved around the car again, still managing to keep his face turned away from the camera. Wendy scooted into the passenger seat and the guy got in behind the wheel, started the car, and backed it out of the parking spot, hiding his face all the while.

"There's something very wrong about this whole thing," Horatio muttered. He had agreed with Calleigh that Sidney Greenfield didn't seem to be acting when they had told him about Wendy's pregnancy. But he had seemed sincere the first time Horatio met him, too.

The more he learned about this case, the more nothing added up. He was going to have to take a closer look at Sidney, and find out more about Wendy any way he could.

Not that he didn't already have enough to do. Police work was like that, though—never really slow, but alternating between ridiculously hectic and slightly more so. This looked as if it would be one of the "slightly more so" weeks.

11

As MUCH AS HORATIO hated the reason the crime lab even existed—he wasn't naïve enough to believe it could ever be done away with, but if for some reason people stopped committing violence against one another, he wouldn't have minded seeking new employment—he liked it when the lab bustled with activity, all of the various analysts and technicians quietly going about their business, white-coated and serious in manner. He enjoyed being surrounded by educated, intelligent people doing what they did best. He liked to walk its halls (slanted, mostly glass-louvered walls creating a sense of motion, an almost underwater sensation that echoed the nearby ocean without literally representing it), checking in on the progress of his people, watching dedicated scientists using their knowledge in pursuit of justice.

He did so now. Calleigh was inside the protected, muffled confines of her firing range, deeply involved in running tests to determine the strength of the explosive materials used at the Greggs house. She had salvaged some objects from the house—a sheet of metal from the side of the oven, a heavy dining room tabletop, and some of the fragments believed to have been part of the bomb's casing, and was pressure-testing those objects to work backward toward learning the *brisance,* or shattering effect, of the explosive materials involved. By pressure testing the objects to find out how much force was needed to cause the dishing exhibited—how much they had been bowed inward—and computing their distance from the seat of detonation, she could get an approximation of the explosive material's shock wave. It wouldn't be definitive, but in court it could back up other findings, building the kind of airtight case Horatio liked to see.

He left her to her work and found Eric Delko and Maxine Valera in the trace lab. They stood close together in their white lab coats, huddled over a printout. "What are we learning?" Horatio asked.

Valera met his gaze, her head bobbing a little, bleached blond hair moving as it did. She was considerably shorter than Eric, and while she usually focused on DNA, she also knew her way around chemistry. "RDX," she said.

"I knew that."

"It's C-4, H," Eric added. "Just like the Baby Boomer uses."

"How much like him?"

Valera fluttered the sheet of paper at him. "We ran GC/MS on the samples from the scene, and compared the results to results from previous bombings attributed to the Baby Boomer, according to the Bureau's records," she explained. "Ninety-one percent cyclotrimethylene-trinitramine, a little more than five percent polyisobutylene as a binder, and di(2-ethylhexyl) sebacate, as a plasticizer to make it malleable. No taggants, which are—"

"Chemical markers used to make the material identifiable," Horatio said.

Valera smiled awkwardly. "—something you already know all about."

"I do," Horatio said. "But I'm interested in the rest of it, especially the match to the Baby Boomer's previous devices."

"It's a perfect match," Eric said. "Either it's the same stuff, or it's at least from the same original source."

"And that source is?"

"Not domestic," Eric said. "Maybe Russia, maybe Iran, maybe one of the former Soviet bloc countries. We just don't know. But it's not from our stockpiles, or there would be a taggant."

"Which could mean that we're dealing with a foreign national, couldn't it?" Horatio suggested. "A terrorist."

"He's definitely a terrorist," Eric agreed. "If you define a terrorist as someone who uses violent acts to send a political or social message. But based on the targets he's chosen so far, he sounds more like the homegrown variety."

"Yes, he does," Horatio said. "But since the C-4 isn't domestic, we can't rule out a foreigner."

"Can't rule much out yet," Eric said.

"But we'll keep at it. Thanks, folks," Horatio said. "Keep trying to pin down the source of that C-4. We find out where it came from, we'll have a better idea of who's using it."

"Got it, boss," Valera said.

In another part of the lab he came across Natalia Boa Vista sitting in front of a computer monitor, her right hand cupping the mouse as she read something on the screen. "Ms. Boa Vista," he said. "Anything interesting on there?"

"I'm actually not doing science for a change," she said. "Just research."

"Into what?"

"Into Wendy Greenfield," she explained. "So far it's involved reading a lot of old society columns and articles in *Ocean Drive* magazine. And golf magazines—they tend to mention her a lot, so it shows up in the search engine listings, but they mostly just show her picture and say that she's married to Sidney. Or was."

"Have you learned anything that might be useful?"

"Well, you never know what will be useful, do you? So far it's pretty much the poor-girl-marries-well story. She grew up in a broken home over in Fort Myers. Her parents were well known to the social workers and the local police, but her dad took off when she was ten. Somehow she managed to get out of there and into Sidney's field of view. The rest, as they say, is history."

"Wendy's history is still being written," Horatio reminded her. "And we're the ones who will write the final chapter. Keep me posted, Natalia."

"Will do."

"Have you seen Mister Wolfe anywhere?"

"Last I heard he was headed down to the garage to process Wendy's car."

"Perfect," Horatio said. "Thank you."

He started that way, but in the atrium he saw a young woman sitting on a leather sofa by the angled glass wall. She was lost in thought, hunched forward a little. Her brown hair was cut short, but she was tall and slender, her arms and long legs pale, as though they hadn't been in the sun recently. A big leather purse sat on the floor at her feet, its strap looped over her knee. She looked familiar, but different, and it took him a few seconds to realize who it was. "Nina?"

She saw him coming toward her and brightened as surely as if someone had clicked on a floodlight. "Horatio!" she cried, jumping up from the bench. She sprang to him and enveloped him in a crushing hug. She smelled like the ocean on a fresh spring day.

He held her for a long moment, then released her and stepped back. Her eyes were just as he remembered, big and brown, drooping slightly at the outer edges, but with a fierce intelligence behind them. "Does Calleigh know you're here?"

"The receptionist paged her," Nina said. "She'll be out in a minute."

"Why don't I take you back to her? How have you been?"

"I'm great," she said, but then her face clouded over. "Mostly great. I mean, I love college, and where I'm living. I've made some wonderful friends there, and Chicago is the most amazing city."

"How's your mother?" he said, leading her down the hall toward the gun lab.

"She's good. Fine. You know, she still worries about me a lot."

"She always will. That's what mothers do."

"I don't know if Calleigh told you, Horatio. And please don't be disappointed in me—"

"Never, Nina."

"—thank you. But I'm a little bit pregnant."

"I thought that was an either/or proposition."

"Yeah, it is."

He stopped and turned to face her again. "And how do *you* feel about it?"

She shrugged. "Honestly? Petrified. I mean, my boyfriend, like, vanished when I told him the news. He's still there at school, physically, but he might as well be invisible. When I run into him around campus, it's like he's made of stone. He just gives me this face that says, 'Don't ruin my life,' and he won't talk to me. So I guess boyfriend isn't the right word anymore."

"It doesn't sound like it."

"And that means it's all on me, right?"

"He can be compelled to do his share, Nina. Financially, at least."

"Yeah, I know. But if he doesn't want to be involved, then I'm not sure I want him involved anyway. Like if he has to give me money, is he going to one day feel like he has a right to interfere in our lives?"

"He may decide that anyway, Nina. People can be unpredictable, especially where families are involved."

"I guess I know that as well as anyone."

"I guess you would."

Horatio couldn't help being impressed by the newfound maturity of the girl he had known as a young teen. It was a maturity tempered by the optimism, and perhaps the naïveté, of youth, but to him it felt reasoned and real in spite of that. She had been through more than most young girls, and the fact that she had survived it at all was a testament to her strength.

"So do you think I'm insane to want to have my baby?"

He took her hand in his and gave it a gentle squeeze. "Nina, I don't think you're insane at all," he said, holding her gaze with his. "I think you'll make the right decision, and you'll do fine no matter what decision you make."

"Thank you, Horatio."

"And if there's anything I can do to help you, all you have to do is ask. You know that, right?"

"I know. Thank you," she said again.

"All right, then," he said. "Let's go find Calleigh, shall we?"

12

BURNED BODIES AND body parts were hard to work with. Human flesh was remarkably supple stuff under most circumstances. But apply intense enough heat to almost any substance composed largely of water and it will dehydrate, turning stiff and brittle. Because about half the body weight of human beings came from the water contained in their cells—called intercellular fluid—the same thing happened to people.

As badly burned as the victims taken from the Greggs house were, Alexx knew they required special care even above and beyond that which she usually gave those entrusted to her. Although their skin was charred, the outer tissue entirely burned away in spots, they still needed to be thoroughly examined. Sometimes fires were set to disguise homicides. She didn't think that was the case here—from what she had heard, she suspected that the fire was a side effect of the bomb, and it was either the shock wave of the blast or smoke inhalation from the fire that had killed these three. But suspecting was different than knowing, and she needed to know.

Beyond that, she had to try to positively identify the victims. They were believed to be Doctor Marc Greggs, his wife Sally, and their daughter Maggie, but that again was supposition, not fact.

She started with the one who appeared to be an adult male, the victim found in the boxer's position, who was the most badly burned of the three. He had been downstairs, where the fire was, instead of upstairs like the two females. His muscles had relaxed slightly since the fire had been put out and he'd been taken away from the scene, but he remained curled in on himself, his arms up in front of his chest. The first thing she wanted to check on, even before trying to identify him, was whether or not he had sustained his burns before or after death.

When a living human suffered a burn, white blood cells, or leucocytes, migrated to the site of the injury and blistered the skin, causing an inflammation called hyperemia. The liquid that caused the blistered tissue could be lab-tested for a positive protein reaction. Postmortem burns tended to be more yellowish, harder, and any liquid present would not produce the same protein reaction.

"What do you have to tell me, darlin'?" Alexx asked the burned corpse. "I know it had to hurt." Finding out if the burns had come before or after death could let the investigators know how many separate crimes they were looking at. It seemed unlikely, but the possibility that the bomb had been set off in order to hide the prior murder of the three victims couldn't be entirely discounted. Setting odds wasn't her job, but she had to take that chance into consideration. "The good part is your pain's over with now."

She found some blistering on his anconeal region—his right elbow, in lay terms—and scraped it into a petri dish, which she set aside on one of the stainless steel counters surrounding her, for closer study. As a backup test, she pried open the victim's mouth and looked at the mucobuccal folds. They were black with trapped soot and ash, almost certainly indicating that the victim had still been breathing after the fire started. His lung tissue would confirm it.

"You died hard, honey," Alexx said, trying not to imagine the terror he must have felt at the sound of the blast, the force of the shock wave driving wood fragments into him, the tumble down the stairs, and finally the roar of the flames as they enveloped him. She had lived through that, hunkered under a fire blanket with Eric Delko while fire blazed around them out in the Everglades, and it had been one of the most horrifying experiences in her life.

She hoped this man was in shock by that point, still breathing but not understanding what was about to happen to him, not experiencing the agony as the heat sapped the moisture from his body and cooked him alive.

She shook away the memory of the deafening roar, the searing heat, and returned her focus to the man on her table. "It's time to start working on figuring out who you are, isn't it?"

There were various ways she could try to do that. Fingerprints, even when the hands were seriously burned, could still retain some of their distinctive ridge patterns. After bad burns, the scars themselves could help in identification, albeit only in the case of someone who survived the burn event. She would try to get a ten-card off this vic, but having glanced at his finger pads she didn't hold out a lot of hope that it would help much. The way his fists clenched would make printing him difficult, and the severity of his burns would make matching his prints to existing databases tricky.

Dental work was only marginally more promising. When she had opened his mouth to look for signs of smoke inhalation, she noticed that a lot of the soft tissue had been damaged by the fire, which would have loosened teeth and allowed them to shift in his mouth. He would no longer match his last X-rays. If there was enough soft tissue left, a full reconstruction might be possible, which would allow her to match X-rays, but without that she would be left with just whatever fillings and other dental work were recoverable from individual teeth.

Likewise, although his skin had been horribly damaged, she might find inorganic parts—implants, pins or stents, or even a pacemaker—that carried serial numbers and could be traced back.

Some bodies, of course, were never identified. That, however, was a rarity, and not something Alexx Woods was willing to concede in this case.

"Just tell me who you are," she encouraged the victim. "We all have secrets, honey. But you don't need to keep them anymore. Not now."

The Mitsubishi Eclipse had been towed to the CSI garage, beneath the lab. Ryan processed the car, hoping to find some evidence of who met or carjacked Wendy Greenfield at the Quick Spree.

The doors and trunk latch held latent friction ridge prints galore. Most were probably Wendy's, some her husband's, while others could easily have belonged to valets and bellmen and car wash employees, maybe even baggers at the supermarket and random people who brushed against the vehicle in parking lots.

Because the car was white, he had dusted the likeliest areas with Sudan black powder. With the latent impressions made visible, he had held up his photographic scale and shot pictures of them. These photos would be uploaded digitally and compared to Wendy's prints. Once those had been eliminated, the others would be run through fingerprint databases to see who they belonged to. Not everyone in the country had their prints in one of the various databases, but many, many people did, including everyone who had been booked by law enforcement, and AFIS, the Automated Fingerprint Identification System, could compare 500,000 prints a second. The process could take time, but when he thought of fingerprint examiners in the old days flipping through individual paper cards and comparing whorls, arches, and loops with nothing but their eyes and maybe a magnifying glass, he was glad he lived now and not then.

What he really wanted was to narrow the field. He knew the guy had been driving the car. In the video footage, it appeared that Wendy might have popped the door open for him, although their bodies were between the door and the camera so he couldn't be sure. It was entirely possible that he had never touched the exterior handle. He had closed the door from the inside, however, so there should be impressions on the inner door.

And he had driven the car out of screen and presumably all the way to where he—or someone—had murdered Wendy and abandoned her and her car. Which meant that unless he had been wearing invisible gloves, the wheel should hold prints. Ryan's favorite way to expose them on that kind of plastic surface was cyanoacrylate fuming. Simple superglue. Japanese police, back in 1979, had accidentally found a print inside the lid of a superglue jar, and since the early eighties, law enforcement agencies all over the world had used cyanoacrylate fumes to reveal latent friction ridge impressions.

In years past, Ryan would have had to dismantle the car, taking the steering wheel into the lab to fume it, or else erect a big tent over the vehicle and fume the whole thing. But he had a Vapor Wand, which, as the name implied, was practically magic as far as he was concerned.

He got the Vapor Wand out and—staying outside the car door so he wouldn't breathe in the fumes—prepared to spray. The wand was just a little bigger than a fountain pen, and consisted of a butane torch fitted with a brass cartridge casing that contained steel wool soaked with methyl cyanoacrylate.

Ryan already had latex gloves on, of course. Now he added a protective face mask and goggles and reached into the car. When he lit the torch, the wand sprayed a fine mist of the fuming agent wherever he directed it. He fumed the wheel and the various dashboard controls, just to be on the safe side, then shut the wand off and backed away from the car. At a safe distance, he tugged the mask away and took a few deep breaths, letting the fresh air dry the sweat that had collected on his upper lip. In spite of the mask's protection, the plasticlike odor of the fumes filled his nose and mouth.

While he recovered from the hot work, the superglue went to work on the prints. The Vapor Wand only took about thirty seconds to reveal them, so he fitted the mask back into place and returned to the car with a portable ultraviolet light. A fluorescent dye had been added to the cyanoacrylate, and when he shone the light on the surfaces he had sprayed, prints glowed back at him, so distinct they might have been textbook illustrations instead of the real thing.

Under the mask, sweating, cheeks itching, Ryan smiled.

"Gotcha!"

Some of the prints were surely Wendy's, but if the killer had been the last person to drive the car, then he had found their first solid lead.

One more thing he wanted to check out quickly. He had been surprised to open Wendy Greenfield's trunk and find shotguns and ammunition. What he wanted to know is if Wendy had put them there. For these objects, which were slightly dusty from their ride in the trunk, he returned to powder, applying it with a magnetic wand that wasn't actually a brush and so didn't touch the surfaces he checked. Using a regular brush might disturb impressions that had been left in the existing dust. The powder he used turned the barely visible prints bright blue.

He was no fingerprint expert, but there were only eight major patterns in prints, different types of arches, loops, and whorls. These patterns were composed of bifurcations, spurs, bridges, islands, and other features, but he wasn't after courtroom-quality comparisons yet. He eyeballed the fumed prints from the steering wheel and the very distinct impressions he had found on one of the shell boxes. After going back and forth a few times, he was convinced that he had found the same prints in both places. He checked Wendy's ten-card, but her prints didn't match.

Which meant—pending a more thorough comparison in the lab—the man who had driven her car had also loaded the weapons into the trunk.

Definitely not a carjacking, then. But it appeared to be the precursor to some bigger criminal enterprise—they weren't dressed for hunting, after all—and the men's clothes in the bag would never have fit the guy in the video, which implied that there was a third person somehow involved.

Ryan needed to document all the prints he'd found on film, then lift samples to preserve.

That could wait a few minutes, though. The first thing he wanted to do was to call Horatio with his results. He pulled off the mask and goggles and reached for his phone.

13

ON THE ASSUMPTION that Wendell Asher was right about the identity of the bomber—the so-called Baby Boomer—Horatio had asked the Denver field office of the FBI to send over any materials it could pertaining to his previous crimes. He knew there would be filing cabinets full, but he also knew the Bureau would not share all of its information with a Miami cop. What he got were abstracts of some of the case files, pertinent information that had been scanned and saved digitally. The Bureau had been undergoing an extensive computer system upgrade since 9/11, and part of that effort involved making its information more easily shared with other agents and other agencies. The transfer of paper files to digital ones made that sharing possible.

According to the data Horatio studied, since 2004 the Baby Boomer was suspected of engineering twenty-two bombings. Sixteen had been at clinics, the rest at the private residences of doctors or clinic staff. Nine had involved fatalities. The fatal incidents had been in Boulder, Reno, Henderson, Grant's Pass, Spokane, Missoula, and Fresno. In addition to those, he had bombed sites in Oakland, Thousand Oaks, Tempe, Trinidad, Twin Falls, and finally Albuquerque. If he was in Miami now, it was the first time he had operated east of the Rocky Mountain West.

Horatio didn't like that. Bombers were precise, cautious people. They had to be, or they didn't generally survive their initial experimentation with explosive devices. Many of them learned their craft in the military, where they were taught not to take unnecessary risks.

Leaving what was obviously a comfort zone was a risky move. Unless there was some truly pressing reason—if, for instance, he knew how close Asher had come to him in Albuquerque—he wouldn't have done it. Horatio wanted to understand this guy, but this inconsistency made understanding more difficult.

He went back to his reading. As Asher had said, the Baby Boomer always used C-4, which meant he had a steady supply of it from somewhere. The FBI hadn't been able to trace it to its origin, which probably meant he got it from some overseas source. The taggants that Valera had mentioned, usually microscopic polymer particles, were added to domestic C-4 in order to identify the manufacturer and batch number in case it was used illegally. Some other countries used the same technology, but it was by no means universal. Finding C-4 without taggants didn't identify the source, but it ruled out some of the possibilities. Much police work was that way: eliminate possibilities until you're left with the truth.

From the couple of unexploded devices that had been recovered (sometimes unexploded bombs were exploded by bomb squads, instead of being rendered safe in a less destructive fashion in order to be analyzed and kept as evidence), it appeared that the Baby Boomer habitually used the same type of timer to detonate his devices. He made it himself, by wiring a digital kitchen timer to a silicone-controlled rectifier, or SCR, to control the current, and connecting that to a nine-volt alkaline battery, then to a detonator. The kitchen timer could be set for any length of time up to several days, but when it beeped at the end of its countdown, a charge ran from the battery to the detonator, igniting the C-4. He used a variety of casings, usually small metal boxes but sometimes wood, plastic, or even briefcases, apparently willing to sacrifice consistency for convenience in that one instance.

The few witnesses who had seen him—or thought they had—described the bomber as a Caucasian male in his thirties or early forties. Average height, weight, and build, which Horatio knew meant that nobody got a good enough look at him—or remembered in enough detail—to be really specific. His hair was dark brown or black. A profiler suggested that he attended church regularly, was outwardly sociable but had few close friends, if any, and probably came from a home with only one parent. Horatio had seen cases in which profilers were right on the money, and others where they might as well have lifted traits out of a textbook by flipping pages and stopping wherever their thumb landed, so he didn't give a lot of credit to this sketchy outline.

The truth seemed to be that no one knew much about the Baby Boomer, Wendell Asher included. The agent had a lot of notes but precious little solid information on the target of his years-long investigation.

At a knock on his office door, Horatio looked up from the screen to see Frank Tripp standing there. "What's up, Horatio?" he asked.

"I've been going over some data on the so-called Baby Boomer, Frank. It's all pretty vague."

"For a case that's been going on for years, that's not a good thing."

"Not at all."

"Got any idea what the problem is?"

"Not so far. I don't know if Asher is a bad investigator, or if this guy is really smart. Or both. He's always a couple of steps ahead, it appears."

"I guess there are special issues with investigating bombing scenes," Frank said, easing himself into a visitor's chair. "I mean, you'd know that better'n anyone, right?"

"There are," Horatio agreed. "The blast itself can destroy much of the evidence. Usually we manage to salvage enough, though."

"You joined the bomb squad right after you came to Miami, didn't you?"

"I did. Al Humphreys brought me on board, trained me, taught me everything he knew. It was a different world then, Frank. We used bomb blankets and jerkus ropes—"

"*What* ropes?"

"Jerkus ropes," Horatio repeated.

"Sounds pretty low-tech."

"The lowest. You tie the rope around a suspected device or package and give it a tug—from a distance, sometimes we used to tie it to a car and step on the gas—and you see if it explodes. If it does, it was a bomb."

"And if it doesn't?"

"Then it might still be a bomb. You can see the drawbacks."

"That's puttin' it lightly."

"A bomb blanket's not much more high-tech. You drape it over the device. When the bomb detonates, the blanket's fire-retardant webbing contains the frag. The top parachutes out to break the pressure wave, gas ports vent the gas, and the sides are weighted down to contain side splash."

"Far cry from robots, and what do you call those things?"

"Now they use robots and remotely controlled devices called wheelbarrows, some of which carry cameras, sensors, and pigsticks, or water-powered disruptors—"

"Yeah, those things. They're impressive as hell."

"And they work well, which is key, while preserving enough of the bomb for us to analyze at the lab. The Andros unit our squad has now is a terrific one."

"You know me, Horatio. I don't really understand anything higher tech than my gun and my gut, but I'm glad there are people on my side who do."

"We'll get this guy, Frank. There's always evidence. Sometimes it's hard to find and harder to interpret, but we will get him."

"I know." Frank rose, went to the door. "Gotta get back over to MDPD. I got a late meeting there."

"All right," Horatio said. "And Frank? You've got one of the best guts in the business. I'm glad it's on my side."

"That's good to know, Ryan," Horatio said. "Thank you."

He ended the call and tucked away his phone. He had walked with Frank to the elevator, and was on his way back to his office when he got Ryan's call. He took it in the hallway, watching the quiet rush of activity around him through the see-through walls.

Now that he was done, he started for his office again but saw Eric Delko walking toward him from the direction of the atrium. Horatio and Eric had been brothers-in-law for the brief time that Horatio had been married to Eric's sister Marisol. Memmo Ferro, a sniper from the Mala Noche crime gang had put an end to the marriage shortly after their wedding—a tragedy from which Horatio hadn't seen how he would ever recover, even though long, sleepless nights and terrible contemplation had brought him to a place from which he knew he could go on. The only lives that never knew heartbreak, Horatio had decided, were imaginary ones. If he had encountered more than his fair share, he could only slough some of it off by trying to help others through their own tragedies.

He had tracked down Ferro almost immediately. But Ferro was just a triggerman following the orders of gang boss Antonio Riaz. Horatio managed to find Riaz as well, but the Mala Noche kingpin made a deal with the Feds and was deported instead of jailed.

A joint crusade to Brazil to bring lasting justice to Riaz strengthened the bond between Horatio and Eric. At a crucial moment, when Riaz was about to end Eric's life with a wicked blade, Horatio made like the cavalry and raced to the rescue.

There had been few people he'd been so happy to kill.

When he saw Eric now, he knew that something had changed between them. A connection had been forged that could not be completely broken; they would never go back to the way they had been before. He offered a warm smile, which Eric returned. "Got a celebrity out there waiting for you, H," Eric said.

"I was just out there," Horatio said. "If it's the ex-governor again, tell him—"

"He just showed up," Eric interrupted. "Think sports,"

"Ahh. Sidney Greenfield?"

"You got it."

"Thanks, Eric." Horatio headed for the atrium. Three times in two days—they were getting to be best buddies. At least this time he hadn't had to fight traffic on the causeway to see the golfer.

"Mister Greenfield," he said as he entered the big open space. Sidney sat leaning forward on the bench, hands clenched together and dangling between his knees, almost in the same spot as Nina Cullen had waited a short while before. The expression on his still unshaven face was one of profound loss. He looked up at Horatio's approach but didn't smile or bound from the bench the way Nina had. Instead, he forced himself to his feet, straining under the effort as though thousand-pound weights pressed down on his shoulders.

"Caine," Sidney said, tugging off his Callaway Golf ball cap and, on the third try, jamming it into the rear pocket of his khaki pants. He glowered at Horatio, as if the anger he had shown at his house had returned. "You got a few minutes?"

"Whatever time you need, sir," Horatio said. A lab tech in her white coat passed through the atrium, and Sidney watched her intently until she was gone. "We can go someplace more private if you'd like."

"That might be good," Sidney said.

"Right this way." Horatio led him to an interview room. Light from outside streamed in through big windows, washing down on the table. Horatio pulled out a chair for the golfer and took one opposite him. Sidney Greenfield sat heavily, with a weary sigh.

Horatio waited. This was the other man's show. He had initiated the conversation, so although Horatio was interested to hear what he had to say, he would let Sidney get around to it on his own time.

It took a couple of false starts and some throat clearing before Sidney finally came out with it. "I . . . ah . . . I didn't mean to intentionally mislead you, but I think I might have done just that. It was . . . I felt like it's nobody's business but mine, okay? But I thought about it all night, and more today after you came to the house, and I think it might be important information that could make a difference to your investigation."

"What is it?" Horatio asked.

"Well . . . it's a little sensitive, you know. Different people have different rules. The way they live their lives, the morality that guides them . . . we each have to figure out what works for us."

"Within certain parameters," Horatio allowed.

"Of course. I'm not talking about hurting other people, or violating their rights or anything. I'm talking about more . . . discreet behavior. Discreet and consensual. It's not something I discuss with most people, because there's . . . well, there's a tendency to pass judgment."

"I don't judge," Horatio said. "It gets in the way of keeping an open mind."

"Good," Sidney said. He rubbed his face with both hands. Horatio could hear the sandpaper sound of his palms scraping against the growth of whiskers. Sidney smelled like old sweat, as if he hadn't bathed since yesterday morning. "I expect you to keep this to yourself, Caine."

"If it's pertinent to the investigation, I'll have to share it with my team, Mister Greenfield. And without knowing what you're going to tell me, I should also warn you that it might come up in court."

"But you'll make every effort to see that it doesn't." He didn't phrase it as a request.

"I'll do what I can."

"It's about Wendy. Like I told you before, she comes from a different world than me. Originally, I mean. I was strictly upper middle class, knocking golf balls around my family's yard when I was six and playing at the country club by twelve. My father probably made more money in a month than Wendy's did in a year, when he was working at all. When he was a father at all, I should say. He had a tendency to disappear for months at a time, the way she tells it, even before he took off for good."

Horatio listened quietly, sitting with his head tilted toward Sidney, hands resting on the table, casual, not rushing or pushing the other man.

"I guess what I'm saying is that she grew up with a different set of standards than me, and a very different life experience. Don't get me wrong, Caine, we love each other. Or loved, I guess. It's hard to start thinking of her in the past tense, but I know I have to. Anyway, a lot of people warned me about her when we first got together. They thought she was a gold digger, a social climber—you know, a young, beautiful woman like that marrying a golfer. We can make some money on the tour, but we're not exactly sexy the way NBA or NFL players are, right? Cardigans and khakis—it takes a certain kind of woman to get excited by that.

"But Wendy was that kind of woman, hard to believe as that might seem. She was ready for a little stability in her life, a little more conservative approach than she had known in her youth. She didn't *object* to the money or the social status, but those weren't the reasons she was with me. She was with me out of love and mutual respect and sexual attraction and all the things that bring any couple together."

Horatio nodded, still keeping quiet. He had a feeling that Sidney was approaching his point, albeit by a roundabout path. Shooting his tee shot into the rough on the left of the fairway, then playing toward the green by bouncing from one bad lie to another.

"What I'm getting at, Lieutenant, is that part of where Wendy and I were different—not from each other, necessarily, because I'm on the road a lot and I've had my share of flings, there are plenty of club bunnies out there happy to polish a golfer's balls, if you get my drift—but maybe from some other people, is that she had affairs with other men. Here in Miami, not on the road."

"And you think she was involved with someone at the moment, and maybe that someone had something to do with her death?" Horatio asked.

"I know that she was definitely seeing someone, as of yesterday. I don't know who. I didn't object to it—that would be kind of hypocritical of me, right? She didn't share the details with me, but she didn't have to lie about what she was doing, and that's how we both wanted it. When I said she was going shopping . . . well, that was a kind of euphemism we used with each other sometimes, and we both knew what it really meant." Sidney paused for a long moment, as if working on phrasing his next statement. "So I wanted you to know, in case it does turn out to be important—I mean, I don't know who the guy was, so I don't know what sorts of things he was involved in. But also . . ."

"Yes?" Horatio prodded.

". . . also, I figured you'd find out sooner or later. And when you did . . . well, there are plenty of guys who want to kill their wives when they find out about extramarital affairs, right? Isn't that the stereotype?"

"It does happen."

"Right. So I wanted to let you know that that's not me. I knew all about it, she had my permission, and I didn't mind. As long as she came home to me at night, right? I was a happy man. Sometimes she even brought home a new trick or two that she'd picked up from her lovers, and that was good for both of us. I just wanted you to hear that from me before you started heading down the wrong highway."

"Of course, if you are guilty, you might tell me this anyway," Horatio said. "Is there anyone who can back you up on this arrangement you and your wife had?"

"Like I said, I didn't really tell a lot of people around here about it. Some of the women I saw on the road . . . but then, I didn't always get their names, either. I could probably come up with one or two who I saw more than once, who I described it to. It'll take some digging."

"I'd appreciate it if you would dig, sir."

Sidney nodded. He looked like some internal

pressure had been relieved, as if holding the secret in had taken a toll separate from the grief of his wife's death. His posture was slightly more relaxed, and his eyes had taken on a bit of a sparkle.

"Is that all, Mister Greenfield?"

Sidney started to nod again, but then he stopped. "No, not quite. There's one more thing I should mention."

"What's that?"

"You said that Wendy was pregnant."

"That's right."

"Well, that part was kind of a violation of our rules. I didn't know about it, so I never had a chance to be upset with her. But the baby . . . well, all I can tell you for sure is that it's not mine."

"How do you know that?"

"I'm sterile. I always have been. It's been kind of a relief, knowing that birth control was never an issue for me. You can check that with my doctor."

"I will," Horatio assured him. He was about to let the golfer leave when he remembered the video from the Quick Spree, and the stills he had asked Dan Cooper to print for him. "Can you wait here for just a minute?"

"It's not like I have any pressing demands on my time," Sidney said. He might have meant it sarcastically—still upset about possibly missing the Masters—but Horatio chose not to interpret it that way.

Horatio hurried to the A/V lab, got one of the

prints from Cooper, and took it back to the interview room. He sat down, put the picture on the
table, spun it around, and shoved it toward Sidney.
"Do you know this man?"

Sidney picked up the picture, studying it intently. "I don't think so, no. Who is he?"

"That, Mister Greenfield, is what I was hoping
you could tell me. He's the last person who we
know saw your wife alive. He drove her car, at
least for a little while. And apparently he put two
shotguns and some boxes of shells in her trunk."

"Shotguns?" Sidney's face looked much like it
had when Horatio and Calleigh had told him about
Wendy's pregnancy—confusion and consternation
warring for turf. "Why would she have shotguns?"

"Again, Mister Greenfield, that's a question that
I can't answer," Horatio said. "Yet."

14

"HORATIO, YOU'RE GOING to want to see this."

Horatio turned around. The elevator doors had just closed on Sidney Greenfield, and Ryan Wolfe walked toward him with a sheet of paper in his hand. "What is it, Ryan?"

"I got a hit off those prints from Wendy Greenfield's Eclipse."

"That's good. And?"

Ryan read off the paper. "Guy's name is Lyall Douglas. Low-rent thug. He's done a few stretches for aggravated assault, B and E, a liquor store robbery, drunk and disorderlies, other miscellaneous misdemeanors. A real loser, it looks like. Strictly small time."

"It looks like he may have raised the stakes now," Horatio said. "Murder is a new game for him."

"That we know of. He's never been charged with one, anyway."

"Do we have an address?"

Ryan read him one near Twelfth and Flagler. Horatio wasn't certain but he thought he could picture the building, a one-story bungalow with an overgrown yard, badly in need of paint. He didn't know every address in Miami, but he had a good sense for neighborhoods and a nearly eidetic memory for places and people. "Let's go," he said, reaching for his phone. Flipping it open, he punched Frank Tripp's number. "Frank," he said when the Texan answered. "I need backup at this address, and I need it now."

Lyall Douglas's house was empty.

As it turned out, Horatio had been right about which house he thought it was. But that hadn't been difficult, since the same general description applied to the majority of the houses on the block. This was a neighborhood where most people worked hard and didn't have a lot of spare time or energy for yard work or the disposable income to hire gardeners or painters. It was also a neighborhood where there were frequent domestic disputes and drug deals. Break-ins were rare because no one owned much more than anyone else, but the police had been to the street often enough for the other things, and Horatio had processed crime scenes in a couple of the houses nearby.

Lyall Douglas's rented house looked like old bones left too long in the ground—faded and dirty, a color that might have been brown once but had become

more a memory of brown than brown itself. The roof
was made of gray shingles, equally faded and water-
stained in spots. A smear of thick black tar showed
where a leak had been hastily plugged. The yard was
thick with grass tall enough to choke a tractor. Two
windows, both curtained, faced toward the street.
The uniformed cops jogging up the alley behind the
house would have a better sense of its rear than Horatio did, but he doubted that it would offer any surprises in design or upkeep. It was just another relic
from the postwar building boom that had housed
one lower-middle-class family after another.

And then Lyall Douglas.

Who, Horatio sincerely hoped, would soon be
moving to a new address for a good long while, as a
guest of the state.

If Wendy Greenfield had been Douglas's first
murder, it didn't say much for his courage. She had
apparently trusted him. No sign of a weapon had
been found on her, if you didn't count the shotguns locked in the trunk, and she didn't seem to
have struggled against him. The crime looked like
one that had been relatively easy for the killer—
awkward, but not dangerous in any way.

Which didn't mean he wouldn't react badly
to the appearance of armed law officers at his
home. It didn't pay to take any such visit lightly,
and Horatio had to assume that where there were
two shotguns, there might be more or some other
equally dangerous weapon. Douglas was probably a

coward, like most murderers, but that didn't mean he wouldn't hit back if he was cornered.

At a signal from the cops behind the house, Horatio, Ryan, and Frank approached the front door. Uniformed cops stood behind them, covering the door and the windows. Horatio rapped on the wooden door. "Miami-Dade Police!" he shouted. "Come on out, Lyall!"

Silence answered him from the inside. He could hear Frank's heavy breathing beside him, and Ryan Wolfe's shallow exhalations. The cops in the yard shifted positions, their gear clinking softly. A gull's raspy croak sounded from somewhere down the block. Blood rushed in his own ears.

But from the house, nothing.

"We're coming in, Douglas!"

He gave that warning a couple of seconds to register, then tried the doorknob. Surprisingly, it turned easily. The latch bolt clicked back and the door swung open when he pushed on it. "Police!" he called into the silence. Third warning. Sweeping his gaze across the room, SIG Sauer grasped in both hands, he entered.

The room was empty. Uniforms rushed in past him, and he heard the sound of a door being broken down in back, the thunder of boots on the hardwood floors.

Empty houses have different smells, he knew, different feels, than other houses. One that has been empty for a long time is musty, the air close and thick. A house that someone has just vacated still feels occupied, as if the person's presence has left behind traces in the walls and floors and furniture.

This house had not been empty for long. Walking through it, listening to the shouts of "Clear!" as the officers checked each room, Horatio could smell spilled beer and trash left under the sink a day too long and, when he opened the refrigerator, leftover pizza with onion and pepperoni. There were a couple of skin magazines on a coffee table in the living room, on top of the TV section from the *Miami Herald*.

But there were also strange voids. In the single bedroom, the carpet had been smashed down in a rectangular shape, as if boxes had been sitting there undisturbed for some time, but whatever had made the shape was gone. There were clothes hanging in the closet, mostly long-sleeved shirts, jeans, and jackets. Horatio glanced into a dresser to make sure, but it appeared that when he had left, Douglas had taken most of his warm-weather clothing with him.

He didn't have a search warrant yet, although one was in the works, so he refrained from looking further for the time being. He had hoped to find Douglas at home, and failing that to be able to quickly determine whether the man had gone on a long trip or just down to the grocery store.

"He's gone," Frank said, as if reading his thoughts.

"Lyall Douglas is in the wind," Horatio agreed. "We need to find him. Any news on that warrant?"

"It's ready," Frank said. "Judge Harrison's clerk has it."

"I'll have Eric and Calleigh pick it up and head

over," Horatio said. "I want this place processed as thoroughly as any crime scene. If there's a hint in here of where Douglas has gone, I want it found."

"I can get started," Ryan offered.

"Not until the warrant gets here," Horatio reminded him. "Then you will definitely get started."

Ryan started to say something, but Horatio's phone and Frank's phone sounded simultaneously, so he kept his mouth shut. Horatio answered first. "Horatio Caine."

"Horatio, it's Calleigh."

"I was just about to call you. What is it, Calleigh?"

"There's been another bombing. In the Gables, at the law office of an attorney named Karen Platt. It sounds like there are several more victims."

"Ryan and I will go right over there," Horatio said. "Grab Delko and pick up a warrant for Lyall Douglas's house. It's empty and we need to find out where he's gone."

"The warrant's ready now?"

"That's right. Get it from Jessica, at Judge Harrison's chambers. Get here as fast as you can. I'll leave a unit here to preserve the scene until you get here."

"Got it, Horatio."

Putting his phone away, Horatio could tell by the scowl on Frank's face that the detective was getting the same news. When he finished his call, he caught Horatio's gaze.

"The Gables."

"Yes. It appears our bomber has been busy."

"Looks like. You going to take it?"

"Mister Wolfe and I will." Horatio turned to Ryan. "Another bomb, in Coral Gables. The offices of an attorney named Karen Platt."

"I've heard of her," Ryan said.

"She's in the news all the time," Frank said. "Takes a lot of pro bono cases, very interested in public affairs and social justice."

"Does she represent abortion clinics?" Horatio asked.

"Not that I remember, but I'll check. You're still thinking about the Baby Boomer?"

"It seems like too much of a coincidence that Special Agent Asher would come to town after him, and then there would be a rash of completely unconnected bombings that happen to share characteristics of the Boomer's signature. I'll admit that the change of targets has me confused."

"When it comes to the Feds, just about everything confuses me," Frank said. "But I get your point."

"Would you call the Special Agent and make sure he meets us at the scene? I think we need to have another talk."

"He's already on his way."

"Good. You'll assign some officers to wait here for Calleigh and Eric and the warrant?"

"I will," Frank replied. "Maybe we'll get lucky and Douglas'll come home."

"Maybe we will," Horatio said. "You never know, do you?"

15

KAREN PLATT'S BUSINESS was a boutique law firm in a boutique town. Her offices were in a former residence—white stucco, red tile-roofed, Mediterranean style—around the corner from Books & Books on Aragon Avenue in Coral Gables, which also made it not far from the local police station, and less than a dozen blocks from where Alexx Woods lived. Officers from that station had been first on the scene, and by the time Horatio and Ryan arrived, they had already secured a perimeter.

Fire trucks jammed the street, but except for a small blaze fire hadn't been a significant issue at this scene. The bomb squad had already gone inside and was working on clearing the premises for the CSIs. Wendell Asher rolled up in his rented car while Horatio waited outside. Ryan looked flatly at Horatio, his eyes a warning not to let his emotions carry him away. Horatio gave him a nod and stalked over to meet the FBI agent.

"Special Agent Asher," he said. "I haven't been inside yet, so I don't know what the situation in there is. But I have to say, two bombings inside twelve hours makes me uncomfortable."

"Welcome to my world," Asher said. He sniffled and pinched his nose as if to shut down his sinuses. "Damn cold. Anyway, I've been living with this guy for two years plus. It's driving me nuts, Horatio."

"So you do think this is the work of your man?"

"It feels like it to me. That's all I've got so far, just a hunch. But I'm pretty deep into his head by this point, and I think it's him."

"If you know him so well," Horatio asked, "then can you tell me why he's changing targets after all this time? My understanding is that Karen Platt involved herself in various causes, but she wasn't known for representing abortion clinics or providers."

"Have you made a thorough check of her client list?"

"I haven't," Horatio admitted. "But I will."

"So there might be some surprises on it yet."

"Anything's possible."

Asher gave a shrug. "I still don't get the doctor. Gregg? No connection at all that I can turn up. You're right, it's a break from his usual pattern."

"There's a lot that I don't get yet, Special Agent.

Why don't you tell me precisely what makes you think the Greggs house bombing was one of his?"

"He's like Jack Benny," Asher replied, a hint of admiration creeping into his voice. "A master of timing. This one's the same thing. He likes to hit when he knows he'll do the most damage. A residence, he hits at night when there will be people sleeping inside, instead of off at work or school or whatever. A business, like this law firm, during the day. When people are working there. Chances are in this case he wanted to kill the lawyer as well as whatever staff members he could, so he attacked her place of business."

"What if Karen Platt had been in court? Or at an off-site meeting of some kind?"

"Then we probably wouldn't be standing here. He tries to find out what people's schedules are. I think he uses public records and close observation for most of it, but there have been a couple of occasions when he has paid people off for the information. Insiders. I interviewed a janitor at a clinic who's probably still having nightmares—he earned a hundred bucks for providing a schedule, and then everybody the guy worked with got killed in the blast. Only reason the janitor was spared was that he worked nights after everyone else went home."

Horatio swiveled around to look at the house. Members of the bomb squad filtered out through the front door, returning to their van to doff their protective gear. "It looks like they're wrapping up," he said. "What else can you tell me?"

"He always uses C-4. I don't know where he gets it—offshore somewhere. But bombers tend to stick with what works for them, and that's his favorite."

"I gathered that from the case files I saw. And he always uses timing devices?"

"Yes. By the time one of his bombs detonates he's far away. Unlike some bombers, he's not one of those guys who likes to watch."

"I see."

"The Baby Boomer uses bombs instead of bullets because he wants his killings to make a statement," Asher continued. "Political, religious, moral, call it what you will. He has a strong sense that what he's doing is right, that he's following a law that's above the laws of men and governments. But he's not a showboat. Make no mistake, Lieutenant Caine. Bombers know their devices will get attention, but if it was *just* about sending messages, they'd use Western Union. Or Yahoo, I guess, to update the old saying. His intent is to kill the people he believes are doing bad things, not just to scare them. That accomplishes two things—it scares the ones he can't get to physically, and it ensures that the ones he does reach stop whatever they're up to."

"Death has a way of doing that."

"So it does."

Jorge Ortiz was walking toward him, so Horatio turned his attention away from the FBI agent and toward the bomb-scene manager. Ortiz was short and sturdy, with unshakable hands and shoulders you could rest the planet on. "We meet again," he said.

"I like to see you, Jorge, but not this often."

"Same goes for me. Give me a lazy day any time, sitting around with nothing to do except polish our robot."

"How does it look in there?"

"One device, seated near the center of the building. Inside the office of the lady who owns it, the lawyer."

"Karen Platt."

"I guess, yeah."

"Victims?"

"Four that I saw."

Frank had been talking softly into his phone, but he put it away and joined the other men. "Makes sense," he said. "I got hold of a part-time legal researcher who said there would have been four people working today. Platt, her legal secretary, and two paralegals. Young lady I talked to would have been here today too, but she's got a cold and stayed home."

"I know how she feels," Asher said, rubbing his nose. "Wish I had that luxury."

"Look on the bright side," Horatio said, barely able to rein in his anger. "At least your place of employment hasn't been blown up, with your friends and coworkers inside."

"I'm just saying—"

"Maybe you'd better not." Horatio walked away from the other men. "Mister Wolfe," he called. "Grab our kits from the Hummer, please. We're going in."

Crime was usually messy. Horatio was accustomed to that—years as a patrol cop, a detective, and a member of the bomb squad didn't leave a person with any illusions on that score. He liked the clean precision of crime scene investigation, the fact that science didn't muddy the waters but cleared them, that it led the way to definitive answers. Science organized things.

Bombs did the opposite.

By the time he crossed the barrier tape for a quick meeting at the command post—a trailer that had been hurriedly brought to the scene—with Jorge Ortiz, Frank, Asher, a paramedic, a city building inspector, a structural engineer, and representatives of the affected utility companies, twenty-two people had already signed the access control log book. A crime scene was supposed to be preserved in as pristine a state as possible, but a bombing scene, in addition to being thrown into disarray by the underlying crime itself, was further contaminated by all the people who had to go in before the CSIs could.

When he finally got inside the law office, he found the expected ruin and wreckage. Someone had carefully tagged potential hazards, like an interior wall that sagged dangerously inward and could collapse at any time. While Horatio did his first walk-through, Ryan busied himself with a camera and Frank coordinated the interviewing of neighbors who might have witnessed someone coming or going from the house.

As Ortiz had described, the seat of detonation had been in Karen Platt's own office. The blast had cratered a hole through the tile floor, exposing foundation below. It had punched out most of the wall separating her office from her law library, and in that room bookshelves had been toppled and books blown from the shelves still standing. Loose pages with torn edges covered the floor, like a blizzard of giant snowflakes had struck.

Horatio established a path that any subsequent visitors to the building would use, getting down on his hands and knees and carefully inspecting a route from the front door to the seat of detonation to ensure that no evidence would be compromised or destroyed by the comings and goings of others. Next he cleared a secondary path, in case the first one was clogged and someone needed to get in or out in a hurry. This secondary path led to a back door. Once that was done, he breathed a sigh of relief, knowing that the evidence still inside the building wouldn't be going anywhere. Time remained a critical factor, as it always was in this sort of investigation, but at least he wasn't fighting to preserve endangered evidence now. The building's roof seemed intact, so even if it started raining, the scene wouldn't be compromised.

In the office where the detonation had occurred, a woman had been sitting at a desk. The blast had been centered on the wall opposite her, the device hidden inside a glass-fronted lawyer's bookcase. The bookcase had splintered, and wood fragments and glass were embedded in all the remaining walls and ceiling, as well as in the victim herself.

The pressure wave had blown her backward, and her head struck the floor, but she was probably already dead by then, Horatio guessed. Her face was ruined, its bones crushed and shattered by pressure that might have hit her at 8,500 meters per second. No one could survive slamming into a brick wall at that speed, and the effect was the same. She had been sitting close enough to the bomb to take the full brunt of the thermal effect, as well, and even some frag.

To make it worse, the blast pressure had flipped her desk onto her with the force of a semi truck, its edge nearly cutting her in two. Blood had pooled around the body and lazy flies helped themselves to it. What was left of her body was curiously shapeless, because the bones, muscles, and organs that dictated structure had been pulped inside the broken bag of her skin. In a blast like this, muscles and ligaments could be ripped from their anchors, bones torn from their joints. Surviving a major explosion could be worse punishment than a swift death.

Horatio scouted around the office and found her purse, butter-soft leather and expensive, thrown from a desk drawer and half buried under rubble. Inside her wallet was a Florida driver's license, showing a picture of a smiling Karen Platt, with neat blond hair and stylish red plastic glasses. He hadn't seen the glasses yet, but the body on the floor had the hair—not so neat anymore but the right color where it wasn't singed—and she looked like the five-seven height and one-forty-five weight probably applied.

Somewhere in the building were three more bodies. Before he got busy processing the scene, Horatio went to look for those.

To remind myself, he thought, *what I'm doing here.*

16

FINISHED DOCUMENTING the scene photographically, Ryan went to work near the seat of detonation, on hands and knees, looking for bomb casing fragments. More than the usual crime scene, bombing scenes challenged his resolve to control his OCD. The chaos gnawed at him like a rat chewing on his nerve endings, and he had to fight to keep his focus on the task at hand.

This one wasn't as bad as the Greggs house, where the firefighters' water had covered the floor in a layer of ashy muck. The only thing worse than crawling around through the detritus left behind by a bomb was doing it in liquid that he couldn't even see through. Although no accelerant had been found at the Greggs place, the old, dry wood of the house itself, combined with antique furnishings and plenty of rugs and curtains, had made it a firetrap. The law office, though, was all tile and stone and stucco, which had retarded the blaze instead of fueling it.

Still, it was a struggle to ignore the mess and concentrate on searching for the minute fragments that could contain valuable evidence.

Bomb casings performed multiple functions, he had learned. First, containing explosives made the release of pressure more . . . well, explosive. Pour a bunch of gunpowder into a pile and light a match, and you got a bright flare-up, some smoke, and some sizzle. Compress the same load into a tight casing and light a fuse, and you got a *boom*.

Casings also helped to disguise the elements of a bomb. A timer might include elements of a digital clock, for instance, and the explosive material might be sticks of TNT—all of which would be extremely noticeable in the average home or office. But combine it all inside a small black box and it could easily sit in the shadows, the box muffling any sounds the timer might make, for hours without being spotted.

Finally, fragments from the casing made the bomb even more destructive, flying everywhere and injuring people or damaging property even if the pressure wave didn't.

Ryan began his search for casing fragments at the seat of detonation—or as close as he could get to it, since the floor had caved in beneath it. Even where the floor was solid, the blast had charred and roughened the surface. There were two phases to blast pressure—positive, the shock front that blew outward from the original explosion, and negative, when air rushed in to fill the vacuum created by the initial outflow. Bomb fragments, tiny and already airborne, were often sucked back by that vacuum, landing close to where they'd started.

With his kit open on the floor beside him, Ryan studied the floor inch by inch. He placed a photographic scale next to each minute piece of unidentified *something* that might be bomb casing and took its picture, then moved the scale and put a numbered cone beside the fragment. He would have to shoot the whole scene again when he was finished with an area, with the cones in place, and plot their locations on a CAD—computer-aided design—program. Wearing the usual latex surgical gloves, he used forceps to lift each piece of jagged black metal and examine it closely. Later he would check each one for prints, or more likely, partial prints that he would try to put together using the puzzle pieces of the fragments. For now, his priority was trying to determine what was probably bomb fragments and what was something less sinister.

A bit of copper wire could have been from a bomb, but it also might have been part of the power cord for a lamp or TV or have been blown out of a wall outlet. A stray battery terminal, on the other hand, was almost certainly from the bomb. Ryan measured, shot, and coned it. The work was the very definition of painstaking, and before long his knees were sore and his lower back aching, and he really, really wanted a hot shower.

Times like this, he sometimes remembered, with bittersweet emotion, that he could have chosen a purely scientific career. He could be standing in a spotless lab somewhere, with the air temperature just right and no aches or pains anywhere.

Then he remembered the pleasure he got helping to put bad guys away.

It's worth the aching back and the shooting pains in my legs, he thought. *And the mess . . .*

It's worth all of it.

17

"THANK YOU FOR COMING in today," Natalia Boa Vista said. "I know it's an inconvenience, and I really appreciate it."

"You said it might, like, help figure out who killed Wendy. If it will, I'll do whatever I can." Bridget Ehrens slouched on a chair in the lab's interview room, a honeycomb pattern from sunlight through the window falling on her. In her early thirties, she had not fared as well financially as her old friend Wendy Mies, who had become Wendy Greenfield. Her jeans were worn at the hem, stained with something black, and her T-shirt had a tobacco company logo on it, probably something given away for free at a bar. She wore cheap fake leather sandals and the wristwatch encircling her skinny wrist was from a discount store. Her eyes showed the telltale creases of a heavy smoker, and even if Natalia hadn't been able to tell from that and her nicotine-stained teeth, the smell of tobacco that clung to her like a coat of paint would have. She had bottle-blond hair showing a couple inches of brown root.

"It might," Natalia said. "You never can tell what's going to crack a case." She was on uncertain territory here. She had been hired on a federal payroll to work at the lab, using contemporary technology to review past convictions and unsolved cases. Items stored in evidence could retain DNA for years or decades—DNA that couldn't have been tested when an original conviction was handed down but could be now. Every innocent person her research set free was a source of great personal pride for Natalia. And the Justice Project grant that brought her into the lab had financed the lab's extensive redesign, so it benefited all of its personnel. But that job had gone away, and now she worked for the MDPD Crime Lab. She was still primarily a lab technician and didn't spend much time in the field or interrogating suspects.

Bridget Ehrens wasn't a suspect, however. More of a witness, although not actually to the crime. Horatio had told Natalia to find out what she could about Wendy, and she had dug around, found a high school teacher back in Fort Myers who remembered Wendy Mies and Bridget Ehrens as inseparable. A little more research had revealed that Bridget now lived in Plantation, in an apartment that she couldn't have paid for on her salary as a manicurist in a Fort Lauderdale beauty parlor. She suspected that Wendy helped her with the rent, but wanted to find out for sure.

"Do you have any suspects?" Bridget asked.

"We're working on some leads," Natalia replied. "What I really need from you is a sense of who Wendy is. I mean, she's in the news sometimes, but it's always as Mrs. Sidney Greenfield, the golfer's wife. There's got to be more to her than that."

"Oh, there is," Bridget said. "Definitely."

"You've known her for a long time?"

"Since junior high." Bridget scratched the side of her mouth with a long nail that had a silver star decorating its tip. "Can I smoke in here?"

"No, sorry." Natalia wasn't really sorry, but she thought it never hurt to be polite.

"Okay, well, in seventh grade, my folks moved to Fort Myers. I met Wendy the first day of school, and we've been tight ever since."

"Do you know any reason anyone would want to hurt her?"

Bridget considered this for a minute, tapping on the tabletop with those claws and squinting toward the window. "Well, she and I, we ran with some rough crowds back in the day, you know?"

"What kind of rough crowds?" Natalia asked. "Tell me about it."

"We were always in some kind of trouble, I guess. Hanging out with older boys, right? I dropped out of high school in tenth grade, and she stayed in, but both of us started, you know, messing around with some drugs and made some bad choices where men and jobs were concerned."

"What kinds of choices?"

"You wouldn't know it to look at me now, but I was a dancer for a while. Stripper, y'know, not like ballet or anything. Wendy didn't do that for long, but she did it for a year or so. Always scored bigger tips than me, too, shaking those moneymakers of hers and all that platinum hair. We met some guys who were on the wrong side of the law, I guess you'd say. Bad boys. I'm no shrink or nothing, but maybe if her dad had hung around, she wouldn't have been looking for love from every male she saw. Then again, my dad was always around and I wasn't so different."

"How did she wind up with Sidney?"

"She always claimed they met at a restaurant, but I think he saw her dance once, and they made up the restaurant story to protect his reputation. Clean-cut golfer dude, right? Couldn't be known as a guy who visited strip clubs. But she stopped dancing right after the so-called restaurant meeting, when they started dating."

"Did he know about all the bad boys?" Natalia asked.

"I don't think she ever told him how bad they were. He knew there had been other men, but probably not that some of them had done jail time.

The few times I met Sidney, she told me not to mention that."

"Done time for what?"

Bridget shrugged and scratched the corner of her mouth again. "Whatever. There were quite a few of them in those days. Small-time wiseguys mostly, you know, but they kind of passed us around, right? Hook up with one guy for a while, then another, and like that."

"Sounds dangerous."

"That was kind of the point."

"Was she still in touch with any of these men?"

"I have no idea. These last five years or so, we haven't really been in touch with each other that much," Bridget said. "She sends me checks, which is sweet as hell, but we don't really talk. It's like she finally decided to put it all behind her and just be the golfer's wife."

"So you don't know if one of those wiseguys you mentioned might have killed her."

"Anything's possible, right? Maybe one of them tried to blackmail her or something, and they fought. Or maybe Sidney found out about them and got pissed off."

Both possibilities had occurred to Natalia, and Bridget hadn't narrowed the options much. "But you couldn't say which one? No particular guy who seems more likely than the others?"

"Can I stand up?"

"Of course," Natalia said.

Bridget rose from her chair and stretched, arms way over her head, until her back popped loudly. She still had a stripper's body, lithe and sinuous. "Ahh," she said. "That's good. Anyway, it probably could have been just about any of them. She wouldn't have told me if she still talked to any of them, much less . . . you know, more than talked. But I wouldn't think so. When she moved to Miami with Sidney she kind of cut off her past, you know? Like she wanted to pretend she didn't come from that background."

"I guess we all do things we're not that proud of." Natalia had her share, including reporting to her federal employers on goings-on at the lab— even though she only reported the positive things her lab mates did, she still felt like an informer, and it had taken the others a long time to forgive her.

Bridget laughed, and the laugh turned into a cough, long and hacking. When she finished, her eyes were watering. "I've done more than my share, sister. Things I'm not proud of, men I'm not proud of. But I don't think I've done any murderers, and if you'd asked me, I would've said the same about Wendy."

"Does the name Lyall Douglas mean anything to you?"

She gave it a moment's consideration, wrinkling her nose while she thought. "It might be sorta familiar, but not really. Doesn't ring any bells."

"All right. If you think of anything else, Bridget,

or remember any particular guys you think might have been especially bad news, please call me, okay?" Natalia put her card on the table in front of the other woman. Bridget palmed it and slid it into her pocket.

"I will," she promised. "You find out who killed her, okay? We were as tight as sisters once, and even if that's in the past, I still feel like someone ripped out part of my heart."

"We'll find out," Natalia assured her. "That's what we're all about here. And we're very good at what we do."

Horatio had stepped outside the house to breathe some fresh Miami air for a minute when his phone rang. He glanced at the caller ID. "Ms. Boa Vista," he answered. "What's up?"

"Horatio," Natalia said. "Like I told you, I was doing some digging around on Wendy Greenfield."

"Yes. You learned something?"

"I think maybe so. She likes bad boys, so on a hunch, I checked out the visitor logs for your guy Lyall Douglas, last time he was in Miami-West."

"And?"

"Wendy visited him there. Numerous times."

"That is interesting, Natalia. I wonder if her husband knows about that."

"There's more, Horatio. I cross-checked under her name, and he's not the only inmate she's apparently friendly with."

"Keep going." He watched Alexx Woods heading into the building to begin her examination of the victims, and tossed her a nod and a grim smile. She wiggled her fingers at him, but he could see that she was bracing herself, mentally and emotionally, for what she would encounter inside.

"She also visited a man named Tony Aldicott, who's currently in jail on a DUI. He's been in for three months of an eighteen-month sentence. He's been inside before, too, and he and Lyall used to be cell mates, a few years ago."

"Very interesting," Horatio said.

"Yesterday, Tony was on a work detail, doing some roadside clean-up. Guess where?"

Horatio wasn't big on guessing games. "Where?"

"About three miles from where Wendy's car was found."

"Fascinating." An image was coming together in Horatio's mind, a picture of how the disparate facts that he knew about Wendy's case might all fit together. It was not quite a guess—more of a supposition based on what he had learned so far. Police work was all about filling in the holes between what was known and what wasn't, then testing the suppositions one had reached.

Either Wendy and Lyall were an item first, or Wendy and Tony were. She met one man while visiting the other, or else in between stints in jail. Whichever way it happened, she started an affair with the second man. Hence the private visits to both of them in prison. One way or another, the three were friends, and Lyall and Wendy had decided that it was time to bust Tony out. Horatio was willing to bet the clothing found in her trunk fit Tony Aldicott and would be used to replace his prison orange jumpsuit after the shotguns were put into play. In case they were caught or observed, she and Lyall faked the carjacking, so she could claim to be a victim and not jeopardize her marriage to her wealthy husband—a marriage no doubt loaded with benefits for her boyfriends as well as for herself.

Probably, he thought, the reason she wanted Tony out was because of her pregnancy. She didn't want the father of her child rotting in jail while she gave birth. Perhaps she hadn't even spilled the fact of her pregnancy to Lyall until the plan had been put together, when she had to explain its urgency. Further, Lyall had probably thought that she was finished with Tony—at least, that way—and that he only had to share Wendy with one man, not two. Not being the husband or the father had probably made Lyall feel like the bottom of the heap.

So he agreed to the plan, while hatching one of his own—one that would leave her a murder victim, patently on her way to commit a crime. Like most small-time criminals, Lyall Douglas likely suffered under the delusion that the police didn't put much effort into finding the killers of their fellow crooks.

If so, he would be in for an unpleasant surprise.

Maxine Valera was already working up the DNA of Wendy's fetus. When they found Lyall they'd get a comparison sample from him. It would be easy to obtain one from Tony Aldicott, still an unwilling resident of Miami-West. Horatio didn't know which one would wind up being the father—probably Tony—but it was entirely possible that Wendy didn't know for sure either.

"Horatio?"

"I'm here, Natalia. That's terrific work, thank you."

"I hope it helps."

"It helps a great deal." He closed the phone and put it away. This had turned into a busy couple of days, and he was glad that they were at least approaching the solution to one of their cases.

He'd be a lot happier when they found Lyall Douglas.

He had a feeling it wouldn't take long now.

18

ERIC DELKO HAD BEEN inside some truly disgusting houses.

Most criminals looked at the rules of house-cleaning the same way they did the rest of society's laws and mores—with disdain and contempt. He had grown accustomed to seeing rats and maggots in their homes, trash strewn around, dirt and dust and grease coating every surface.

He was happily surprised to learn that Lyall Douglas was a better housekeeper than most, relatively speaking. The front yard gave no indication that the interior would be cleaner than any other thug's home, but inside, while the place was far from neat, at least it wasn't god-awful. Douglas appeared to own a vacuum cleaner and a broom and maybe even a dust rag, and he knew how to use them. The house smelled like last night's din-

ner, and compared to what Eric had expected, that
wasn't a bad thing.

"I'm surprised," Calleigh said as they walked inside, echoing what Eric had been thinking.

"I know, huh? Place isn't too filthy."

"We've definitely seen worse."

"I like those crime scenes in rich neighborhoods,
where the housekeepers keep the place so spic-
and-span that the lemon scented cleansers over-
power the blood and bodily wastes." Eric smiled at
Calleigh. "Too bad they don't crop up that often."

"If we wanted to surround ourselves with that
kind of environment, we could always marry rich,"
Calleigh suggested. "Or become housekeepers."

"The latter seems more likely in my case."

"My luck hasn't been much better," Calleigh
said. "Anyway, I didn't think your problem was
that you couldn't find women, it's that you don't
want to . . . you know, learn their names and ad-
dresses. Or have conversations. Both of which are
pretty much prerequisites for marrying, rich or
otherwise."

Eric glanced away from her. Calleigh knew him,
all right. Well enough to know where his buttons
were. He liked to play the field.

That's putting it mildly, he thought.

*Truth is, Delko, you like to get your rocks off and go
home.*

There was, he believed, nothing wrong with that
as long as everyone knew the score. The times he

had deviated from that pattern, like with Boa Vista, things had turned scary. A pregnancy scare with her—a false alarm, as it turned out—had given him nightmares of parenthood, commitment, a lifetime with just one woman.

He shook his head, keeping his wry smile away from Calleigh's gaze. She might well know what it meant, and it would launch her off into another diatribe about his personal life. She accepted him, but that didn't mean she thought much of his choices.

"You're right, Calleigh," he said. "I guess I can write off the idea of marrying rich. There's always Powerball, right?"

"Sure, Eric. And there's also the chance that one of the drug kingpins we arrest will reward you with a million bucks for turning his life around. Odds are about the same."

Lyall Douglas's house was not, as far as they knew, a crime scene. But they had to put similar effort into processing it. Most people who left a house behind—especially if they left in a hurry—also abandoned clues to their next destination. They weren't after evidence to put him in jail, necessarily, they just wanted to figure out where he had gone. They carried their crime scene kits and had come fully prepared to process the scene as they would any other.

"I'll start in the bedroom," Calleigh said, glancing at the nudie magazines on the coffee table in the living room. "With any luck all his porn and biologicals will be out here."

Eric followed her gaze, saw what she meant. "Sure," he said. He didn't want to deal with Douglas's spilled semen either, but they did need DNA to compare to Wendy's fetus. Anyway, it wouldn't hurt to know where it was so he could avoid stepping in it.

Before he got involved in that, however, he took a good long look at the living room, hoping something would call out to him as a likely starting point. He didn't see any handy notepads on which Douglas might have written down a forwarding address, bearing down so hard that Eric could decipher it by rubbing a pencil across the next page down. Come to think of it, he had never been quite that lucky. Maybe he had found something that had worse odds than Powerball after all.

What he did see was mud on the carpet.

The mud was dark brown, rich looking, fertile. It was dry but maybe hadn't been for long. Some of it was stacked in a curve that looked like the edge of a shoeprint. More was simply scattered across the floor as if it had fallen from a shoe or from some other object carried through the room. It had been ground into the carpet, but there was what Eric considered a statistically significant amount of it around. He crumbled some between his fingers, finding it soft and moist inside.

And it hadn't rained all week.

He went back out to the department Hummer and fetched the forensic vacuum, a small hand-held vacuum cleaner with a long wand-type neck and a chamber that held a paper filter. The filter collected microscopic particles of soil and held it for examination at the lab. Usually that meant analyzing it with an optical comparison microscope or a scanning electron microscope. If the mud turned out to be evidence of a crime—if, say, the mud matched that at the location where Wendy Greenfield's car had been found—then it would go that far, but at this point Eric didn't think that would be the case.

But he thought the mud might offer a clue as to where Douglas had gone—if it was rare or unusual mud, that was, and if in fact it had come from wherever the guy had taken off to instead of a gardening project he'd been working on in the front yard before he left.

Then again, Eric had seen the front yard. The guy was no big-time gardener.

"Not much to see in here," Calleigh reported from the bedroom. "Lyall Douglas sleeps *au naturel*, judging from the hairs and epithelials in his bedding. And from the fact that his dresser contains no pajamas. And there's not much underwear for a guy with no washer and dryer in the house."

"Thanks for that update," Eric said. "I might have something here—not sure yet."

"Let me know," Calleigh replied. "The sooner I

can stop poking around in this guy's personals, the better I'll like it."

"I'll keep you posted," Eric muttered to himself. A hunch had started niggling around in his brain, and he turned his attention to that, trying to tease it into fully revealing itself.

He followed the dropped mud through the living room and kitchen (where it had been stepped on, smearing it against old, faded linoleum tile flooring, yellow and black that matched the appliances and the ceramic tiles of the backsplash behind the sink—the kind of kitchen, Eric thought, where he'd expect to see pot holders shaped like honeybees). A back door led out of the kitchen into the backyard, which was not quite as overgrown as the front. Maybe Douglas owned a mower after all.

Standing in the doorway, at the top of three raw wooden steps that descended down to the yard, Eric scanned the grassy swath. A couple of trails had been beaten down through the grass. One led to a wooden enclosure in which Eric could see the lids of aluminum garbage cans. Presumably the cans were beneath the lids, but the fence hid them from view. Another trail led all the way to the back of the yard, where a line of trees and taller growth probably marked the property line. The grass back there was greener than in the yard, possibly indicating a water source.

He stepped off the stairs and into the grass, watching before he put down his feet so as not to crush anything that might be important. There didn't seem to be anything in the yard, though, *except* yard. But then he found traces of mud—mud that looked like the stuff he had found inside. He kept going.

At the tree line, he peered through leaves and tall grass and low brush and spreading ferns. He was right. There was a creek back there. At the point where the trail across the yard met the tree line, he saw signs of disturbance. A broken leaf stem on a fern, a leaf that had been trampled into the ground, that kind of thing. Like someone had passed through carefully—just not carefully enough to fool a CSI.

Eric stepped through, even more carefully, and followed the path to the creek's edge.

Where the ground was muddy. Rich, black mud, easily tracked into a house.

He checked for alligators before he went any farther. In Miami, it wasn't smart to ignore the possibility that gators might be lurking inside any body of water, mostly submerged, just their nostrils and eyes floating above the surface. He had seen them in residential swimming pools, streams, swamps, golf course water hazards, once even in the fleeting pond made by a broken hydrant.

On the other side of the creek was a similar line of trees and brush, then another yard and another house. That one was smaller, almost entirely engulfed by trees and tall growth, like a rustic fishing cabin. He could see only glimpses of the road that led to the little house, just enough to tell that it was dirt, and rarely traveled.

Which might make it a good hideout.

He thought about calling Calleigh but didn't want to disturb her for nothing. He'd just have a quick look at the place. If Lyall was there—simply relocated by hauling some of his stuff across the creek—he should be able to tell easily enough, and then he could go back and get Calleigh and call for backup.

Still, he wouldn't take any stupid chances. Just in case, he drew his service weapon and continued forward cautiously, gaze shifting between the windows that faced the rear of the cabin. He didn't see anyone appear at either of them, no shadows or shifting reflections.

When Eric reached the cabin he pressed himself against the rough wood-sided wall and slowly, carefully approached the nearest window. It had a crude curtain, really just what looked like a piece of a sheet nailed or stapled above the window, but it was pulled aside and Eric could see a cluttered room, with cardboard boxes and plastic garbage bags stacked on and around the cheap furniture. It looked like someone had moved in quickly and hadn't taken the time to unpack.

Maybe from the house across the creek.

He risked a longer, more thorough look. The floor was wood, with the passageway between the room he could see into and what must have been a hallway worn in the center by years of foot traffic.

In the smooth spot Eric could see mud, like the mud from inside Douglas's house.

Has to be him. He didn't go far, just grabbed the stuff he thought he'd need and hauled it back here. Maybe he didn't think we'd bother searching the neighborhood—who would assume that someone wanted for murder would hide out right behind his address of record?

What he couldn't tell was if Douglas was inside. Maybe the other window would offer a better view. He ducked under the first one and hurried to the next.

Once more he drew his head slowly to the window, ready to react if he was spotted. He brought his left eye to the window's edge, peered in enough to make sure that no one was in sight.

And heard a distinctive click. Outside, not from the cabin. *Calleigh might know what kind of gun that is, just from the sound,* he thought stupidly, his muscles tensing, adrenaline surging through his body.

Then he heard a voice.

"You wanna drop that piece, hoss?"

19

Back from Karen Platt's law firm, inside his glassed-in corner office, Horatio scanned news reports online, using a laptop computer that rested on his sleek desk.

He knew that there had to be some connection between Marc Greggs and Karen Platt. The similarities between the two bomb attacks had demonstrated that. Which meant that the key to finding the bomber was figuring out what they had in common.

Once he reached that conclusion, the rest was easy.

Both had been important figures in a high-profile right-to-die legal case that had consumed the Miami papers, even reaching the national news, eight months ago. He remembered the case well, but now he studied the newspaper accounts from the time because he wanted to refresh himself on its details. He especially wanted to identify any other potential victims.

Sadly, that was not a small pool.

Hector Ibanez was a Cuban émigré who had been rising fast in Miami's rough-and-tumble political world—a particularly bloodthirsty subset of government that had a history of chewing up politicians and spitting out their bones. Maybe it was the heat, maybe the humidity, maybe Miami's unique mix of nationalities and lifestyles—and probably, Horatio believed, some of it stemmed from Miami's long connection to the drug trade (studies had shown that virtually all the currency in use in the city had cocaine on it, in fairly substantial quantities)—but things went on here that wouldn't be tolerated by any other city's political leaders.

Ibanez had been smart, shrewd, tough, and connected. As a young man, he had come out of Cuba with money, and with a circle of friends who enabled him to amass more in a hurry. His rise to prominence was fast, fueled in part by the Elián González case, which he had ridden to notoriety in Miami's Cuban-American community. The six-year-old González boy had been smuggled over from Cuba by his mother, without his father's knowledge. During the difficult crossing, she and most of the other would-be émigrés on their boat died. Fishermen found Elián floating in an inner tube and handed him over to the Coast Guard. He was put temporarily into the custody of his great uncle in Miami, but his father wanted the boy returned to him in Cuba. Relatives in the United States wanted him to be allowed to stay, but the law demanded otherwise, and it was enforced by a SWAT team's raid on the Miami house where he was staying. The child was taken, over mass protests, and returned to his father's care. When young Elián had been sent back to Cuba, Ibanez's reputation as one of the boy's staunchest defenders had not gone with him. It was said that Ibanez couldn't buy his own drink or meal in Little Havana for a year after that.

But Hector Ibanez had not been satisfied with being a prominent player in Cuban-American politics. He had his eye on bigger prizes, and his support in the Cuban community catapulted him easily onto Miami's City Council. There, his genuine political skills became apparent. Supporters started to talk openly about a future Mayor Ibanez, and to whisper his name in connection with the word "governor." No one expected it to take him long, either.

All that changed the night he was driving his brand-new Dodge Stealth on the Venetian Causeway (after, some claimed, visiting the married girlfriend on Belle Isle who had paid for it—but this was Miami, after all) and, in passing a slow-moving tourist's Camry, had slammed into an oncoming eighteen-wheeler.

Ibanez had been airlifted to Dade Memorial Hospital, where he spent the rest of his life. The doctors who treated him declared that life over almost as soon as he arrived. His brain had suffered severe trauma, and he was brain-dead, they said. Although his body still functioned, it was only marginal function, and that with the help of the latest medical technology. Left to its own devices, it would shut down and join his brain in permanent slumber. Everything that had made Hector Ibanez who he was had gone away and wasn't coming back.

His supporters and fans refused to accept that diagnosis. Their ranks included his adult son Esteban, and they wanted him kept alive by any means necessary. Doctors had been wrong before, they pointed out. Miracles could still happen. Hector Ibanez was a force of nature, they said—he had been counted out before but had always emerged from any challenge stronger and more successful than before.

His wife and daughter took the opposite view. Ibanez had been an exciting, charismatic, powerful man. He wouldn't want people to see him sitting in a hospital bed, unable to eat or speak or even change himself. They didn't want people to know that their hero had to be moved around by orderlies to avoid bedsores, had to be washed by nurses. His sharp intellect had vanished, as had his sense of humor, his unerring memory for names and faces, the instincts that had made him an opponent to be feared or a friend to be cultivated. He was nothing but an empty shell, kept breathing only through profound medical interference, and every day his wife Carmen and daughter Antonia had to see him that way was agonizing for them. Besides, they argued, he had always said he didn't want to be saved through heroic measures, and he feared brain death more than anything. To keep him alive was torture for everyone, especially him.

So the legal lines were drawn, lawsuits and countersuits filed. Ibanez had a living will, but its authenticity was contested. Esteban testified against his mother and sister, and they returned the favor. Each side won some victories, but the side favoring Ibanez's death won more. The case went to the state's Supreme Court, which sided with Carmen and Antonia. Esteban made an appeal to the governor, but he, leery after the backlash in the Terri Schiavo case, refused to intervene. Esteban went to Congress, where the issue was debated, but ultimately the decision was left up to Florida's courts.

Finally, after three years of struggle, the plugs were pulled. Eight months ago Hector Ibanez drifted off to a sleep that didn't look much different than his last three years had, and he never woke up.

Doctor Marc Greggs had been Hector's chief neurosurgeon, and ultimately had been the one who turned off the machines that kept him alive. Karen Platt had represented Carmen Ibanez and her daughter through the various suits and coun-tersuits. The connection, Horatio decided, couldn't be clearer.

The Baby Boomer had shifted his focus from abortion providers to the people involved in Ibanez's death.

A clearing throat drew Horatio's attention away from the computer. He swiveled in his black office chair to see Wendell Asher standing in his door-way. "You wanted to see me?"

"Special Agent Asher, yes, I did. Thank you for dropping by. I want to tell you what I've just learned."

"I'm all ears, Lieutenant," Asher said.

Horatio filled him in. "What I don't understand," he finally said, "is why your bomber has changed his obsession. Isn't that rare?"

Asher didn't answer right away. He cleared his throat again and blew his nose on a tissue as he tried to compose his response. Wadding it up, he held it gingerly until Horatio scooted a waste-basket toward him. Asher tossed the tissue inside. "Thanks. And you're right," he said after a while. "It is rare. I don't think it's unheard of, but it's unusual. Then again, if this guy was your usual nut job, I'd have caught him years ago. He's smart enough to dodge me, so maybe he's smart enough to know that switching things up once in a while will help him stay free. Maybe he's even smart enough to have varied interests. A lot of religious conservatives see euthanasia as usurping God's authority, right? Just like abortion, they see it as a form of state-sanctioned murder. When you look at it that way, it's not such a big change after all."

"I suppose that's true," Horatio said.

"I mean," Asher continued, "it's really not so different. An unborn child is unable to speak up for his rights, isn't he? So is a guy who's been declared brain-dead. We don't really know what might have been going on in his head, or in Terri Schiavo's or anyone else's in a similar predicament. We know what the electrical impulses show on medial equipment, but that's not the same as truly knowing what's in the heart or soul. But again, that person can't speak up, can't defend his right to live. So the state reaches a decision and yanks the plug, right? Game over."

"Game over," Horatio repeated noncommittally. His job was to enforce existing laws, not to second-guess them. He'd let others worry about right-to-die issues while he worked on preserving the right of potential murder victims to keep on living.

"Sorry to yammer on like this," Asher said, as if picking up Horatio's mood. "I have a tendency to run my mouth, especially when I'm talking about this case. I think maybe I've been living inside this guy's head for too long, you know?"

"That's an occupational hazard, isn't it?" Horatio said. One with which he, by virtue of his brother's experience undercover, was far too familiar. Ray had gone so deep into his drug-using persona, he had almost lost track of who he really was. Once he had been able to shed the cover story—and come back from a faked death—he took his wife Yelina and their son and went into hiding.

"Tell you what, Horatio. When all this is over, before I head back to Denver, I'd love to buy you a cup of coffee or a steak dinner or something. We can sit down together and really get acquainted, all right?"

"I'd like that," Horatio said. Which wasn't necessarily true but seemed like the polite thing to say. He still had to work with the guy, after all, and didn't think it would help their working relationship to point out that he had no interest in getting acquainted with an out-of-town Bureau drone.

When he got Asher out of his office, his next call was to Frank Tripp. Once again, he had to outline his thoughts, although Frank had lived through the whole story and remembered it well, so the process went faster than it had with Asher. And Frank didn't interrupt as often.

"Sounds like you've nailed it," Frank said at the story's end.

"Which means that what we need to do is put bodies around everyone else associated with the case," Horatio said. "The judges who heard it in its various trials and appeals. The other doctors who testified. *Their* lawyers. Journalists and pundits who wrote opinion pieces in favor of letting Ibanez die. It's a big list, Frank."

"That's what overtime's for," Frank said. "I'm on it."

"And Frank?" He hadn't told Asher this part, had barely wanted to believe it was true. The news accounts, though, had reminded him that it was.

"Yeah?"

"Alexx Woods did the postmortem on Ibanez."

A moment's silence. Horatio could hear the faint hum of the line. "She still at the morgue?"

"Yes."

"I'll get someone over there."

"Do it. And get a car to her house, pick up her husband and kids. I'm going to put in a call to Jorge Ortiz, have him check that location first."

"Got it," Frank said. "And I'll get someone over to Ibanez's wife's house, too."

"Good. I'm on my way there after I check in with Alexx, and I'll feel more comfortable if there's a uniform outside when I get there."

"Horatio," Alexx said. As he approached he noticed that her eyes were moist.

"Are you all right, Alexx?"

"I'm fine, Horatio." She gestured toward the ruined corpse of the lawyer, on her table. "It's just . . . I knew Karen Platt. Her son goes to school with my kids. We're not friends, but I see her at PTA meetings, the market . . . it hits close to home."

"Maybe closer than you think, Alexx." He had stopped off at the morgue before driving out to Carmen Ibanez's house, but he couldn't spare a lot of time. Mostly he had wanted to check in, to see with his own eyes that she was safe.

"What do you mean?"

"What I mean, Alexx, is that we believe the bomber is targeting people connected to the Hector Ibanez case. You did the post in that one, right?"

"Yes, of course I did."

"Even though there was no doubt as to the cause or circumstances of his death."

"Not at all. But in a high-profile case like that, especially with questions remaining about his exact medical condition, there's almost always a postmortem examination. I happened to catch that one." She considered for a moment, staring into space, as if trying to read her own notes from the time. "I found extensive, permanent brain damage. Mister Ibanez was totally deaf and blind, nonresponsive to any external stimulus, with almost complete impairment of every mental process. There was no medical chance that he would have recovered brain function." She paused again, then caught Horatio's gaze, her eyes bright with fear, and steadied herself with one hand on the table. "Do you think I'm a target, Horatio?"

"It's possible. Frank has already dispatched a car out to your house to pick up your family. Jorge Ortiz is going in with the bomb squad to make sure the bomber hasn't been there yet." He ticked his head toward the door. "There's an officer outside that door, and until we catch this guy, you and your family will be protected at all times."

"Okay, Horatio. We'll do whatever you need us to. Just find that bastard."

He offered her a comforting smile. "I intend to do just that."

"You really think he'll go after her? The grieving widow?" Ryan asked en route to Bal Harbour. They were headed north on Highway 1, and would cut across the northern end of the bay on 922.

"I think he'd like nothing more than to kill her. She was the one who pressed the hardest. She was the public face of the right-to-die side of the debate. And she was the wife. In the killer's mind, of all people, she should have stood by her man, shouldn't she? No matter what."

"Yeah, you're probably right, H." Ryan looked out the windows at the traffic falling behind them. "And people say I drive fast."

"You do," Horatio said. "Right now there's a reason for it."

"A reason? You think he's there now?"

"I don't know where he is. But I don't want to take that chance. The thing about this bomber is that he needs time to prepare his attacks. He plants his devices carefully, conceals them well, and makes sure they'll hurt the people he wants hurt. All of which requires him to spend a certain amount of time on the premises. He's got to know that we'll figure out the connection between Greggs and Platt soon enough, if we haven't already, which means he has to hurry up and get to whatever other victims he wants to hit right away."

"Makes sense," Ryan said. "But what if he's done? What if the lawyer and the doctor were his only targets here? Or he figures out that we're on to him and decides to cut his crusade short?"

"Then he moves to another city, another set of targets. I don't think this is a guy who'll stop what he's doing until someone stops him. If he leaves town, he'll still be Special Agent Asher's problem, but not ours."

"In some ways that'd be a relief, huh?"

"In some ways," Horatio said. "But I don't intend to let that happen."

20

CALLEIGH BAGGED A long blond human hair, hoping it wasn't one of hers. She didn't think it was—hers was pulled back and banded to keep it in check, and she had found this near the center of Lyall Douglas's bed, where she hadn't been. A close look revealed that it still had its follicular bulb, which meant DNA could be extracted from it. Chances were it belonged to Wendy Greenfield. If it did, it wouldn't help locate Douglas, but it would be one more thing connecting him to his victim.

If he went to court, that would aid the case against him. The idea was to have an overwhelming amount of physical evidence at the disposal of the State Attorney. Sometimes people would buckle under the weight of it and plead guilty without going to trial. Those who did offer defenses often found that juries might believe that one or two bits of physical evidence weren't convincing, but that one after another after another stacked up like bricks built a solid wall of proof.

The trouble was, if they didn't find him, they'd never get him into a courtroom. She hoped Eric was having better luck at that than she was.

"Eric?" she said. "Are you getting anything useful?"

He didn't answer. *That's weird,* she thought. *He was just in the living room a few minutes ago.*

Or was he? Maybe it had been longer than she'd thought. Sometimes when she was scouring a scene for the tiniest bits of evidence, she lost track of time. Her mind went into its collecting groove and didn't pay attention to the passage of minutes, or even hours.

"Eric?" she said again, a little louder. "Hello?"

The stillness of the empty house answered her.

She went back into the living room. Eric's kit was still there, and so was the forensic vacuum. She saw the mud on the floor near it. Probably why he had brought it in, she guessed, to suck some of that up and get it back to the lab.

But no Eric.

She glanced at the bathroom door, but it stood open, the lights off. Even if he had used the bathroom—a big no-no at a crime scene, and they were treating this like a crime scene—he'd have heard her and responded. The house wasn't that big, so it only took her a minute to check all the rooms.

After that, she went back out to the Hummer. Maybe he was napping in the back. Unlikely—Eric Delko was a professional, and wouldn't pull a stunt like that. _Unless he's sick or something . . ._

He wasn't at the vehicle, though. She looked up the block, then down it. Had he gone to a neighbor's house to use a bathroom there? But why wouldn't he have said something?

This, she thought, _is_ really _a mystery._

And as with most mysteries, evidence would reveal the answer.

She went back inside, trying to look at the house with a fresh eye. Now she wasn't trying to determine where Lyall Douglas had gone, but what had become of Eric. The clues might be the same and they might be entirely different.

She looked at his crime scene kit. At the vacuum. At the mud.

Mud?

She remembered the last day it had rained in Miami. She'd been off duty, helping a friend move from an apartment into a condo of her own. At the apartment building, Becky had lived on the second floor, and the staircase was an exterior one.

So, of course, rain. They had tried to wait it out, but the clouds settled in over the city like they didn't plan on going anywhere. Every now and then the rain lightened up, but it wouldn't quit.

Finally, they had decided that they had to go for

it, or they would not only be moving in the rain but also in the dark.

It had not, all in all, been Calleigh's favorite Miami day.

And it had been nine days ago.

She crouched beside the mud on the floor, looked at it. With her gloved hand she picked up a small clump, turned it over. This had definitely been wet more recently than nine days ago.

Rising, she followed the trail of mud through the kitchen to the back door. From there she could see recent tracks in the grass, blades of it smashed down, trying to stand up again. Big footprints. Eric was no NBA center, but he was a tall man, and to her his feet had always seemed huge.

At the back of the property, the footprints disappeared into thick foliage. The kind that might grow up around a stream. Where mud might come from.

Maybe Eric had found something in there. Calleigh followed his path. As she went, she hoped for a quick end to this particular mystery, so they could get back to the larger one.

Wendy Greenfield's killer was out there somewhere. Every minute not spent finding him was a minute he could be increasing his lead.

That wouldn't do at all.

Time slowed down.

Eric's mind raced. He stared at the man who

could only be Lyall Douglas, physically and in his posture identical to the man he had seen on the Quick Spree surveillance tape. His narrow face, with hooded eyes and a cruel, thin-lipped mouth surrounded by a brown mustache and goatee, framed by longish brown hair, was the same as the one in Douglas's mug shot.

But Eric also saw a sparrow flitting from a low branch to one slightly higher up, its individual wing beats distinct, frozen in space, as if photographed under a strobe light. A shred of leaf fell from the branch the bird landed on (branch vibrating under its miniscule weight), twisting and turning on a gentle breeze as it wafted down. High overhead, an airliner, not much more than a spot of silver against the azure sky, passed behind a white cloud as it arched out over the Atlantic.

Sounds, too, came at him distinctly, amplified by whatever in his brain had slowed the world down to this degree. He could hear the beating of the sparrow's wings, Douglas's ragged breathing, his own pulse pounding. He smelled sweat: his and Douglas's, twisted in a blend of fear and anxiety, and the rich, dank odor of the creek, and the oily stink of Douglas's gun.

While all this was happening, Eric tried to figure out how to react. Douglas had come around the far corner of his hideaway cabin holding a Taurus 9 semiautomatic pistol. Catching Eric peeking through his window, his hands against the cabin wall to steady himself, Douglas had aimed his weapon at Eric's chest while Eric's gun dangled uselessly from his fingers. He hadn't just opened fire, which was good. But he had killed once—at least—and Eric didn't doubt that he'd be willing to do so again. The only reason he hadn't already been shot, Eric guessed, was that Douglas wanted to know what was going on before he killed again. If Eric had still been at the other window, closer to the corner Douglas had rounded, Douglas might have been startled enough to shoot immediately.

As it was, Eric had only seconds to come up with a plan.

Douglas had ordered him to drop his weapon. He could do that, hoping to stall the killer for another minute or two, while he figured out that Eric was with law enforcement. But he knew that cops who surrendered their weapons usually didn't live long enough to regret it. Or he could hang on to the weapon, see if Douglas was really willing to shoot, and hope for a chance to get a shot of his own off.

Either scenario could easily end with a hole in Eric's heart and a trip to Alexx's morgue.

So Eric chose option number three, without even thinking it through.

Although he'd been caught with his gun pressed up against the cabin, when Douglas had startled him, he had dropped his hands away from the wall. He hadn't aimed the weapon, assuming that would be taken as a threat and would bring an immediate response, but it was held more or less pointed at the ground several feet to Douglas's left.

He squeezed the trigger.

The gun roared, and with it time sped up again, to normal speed and then some. Even as the gun bucked in his hand and the bullet hurtled in Douglas's general direction and Douglas reacted by yanking on his own trigger, Eric was airborne, diving toward the near corner of the cabin. He launched himself into the air and flew, arms outspread, around the corner. He hadn't been able to see what was there, but now tall grass with a couple of loose cinder blocks in it zoomed toward his hands. His feet were the last to clear the corner, and before his trailing right made it around, he felt an impact like someone had kicked his shoe, hard.

Then he was rolling, tumbling, a chunk of concrete block tearing at his shoulder, grass spiking at his face. He found his balance and rolled to his feet, aiming the weapon at the corner for what he assumed would be a fairly immediate appearance by Douglas. Whipping his head around to check the far corner, behind him, he knew that this situation wouldn't be acceptable for more than a few seconds. Douglas could go around the house in either direction, or he could go back inside and fire through a window. Either way, Eric was out here alone, on unfamiliar turf, with no escape plan and no backup.

Stupid. Just stupid, Delko. What the hell?

He risked a glance at his foot. A bullet had grazed his shoe, ripping off a chunk of tread. At least it had not passed through an inch higher, which would have shattered some of his cuneiform bones and crippled him.

He heard the rustle of grass. Douglas making his move. Eric's finger tightened on the trigger. This shot would be make or break. Life or death. He blew out a long breath, trying to steady his hand.

And he heard Calleigh's voice, loud and commanding. "Miami-Dade PD! Put that weapon down on the ground and kick it away from you, then lock your hands behind your head!"

Nothing had ever sounded so sweet.

Eric rose and went back to the corner. Calleigh had just come through the brush by the creek, her service weapon gripped in both fists and pointed at Douglas. Her arms were as steady as her gaze. "On your knees!" she barked.

Douglas complied, lowering himself to his knees, hands behind his head. His balance was precarious.

"You have handcuffs, Eric?" she asked.

"Not on me." They were back in the house, with his evidence kit. *Also stupid,* he thought. *This has not been your best day, Eric.*

Calleigh released her gun with one hand, reached behind her, and brought out a pair from her belt. Her gaze remained riveted on Douglas the whole time and her weapon didn't waver. She tossed the handcuffs toward Eric.

"Thanks," Eric said, holstering his weapon and picking them up from the grass. They had fallen well short of him, but he couldn't blame her for not focusing on her throw. Passing between Douglas and the cabin so he didn't block Calleigh's shot for even a moment, he went behind the man, and closed one of the manacles around his right wrist. "Lyall Douglas," he said, "you're under arrest for the murder of Wendy Greenfield." He closed the other manacle over Douglas's left wrist and pulled him to his feet.

"You might as well add the attempted murder of CSI Eric Delko," Calleigh suggested. "Just for good measure."

"Why not?" Eric asked. "And what she said. You have the right to remain silent. . . ."

21

WHEN THEY CROSSED into Bal Harbour, it was apparent from the scenery—neatly manicured topiary, spotless streets, a stretch limo the length of a football field or two idling outside a high-end pet groomer's. "You'd better not speed here, H," Ryan cautioned. "They don't care who you are."

Horatio was already driving within the legal limit, but he double-checked the speedometer at Ryan's warning. He was right—Bal Harbour's police took great pains to prosecute speeders, and any other violator of the law, to the fullest possible extent. Their efforts kept the tony community safe, if a little on the bland side.

The Ibanez family had lived in Little Havana originally, just a couple of blocks off Calle Ocho. With the neighborhood's transition from original Cuban families to those from Central America and Mexico—and with their growing wealth—the Ibanezes had moved to Bal Harbour, while many of their Cuban neighbors chose Hialeah or the Gables or even the southern suburb of Kendall. Little Havana was nowhere near as Cuban as it had once been, but some families of Cuban descent still lived there, and you could still find a good *ceviche* or *arroz con pollo* there if you knew where to look.

Their Bal Harbour home was a startlingly modern structure, stark white with angles and planes that seemed almost randomly chosen instead of designed—which could only mean that its design had been carefully thought out, and expensive. Huge windows took full advantage of sun and views, and mature palms offered shade from the worst of the afternoon glare (even now, the sun hammered down on the west side, but behind the trees the house looked cool). The grounds were as carefully maintained as the rest of Bal Harbour. Horatio thought that to fail to mow one's lawn here might cause the neighbors to rise up in a mob as angry as any that ever stormed Doctor Frankenstein's castle, but he didn't know if that theory had ever been tested.

A cruiser sat outside the house. The officer at its wheel had made Horatio and Ryan for cops even before they came to a stop, and was out of his car by the time their feet hit the pavement. "You Lieutenant Caine?" he asked. He was tall and trim, with a bushy mustache and eyes that never slowed down.

"I am," Horatio said.

"Was told to expect you." He checked Horatio's ID badge carefully, leaving nothing to chance. Horatio appreciated that.

"I'm here now. Can you stick around? I'm not sure how long we're staying."

"I'm not going anywhere," the officer said.

"Family inside?" Ryan asked.

"Mrs. Ibanez is home with a couple of household servants, and there's a gardener working in the back."

"That's fine," Horatio said. "Thanks for your help."

He and Ryan proceeded up a concrete walkway flanked by yard lights—handy, since otherwise he'd have had no clue where the front door was. It turned out to be recessed into a shady alcove bursting with greenery in elevated pots. A maid opened the door before he knocked, a slender woman with jet-black hair and a bashful gaze.

"I'm Horatio Caine with the Miami-Dade Crime Lab," he said. "I'd like to see Mrs. Ibanez, please."

"Yes, come in," she said. Even with those few words Horatio could detect a strong accent. Not Cuban, but maybe Nicaraguan, he believed, or Salvadoran. She hadn't been in the country long.

She led them into a library, which seemed to be the only room that didn't have floor-to-ceiling windows on at least one wall. Instead, it had floor-to-ceiling bookcases. The books on the shelves didn't look like your typical magazine layout array purchased by the foot, but instead appeared to have been read and shelved in ways that made sense. Mostly nonfiction, with lots of Latin American history and biographies, there were also pockets of fiction best sellers and a wide assortment of books in Spanish. Paperbacks had been shelved in with hardcovers, another indication that this library was meant to be used rather than merely admired.

In the library, a woman in her midfifties, Horatio guessed, sat in a comfortable leather chair with her feet tucked up under her, reading a book. Beside the chair, a small round table held a reading lamp and a cup of coffee or tea. She looked up when she heard footsteps on the tile floor, tilting reading glasses down on her nose and eyeing the newcomers over their rims. Her eyes were dark and direct, her face open, angular but quite lovely. A few threads of silver accented her black hair, as perfectly placed as if they had been painted there by a master. Her pose was entirely casual, but there was an air of entitlement about her that could only mean she was the head of the household.

"You are the lieutenant," she said. It wasn't a question.

"I am, Mrs. Ibanez," Horatio said. "Horatio Caine. This is CSI Ryan Wolfe."

"A CSI. And the officer sitting outside, frightening the neighbors. He said you're from the crime lab?"

"That's correct."

"Don't you usually show up someplace *after* a crime has been committed?"

"That's right, ma'am," Horatio said.

"Do you think that one has been committed here?"

Horatio glanced around. The maid who had brought them in still waited by the door, in case someone ordered a drink, Horatio guessed. Now he could smell Carmen Ibanez's café Cubaño, and he wouldn't have minded a cup, but she didn't offer and he didn't ask. "I don't know yet," he said. There was no gentle way to phrase the next thing he had to say, but he kept his tone as soft and comforting as he could. "Mrs. Ibanez, I'm afraid that someone is killing people who were involved in the legal case surrounding your husband's hospitalization and death. So far, Karen Platt and Doctor Marc Greggs have both been murdered. I don't know who's next, but I believe that you might be in danger."

Carmen Ibanez bit down on her full lower lip, and moisture showed in her eyes. "I saw Marc at a charity luncheon just a few weeks ago," she said. "I'm afraid I haven't spoken to Karen in months."

"I'm very sorry," Horatio said. "I know this has been a terrible year for you, and now this is just making things worse."

"And you think I might be a target?"

"You, and possibly your daughter," Horatio said.

"Who could be behind this?"

Horatio's first thought, after the obvious idea that the Baby Boomer had simply switched gears slightly, was that Esteban Ibanez, Hector and Carmen's son, might be involved. He didn't want to broach that idea without some evidence, though, so he didn't mention it to her. "The FBI believes that a man who has been bombing abortion providers in other states has come to Miami and taken on a new cause."

She rose from her seat and walked toward Horatio. She projected calm command, but he could tell her knees were rubbery. "I didn't understand why people in Washington would debate our private family matters," she said. A single tear had started down her cheek. "And I certainly can't understand why someone would kill over them."

"People kill for strange reasons," Horatio assured her. "And sometimes for none at all. In this case, we're not sure if the motivations are religious or political, or both, but the killer appears determined to make a point. He's taken many lives and we don't want one of them to be yours. Is your daughter at home?"

"No, she's in Spain for a month," Carmen said. "Is she safe there?"

"I'm sure she is," Horatio said. "That's a good place for her right now. Can you gather whatever servants are on the premises now?"

"Lupita," Carmen said sharply.

"*Sí,*" the maid said. She vanished from the room.

When she was gone, Carmen caught Horatio's gaze again. "I notice you didn't ask if my son was home."

"I know he doesn't live with you. And frankly, considering what we believe to be the killer's motives, I doubt that he's in any danger." He had every intention of talking to Esteban, and very soon, once he was finished here.

"You have done your homework, Lieutenant Caine."

"I always do."

Lupita returned with two more servants, an older man in a cotton jumpsuit who looked like a handyman, his hands nicked and scabbed by his work, and a woman in a white uniform who smelled of ammonia-based cleaning products from across the room. All of the household staff were Hispanics. "This is everyone," Carmen said. "You've met Lupita. This is Jesus, and Hilda."

"And there's a gardener?" Horatio asked, remembering what the officer outside had reported.

"I meant to ask you about that," Jesus said. "I never saw that gardener before, ma'am. Did something happen to Guillermo?"

Carmen froze in place, her expression one of shocked dismay. "I didn't hire any new gardeners."

"It's okay, ma'am," Horatio said quickly. "You just stay right here, and CSI Wolfe and I will check it out." He nodded toward Ryan. "Let's go."

22

JESUS SHOWED THEM the way to the backyard, where he said the gardener had been working last time he had seen him. Jesus's face was deeply lined, his hair no more than a few dark strands combed across his scalp, but his eyes were lively and bright even though he was deeply afraid.

Some gardening tools had been abandoned near a flower bed, but the person who had left them there was nowhere in sight. Horatio scanned in every direction, then made a decision. "Here's what I need you to do, Mister Wolfe. Go back inside and quietly get everyone out the front door, and then a thousand feet away from the house. Not an inch less, all right?"

"Got it," Ryan said. Without another word he took Jesus and hurried back into the house.

Horatio followed as far as the back door.

From there he was on his own.

He didn't think the bomber would have been able to plant anything in the library, since Carmen Ibanez had clearly been there for some time sipping coffee and reading.

That only left the entire rest of the house, which had somewhere north of five thousand square feet of floor space and a layout only slightly less confusing than the schematics for a space shuttle.

From what Asher had said—and from his own limited experience of the Baby Boomer—the man would be most likely to plant his device near Carmen's bedroom. She was the target, not her staff. He should have had Jesus show him where her bedroom was, but he didn't want any extraneous bystanders in the house an instant longer than absolutely necessary.

The house had two stories, and he was sure the main bedroom would be upstairs, so that narrowed things down. Gun in hand, Horatio crossed from room to room, kitchen to formal dining room to living room to home theater, until he found a staircase that wound up. He climbed carefully, making sure to keep his SIG Sauer at eye level as he ascended in case the Boomer was waiting for him.

At the top, the stairs fed into a kind of star-shaped foyer, with hallways branching off in three different directions. Horatio listened but heard nothing except bird sounds and the distant rumble of a car on a roadway. The floor here was thickly carpeted, but the passage of many feet had crushed the pile enough so that there was no way of telling which hall had been traveled most recently.

He decided to try the one that led to the east. Since the landscaping had clearly been designed to limit sun from the western exposure, he doubted if the master suite would face the west. More likely, it would look east, toward the sunrise and the ocean.

He glanced into each room as he passed, turning doorknobs silently, opening them only far enough to determine if they appeared to be a master bedroom.

The third door was the one.

And when he opened that door, a flash of movement inside convinced him that he'd made the right choice.

"Police!" Horatio shouted. "Freeze!"

The person who had been in the room, squatting near the big four-poster bed, darted through another doorway. As he went, he whipped a handgun out and fired a wild shot that slammed into the wall near the doorjamb. Too close for comfort, considering he had taken no time to aim. Horatio squeezed off a shot in return, but the target was gone by the time his round plowed into the far wall.

All Horatio had seen was a dark blur, with no distinguishing characteristics at all. He thought it was an adult male, but that was really more of a sensory impression than any kind of certainty.

"I'm coming in," Horatio said. "I'm armed, and

there are more officers outside. You're trapped, so it's time for you to surrender before someone gets hurt."

The man inside didn't respond. Horatio walked far enough into the bedroom to see that the intruder had ducked into a dressing alcove as big as Horatio's entire office back at the crime lab. Luxurious women's clothing hung everywhere, along the walls and from floor racks, and a dressing table with an illuminated mirror sat against one wall.

But he couldn't see the man who had run this way. He checked below the hanging clothes, looking for legs. His heart pounded, but the weapon was steady in his hand.

With another step closer, he could see that the alcove led into a bathroom, full of gleaming tile and gold fixtures. Firing a shot in there would risk ricochets, but he would do it if he had to. He just had to make sure he didn't miss.

He had taken two steps into the dressing alcove when the bomb went off.

Horatio heard the click of the detonator, even realized what it was, but that realization was simultaneous with the blast. A ball of bright white light with a fiery core flashed in front of his face. A pressure wave hit him an instant before the heat and knocked him backward, stunning him. The sound slammed into him at the same time as the heat wave, but the worst of the heat scorched the air above him, and he was already rolling away, pressing his face against the plush carpet, turning it away from the burst of flame. Debris rained down on his back.

Although he knew in what order the various effects of the blast reached him, in the moment it came all at once, pressure and heat and noise, and it felt like someone had shoved a lit firecracker in his mouth, like it was all happening inside his head and outside at the same instant.

When the rain of plaster and fabric and debris had settled, Horatio rolled again. His muscles seemed to work, his bones weren't broken. Blood trickled from ears (the ringing in them so loud he wasn't sure if he could hear anything, until he snapped his fingers as a test; that he heard, but far away, as if he were underwater with his hand above the surface) and his nose.

Blinking away the slivers of light burned into his retinas, Horatio found his gun, a couple of feet away from where he had landed. The bomber had apparently fled the scene, or at least had not taken advantage of Horatio's defenseless state. Maybe he thought his bomb had done the trick.

A small fire blazed in the closet, some of Carmen's clothing having been ignited by the blast. Horatio kicked the clothes to the floor, yanked a duvet off the big bed, and threw it over the flames, stomping on it until he was sure they were out. Then he stepped over the mess and into the bathroom, his weapon at the ready in case the bomber had taken refuge in the tub.

A glass shower enclosure was cracked and the bomb had left scorch marks on the white tile floor, but otherwise the room was clear. Another door, wide open, led out into a hallway. Horatio passed through it. Outside, he heard a car engine abruptly catch, and he raced to a window just in time to see a dark green sedan speeding away on the street behind the property. Through the trees he couldn't identify the driver or even the make of the car.

He was back in the bedroom, looking for a secondary device, when he heard someone on the stairs.

"Horatio!" Ryan sounded almost panicked.

"I'm fine, Ryan," he said. "I'm in the bedroom."

"Keep talking," Ryan said. "This house is like a maze."

"You're almost here," Horatio said. A moment later, Ryan appeared. When he saw Horatio, the relief was clear on his face.

"Are you okay? I heard—"

"We traded shots, and there was a small detonation," Horatio said. "Not enough to kill me, maybe even just a blasting cap or a little flash-bang. Here"—he pointed a small Maglite at a black box on the floor beneath the head of Carmen Ibanez's bed, about eight inches long, four wide, and three tall—"is the real bomb."

"Is it live?"

"It is. That's why I wanted everyone out of the house. Including you."

"Can you disarm it?"

"I might be able to," Horatio said. "Then again, opening the casing might set it off. Our man usually uses timers, but 'usually' isn't the same as always, and we don't know that he hasn't set a backup detonator that's triggered by vibration. We'll let the bomb squad render it safe remotely."

"Is there time?"

"The bomb that caught me was a quickie, and tiny," Horatio said. "More sound and fury than actual destructive power. I suspect it was something he had handy, that he could detonate on the run, meant to be a distraction if he needed one. If he could have detonated the big one remotely, he would have, since he knew that once the little bomb went off, even if it killed me, someone else would find the real one before Mrs. Ibanez slept here again. So the real bomb is on a timer, and there's no remote override. And it's set to detonate late tonight, when there's the best certainty that she would be asleep in bed."

"You're bleeding, though, H. You should get to a hospital, get checked out."

"I'm fine," Horatio said again. "Let's get out of here and get the bomb squad rolling."

23

AFTER A RADIO CAR took Lyall Douglas to be booked, Calleigh and Eric were left standing on the dirt road that led to Douglas's cabin hideout. "You think we've been processing the wrong scene?" Eric asked.

"I'm not sure there's any such thing," Calleigh said. "There are scenes that are helpful and scenes that aren't, but you don't know which is which until you look."

"Good point."

"I wasn't finding much of interest in his house, though. If you think we should have a look inside the cabin, I'm game."

"That's what I was thinking," Eric said. "If he moved over here because he had killed Wendy Greenfield and didn't want to be found—"

"In which case, he might have wanted to move farther away," Calleigh interrupted.

"No one ever said he was a genius."

"Most criminals aren't."

"Anyway," Eric went on, "he probably would have taken anything incriminating with him, or dumped it. There might be transfer from Wendy Greenfield at the house, but anything like blood-stained clothes would have been moved."

"That's probably true, Eric. I left my kit back at the house, and I believe you did too."

"With my common sense inside," Eric said. One of the things she liked about him was that he was willing to admit to making mistakes. Sometimes it took a while for him to see them as mistakes, but once he did he wasn't reluctant to acknowledge them.

"You were following the evidence," she said, letting him off the hook to some extent. "The mud pointed to the creek, and the creek pointed to the cabin. You just should have let me know before you followed the trail all the way to the cabin."

"You're right," Eric said. He tossed her a smile that let her know that he knew she was dressing him down, but doing it in her patented Duquesne fashion. She supposed it came from growing up with an alcoholic father who she loved dearly—she had plenty of practice expressing disapproval of her dad's actions without attacking his character, and she employed the same technique with the members of her CSI "family."

"Let's get our kits, then," she suggested, "and see what's inside that cabin."

As Eric had observed through the window, the cabin was a disorganized mess. Douglas had apparently hauled his things over from the house and dropped them wherever he could, but had not had time to go back through and put them away. He was a haphazard packer, too; one box Eric opened contained kitchenware, plates and mugs and silverware, none of it wrapped or separated (and most of it, as a consequence, chipped or shattered) and on top of it he had packed tools, a hammer and some pliers, wrenches and screwdrivers. On top of those he had added a layer of underwear, which might have served to protect the dishes if he had put it between them and the tools.

Douglas hadn't moved much into the cabin, but it was tiny and couldn't hold much anyway. It appeared to have already been furnished, in a manner of speaking. There were a couple of folding chairs and a card table in the main room, a TV set, a single floor lamp, and boxes. One end of this room was the kitchen, consisting of a sink, a small refrigerator, and a wooden counter that held a two-burner hot plate and a toaster oven. A bare lightbulb was mounted above the sink. The other room was a bedroom with a bathroom separated from it by a thin curtain, and it contained a twin bed, another lamp, and more boxes. The place smelled dusty and close, like it had been empty for a long time and Douglas hadn't had a chance to air it out.

"We should clear a path," Calleigh said when they went in the front door.

"I agree," Eric said. Clearing a path was important at any scene, because otherwise evidence could stick to an investigator's shoes and be walked right out of the case. With a cleared path, everybody knew what they were stepping on, and if anything was tracked into the path its origin could be retraced. "But to what?" There was no system at all to the placement of the boxes, and some of them had had things pulled out and set aside, which meant any path would include stepping over some of Douglas's things. And there had been no particular crime committed here, so it wasn't like they needed a path to a specific point. They needed to look at everything.

"You're right," Calleigh said. "Let's just get started, and be careful where we step."

"I can start in the back room," Eric suggested, "and we can work toward each other."

"Works for me."

Stepping carefully, checking the floor before he set either foot down, Eric worked his way through the mess into the cabin's bedroom. He could almost stretch his hands from wall to wall; for sure, if he tried to lie down, his head and feet would touch them. The other direction, the way the bed was arranged, there was a little more space—almost two feet separated the foot of the bed from the curtain that delineated the bathroom.

He started with the piles of dirty clothes on the floor. Keeping in mind the image he had seen of Lyall Douglas at the crime scene, in what looked like a solid color short-sleeved shirt and faded jeans, he picked up each item of clothing, one at a time. He scanned each one for suspicious stains, compared it to his mental image of what Douglas had been wearing that day, and looked for anything else out of the ordinary, including checking every pocket he came across. He found plenty of pocket lint, a few coins, a pebble, and a single rusted key, but nothing genuinely helpful. *It's like checking the pockets of an eight-year-old,* he thought.

When Eric had finished with the clothes on the floor, he turned to the boxes. There were three of them in a stack beside the bed. Eric folded back the flaps of the top one and saw yet more clothes. From the smell that wafted out, these were dirty too. Maybe he had been seeing Wendy because she had money, and he preferred buying new clothes to washing his old ones. As Calleigh had noted, there hadn't been a washing machine at his house, and this cabin barely had space for a washboard to use at the creek.

"Eric!" Calleigh's shout held undeniable urgency, and Eric grabbed his weapon as he rushed back out to the living room.

"What is it?"

"I think I might have found our murder weapon," she said. She stood in the kitchen area, behind the wooden counter. "In the drawer here."

He came around beside her. "Let's see."

She trained her Maglite on a folding knife, in a drawer full of kitchen utensils that could have been purchased at a thrift shop. Most looked like they had been new sometime in the seventies. The knife was newer, resting on top of the other utensils like it had been dropped in recently.

"That's not exactly a kitchen knife," he said.

"No," she said. "And it's got a six-inch blade on it. Not a Boy Scout knife, either." She put the flashlight down and took a camera from her kit, photographing the knife where it lay in the drawer.

"Any blood on it?" Eric asked.

"Let's find out." With her latex-covered fingers, she tore loose a paper towel from a roll and put it flat on the counter, then plucked the knife from the drawer and set it on the towel. She opened the blade partway, revealing a dark patch of something crusted near its back, where it would be hidden with the blade either fully open or fully closed. "Looks like maybe."

Eric reached into his crime scene kit, and found a small spray bottle of Luminol. He stopped himself, though. Luminol was handy and easy to use—a simple spritz on the questioned surface, and they could turn off the light. If the dark stuff was blood, it would glow a bright blue-green color.

On the other hand, it also might react to copper or iron compounds, and other substances. It could also cause the loss of certain genetic markers, which might make the identification of the blood donor more difficult. And it could cause the blood to run and obscure any potential prints on the knife, although he couldn't see any now. He had to train himself not to grab for it every time just because it was easy.

Instead, he brought out a sterile swab, a tube of Hemastix Reagent strips, and a small bottle of distilled water. Opening the water, he used a drop to moisten the end of the swab. As Calleigh put away her camera, he touched the swab to the dark spot on the blade, just brushing the edge of it and leaving most of the substance undisturbed for later analysis back at the lab.

Calleigh opened the bottle of Hemastix strips, which contained tetramethylbenzidine, or TMB, a chemical that reacted to the presence of blood by changing color, and removed one. She held it out for him, smiling like she was handing him a gift, and he applied the swab gently to the end of the strip, rolling it to be sure any transfer from the knife blade came into contact with it.

Sure enough, the strip's treated end turned blue-green immediately.

"We've got blood," Calleigh said. "No way to know until we get it to the lab if it's human. But my guess is that we'll find out that it is, and that it belongs to Wendy Greenfield."

"I'd like that," Eric said. "Be good to get this one wrapped up tight."

"Maybe no one told Lyall that it's hard to wash all the blood off any surface," Calleigh said. "Without using chlorine bleach, he was bound to leave traces."

Eric looked over the kitchen as he put the knife into a paper evidence envelope. The floor was dirty, the appliances covered with a film of grime. "He's not the world's biggest slob, but he hasn't had a chance to clean up this place. I figure he eats out most of the time, and that's probably for the best."

Calleigh nodded her agreement. "Let's finish up here, Eric. This place is making me lose my appetite."

24

ESTEBAN IBANEZ'S ADDRESS wasn't in Bal Harbour like his mother's, but that didn't mean it was in a poor neighborhood. He owned a condo on the twelfth floor of a building on Bay Avenue, with a view that looked back across Biscayne Bay toward the Miami skyline. When he opened the door and let Horatio in, the sun was lowering in the western sky, framed in a floor-to-ceiling window that silhouetted the young man's form.

"Esteban Ibanez?" Horatio asked.

"That's right."

Horatio's ears still rang like he carried a hive full of angry bees around in his mouth, and he had to strain to hear Esteban's soft voice. He had taken a quick shower and changed clothes, putting on a soft blue-and-white-striped silk shirt with a navy suit, but he had refused all suggestions that he seek medical attention. There might be time for that later, but not yet. "I'm Lieutenant Horatio Caine, with the Miami-Dade Crime Lab," he said. "I've just paid a visit to your mother's house. Someone planted a bomb there today."

"She called and told me," Esteban said. "She said you might be coming over. Would you come in?"

Esteban stepped sideways and swept his arm toward the big window. Horatio nodded and went past him, into a big room with a wooden floor polished to a high gloss, modern black furniture with silver and glass accents—some of which wouldn't have looked out of place at the lab—pricey-looking abstract paintings hung on the walls, and that million-dollar view. Esteban had not done badly for himself at all.

Hector Ibanez's son looked much like the photographs Horatio had seen of Hector as a young man. He was whip-thin, with a casual manner and a relaxed stance belied by sharp, interrogative eyes that Horatio had felt boring into him from the moment the door swung open. His dark hair was combed straight back from a high forehead, and it curled over the collar of a dress shirt worn with the tail untucked and the first three buttons opened.

"Mother said you almost caught someone at the house," Esteban said. "But there was a gunfight, an explosion, and the criminal escaped."

"That's right."

"And yet here you are, barely an hour later. You're not injured?"

"I'm fine."

"I'm pleased to hear it. Have a seat, Lieutenant Caine."

Horatio lowered himself into a comfortable leather chair, realizing as he did that his balance wasn't what it should be. He caught himself on the chair's arm and steadied himself, then sat.

"Thank you for saving my mother's life. I am in your debt."

"Not at all," Horatio said. "That's the job. I'm glad I got there in time."

"As are we all. My mother and I have been . . . estranged, you might say. But she is a good woman, and in spite of our serious differences, I wish her no harm."

"Can you think of anyone who might?"

Esteban settled onto a leather sofa across a steel and glass coffee table from Horatio's chair. The area was defined by an elegant kilim rug in colors that would echo the coming sunset. "I'm sorry, I thought you already had an idea on that score. She said other people involved in the case against my father have already been targeted."

"That's right," Horatio replied. "I hoped you might be able to narrow the field a little. Where were you an hour ago?"

Esteban's face took on an expression of surprise, his eyes going wide, mouth dropping open, the color blanching from his cheeks. But he recovered quickly and smiled a wolfish grin. "You can't genuinely believe I would have anything to do with an attack on my own mother."

"I don't know you well enough to rule it out, do I, Esteban? So why don't you help me?" He had caught the barest glimpse of the bomber, but the man had looked bigger than Esteban, stockier, carrying at least thirty or forty more pounds. But that didn't mean Esteban wasn't involved in some way.

"An hour ago, I was here. Entertaining a . . . a guest."

"Business, or pleasure?"

"Oh, entirely pleasure," Esteban said. "At least, on my part. I hope she got pleasure out of it too. She said she did."

"A young lady, then."

"Indeed."

"I'd like her name and address," Horatio said. "So I can confirm your account."

"Of course. I'll have to ask for your discretion, though. She is the fiancée of a business associate of mine."

"I see," Horatio said. "And what business is that?"

"Postcards."

"Postcards?"

"I own a publishing company. Postcards, calendars, those tourist booklets printed in eight languages. It's a competitive business, Lieutenant, but it can be quite lucrative. These past few years, tourists have been buying DVD postcards by the truckload."

"I can see that you've done very well, Esteban. And apparently you can set your own hours. How long was the lady here with you?"

"Since noon. We had lunch, and then . . ."

"You don't need to paint me a picture," Horatio said. He changed the subject abruptly, hoping to catch the man off guard. "The rift between you and your mother came about because of the court case?"

Esteban's eyes flickered toward the window as he mentally caught up with Horatio's conversational leap. "For the most part, yes. Before that . . . well, you know, there are always issues between sons and their parents, even after we are no longer children. Particularly when a mother is as controlling as mine."

"Your father was a powerful presence, right?"

"Yes, of course. A vital man. My hero, in so many ways. But Mother—behind the scenes, of course—ran everything. The household, his career. She is made of steel, that woman. Had you stood behind her, you needn't have worried about that bomb."

"Was this well known? Would your father's political enemies have any reason to target her now?"

Esteban shook his head. "His goals were political, not hers. To her, the politics was simply a means to an end. Material comforts, good schools for her children, a fresh start in life. She achieved her goals long ago."

"Which brings us back to the court case," Horatio said. "You took the opposite side, literally sued your own mother."

"She wanted to kill my father. How could I not?"

"The doctors say he was already dead in every way that mattered. His brain would never have functioned again. The man you loved was already gone."

"Doctors say many things. They tell us that diseases are incurable, and then they discover cures, the next year or the year after that. Meanwhile, anyone who gave up is already gone."

"So you wanted him to be kept alive, on machines, in case some experimental treatment came along that might have brought him back."

"Experimental treatment was one option," Esteban said. "A miracle was another."

"You were hoping for a miracle?"

"I prayed for one every day. During the trial and the protracted period before we actually went to court, I was surrounded by others who prayed with me, who insisted that a miracle was not only possible, but almost inevitable."

"Who were these people, Esteban?"

"I've never been a particularly religious person, Lieutenant. I'm a believer, I go to Mass and confession, but that's about the extent of it. These people—their faith was phenomenal. It guided every aspect of their lives, and they sought me out, offered me support, both financial and spiritual, during that difficult time."

"Were there any who you remember as more radical than the others?"

"If you think . . . no, I'm certain that they weren't the kind of people who would murder. They value life, above all. Causing anyone's death, even someone they disagreed with, would go completely against everything they stand for."

"I'll need as many names as you can remember, Esteban, just the same. Are you still in touch with them?"

"Some, of course. Not as frequently as I was then."

"Whoever tried to kill your mother won't give up easily, Esteban. She dodged one today, but she's still a target. It's very important that you try to think of anyone who might be part of such an attempt."

Esteban thought for a moment, chin resting on his loosely curled fist. "Families are strange beasts, Lieutenant Caine. We love our family members simply because they are who they are, when, if we met the same people under other circumstances, we might want nothing to do with them. We choose friends, we choose spouses, but sometimes those we remain closest to for our whole lives are those we never chose at all. That's how it is with my mother and sister. I would never befriend someone who argued in court for her husband to be killed. By the same token, I wouldn't have anything to do with people who would murder anyone. The people I have befriended, they value life, and in that way they're unlike my mother and sister. Strange, isn't it?"

"It is strange, Esteban," Horatio agreed. Most families, in his experience, were far less ideal than they might appear, once you scratched beneath the surface a little. Few, though, had been quite as dysfunctional as his own. "But there's someone after your family who claims to value life by destroying it, and I intend to find out who it is."

25

Frank Tripp had paged Horatio to MDPD headquarters to sit in on the interrogation of a suspect in the murder of Silvio Castaneda. Horatio would rather have stayed focused on the bombing case, but for the moment everything that could be done was in progress, and protection had been put into place around all the potential victims. Eric Delko had just called with news of the arrest of Lyall Douglas and the discovery of a possible murder weapon, which had brightened Horatio's spirits considerably, and as he walked into the police station he felt as if some measure of the week's bad news was finally turning good.

Frank met him outside the interview room. "You okay, Horatio?"

"I'm fine."

"Look a little singed is why I ask. Heard about your close call."

"Close calls don't count," Horatio said. His head still throbbed and his ears rang, but the nosebleed had stopped and he was sure he wasn't seriously injured. The bomb squad had defused the device rather than exploding it, which would provide invaluable insight into the bomber's technique when he finally had time to analyze it. Night squad CSIs had been called in early to process the Ibanez house. His team was pressed to their limits, working the cases they already had. On his way over, he'd had another call, about a gardener found dead in his downtown home, shot in the head with a nine-millimeter. It was his truck that had been found in front of the Ibanez home. "Where's your suspect?"

"Got him coolin' his heels," the detective said. "He's a real piece of work, I'll tell you that."

"Why did you bring him in, Frank?"

"We squeezed some of our gang contacts around Overtown. A CI told us that this guy"—he jerked a thumb toward the closed door—"had a run-in with Silvio a few days back. Something about him insulting Silvio's little sister."

"Faustina, yes, I met her. Talk about a piece of work."

"Guess it goes with the territory."

"Is this suspect a gang member too, Frank?"

"Yeah. Kuban Kings."

"One of the chief rivals of Los Danger Boys."

"That's right. This guy's Little Willy Garza. I figured you know the case as well as anyone, so I thought if you sat in on the initial interrogation it might come in handy. Little Willy hasn't lawyered up yet."

"Well, that's something, right?"

"Best time to get the truth out of 'em," Frank said. "You ready?"

"As I'll ever be."

Frank opened the door and led Horatio inside. The interview room in which he had parked Little Willy Garza was about fifteen by fifteen, its block walls painted industrial green. It was a far cry from the light, modern interview rooms at the crime lab. A mirror hung on one wall, and a small video camera was mounted high in a corner; no one could fail to understand that they were being watched intently while they were in here.

Little Willy sat at a steel table, scowling. Horatio knew two things at once. The young man's name, Little Willy, was meant to be ironic. Even seated, he was tall. Horatio guessed his height to be at least six-four, and his weight to be somewhere north of three hundred and fifty blubbery pounds.

The other thing he knew was that while Little Willy might conceivably have been the fatal shooter, he wasn't the other one. Eric and Ryan had demonstrated that the nonfatal shot had been fired from a low angle. Little Willy didn't look like the kind of guy who would get on the ground during a firefight, because getting up again would require enormous effort, if not a crane. Unless he fired from the hip, which would also be awkward given his build, he had not been that shooter.

Which didn't mean he had not fired the fatal shot. But at the killer's position, Eric and Ryan had discovered cotton fibers from a pair of Wrangler brand jeans. Looking at Little Willy, clad in a loose white T-shirt and baggy black pants festooned with what seemed like dozens of zippers and pockets and loops—all size XXXL, no doubt—Horatio didn't get the sense that the Kuban King was much of a jeans guy.

He wasn't quite ready to rule Little Willy out—he would let the evidence do that, not his own first impression—but the suspect didn't look promising to him.

"Little Willy," Frank said, scooting back a chair on the other side of the table and lowering his bulk into it. It was rare that anybody made Frank look svelte, but Little Willy accomplished that task. Horatio leaned against a corner, crossing his arms over his chest. "Little Willy," Frank repeated. "What are we gonna do with you?"

Willy rattled the handcuffs holding him to the table (the manacle, at its widest setting, still biting into the flesh of his thick wrist). "Try cuttin' me loose?"

"Can't do that," Frank said. "I got a dead kid in the morgue. And you had an argument with that kid just a couple of days ago."

"I argue with a lot of people," Willy said. "Don't mean I cap 'em."

"Don't mean you *didn't* cap this one. You wanna tell me about it?"

"I don't even know who you talkin' 'bout, *ese.*"

"Name Silvio Castaneda mean anything to you?"

Willy touched the stud in his right eyebrow with a pudgy finger. His face was thick, fleshy, his head almost as round as a beach ball. He kept his black hair cut short, and what looked like the ghost of a mustache floated above his upper lip. "Maybe."

"He's Los Danger Boys," Frank said.

Willy's response was to spit toward the corner.

"You do that again, and you can clean it up with your tongue," Frank said, an edge of menace in his tone. "I don't know about where you live, Little Willy, but here we got rules. No spitting, no back-talk, and you tell me the truth."

"Sorry," Willy said. "I just hate those *putas.*"

"You hate Los Danger Boys? Way I hear it, they feel the same about the Kuban Kings."

Willy shrugged. "How it goes, right? Everybody hatin' on everybody."

"Not here," Frank said. "In here there's nothing but love. Long as I get the truth."

"Right," Willy said. He didn't look convinced.

"Tell me about your fight with Silvio."

"Wasn't no fight," Willy said. "More of a dis-agreement."

"Don't define it, just tell me what happened."

Willy shrugged again. "I might have said something to his sister."

"What'd you say?"

"I thought she was kinda hot, you know. Little and all. Told her I thought it'd be fun, we hooked up, her and me. Big man, little girl."

"Girl is right," Horatio said, unable to contain himself any longer. "She can't be more than fifteen. You know about statutory rape laws, right?"

Willy shrugged for a third time. Horatio hoped the guy didn't keep that up, or he would quickly lose his patience. "No girl been with me ever complained about it to anyone."

"She doesn't have to complain for it to be a crime," Horatio said. Frank shot him a look, and Horatio folded his arms again, going back to his corner to let Frank continue his interrogation.

"Okay, Casanova. You hit on the girl. Where was this?"

"Parking lot of the arena."

"And what happened?"

"She turned me down." Little Willy gestured toward his own physique. "You imagine that?"

"Not in a million years, Little Willy. Then what?"

"I told her what a mistake she was making."

"In the nicest possible way, I'm sure."

"I might have called her something."

"Like what?"

One more shrug. Horatio felt his hackles rise, willed himself to stay calm. "I might have said something like she was a stupid, useless ho that didn't know quality when she saw it, and when she changed her mind she'd have to beg for a piece of me."

"You got a way with words," Frank said. "Toast-masters?"

"Huh?"

"Never mind. What happened next?"

"I didn't know this punk-ass dude was her brother. He come over to me, got all up in my grill, wavin' his hands and sayin' don't nobody talk that way about his sister, and he'd put a cap in my ass next time he saw me."

"There you go," Frank said. "When you shot Silvio, it was self-defense, right?"

"I didn't freakin' shoot him! What I'm tryin' to tell you."

"But he was going to shoot you."

"He's so full of it his eyes are brown."

"So are yours," Frank pointed out.

"Latino curse, right?" Willy said. This time his shrug was more abbreviated, just a slight wag of one shoulder. "Anyway, Silvio ain't man enough to back that up. And me? I'm a lover, dog, not a fighter, 'cept when I gotta be. I wasn't scared of him, and I didn't have no other reason to cap him."

"Looks like reason enough to me."

"The victim was killed between two and four yesterday morning," Horatio interrupted. "Can you tell us where you were at that time?"

"Shit," Willy said. "Why didn't you ask me that right off?"

"We're askin' you now," Frank said.

"I was at this club," Willy began.

"What club?"

"Didn't have no name. In some warehouse in Opa-Locka."

"Break-in party?" Frank asked.

"I guess."

"Then there won't be anything like surveillance video to back up your story, will there?" Horatio asked.

Willy smiled. "No surveillance video. But plenty of other video. I got friends who was playin' with their phones all night, shootin' flix. Must have hours on me. I got some moves, yo, I get on that dance floor."

"I'll just bet you do, Little Willy," Horatio said. "Can you put your hands on some of that video?"

Outside the interview room, Frank looked abashed. "You think we should kick him?"

"You might want to wait until you see the video," Horatio said. "But my guess is that he really was at that break-in rave. And from what I've seen here, he doesn't match up to the physical evidence we took from the scene. Besides, if the shooting was gang-related, do you honestly think the shooter would have taken shell casings and left the drugs behind?"

"Probably not," Frank admitted. "I guess we're back to square one, then."

"Maybe not, Frank," Horatio said. "Maybe we're getting somewhere after all . . ."

26

Horatio didn't really spend two-thirds of his time behind the wheel of the Hummer, but there were days it felt like he did. This was one of them. With Eric riding shotgun, he drove up North Miami Avenue again. Back toward Overtown and the Castaneda house.

Sitting in on Frank's interrogation of Little Willy had been helpful in two ways, he decided.

Potentially helpful, at any rate. He wouldn't know for sure if that potential would be realized until he checked some things out. The lot of a police officer—evidence led to making mental connections that might answer the problem, and then the answer arrived at had to be confirmed with yet more evidence.

Much like doing science, he thought.

He opened his phone, steering one-handed,

punched up Ryan's number. The call was answered on the second ring. "What's up, Horatio?"

"I need you to do something for me, Ryan. You won't like it."

"So what's new?"

"Ryan, I need you to go into my office. In the wastebasket by my desk, you'll find a used tissue. There should only be the one. I need you to collect and process it. By the book, please—it may be evidence."

"Today's not April Fool's Day, is it?" Ryan asked.

"No, Mister Wolfe, it's not, and this is not a joke."

"And it's got to be me."

"I would like it to be you, Ryan."

"Got it, H. One used tissue, coming up. Am I looking for anything in particular?"

"I'd rather not predispose you in any special direction," Horatio said. "Just let me know what you find out. And right away, please."

When he put the phone away, Eric was looking at him with a big grin on his face. "Something's funny?"

"Making Ryan go fishing for used tissues. Might as well ask him to jump in a sewer."

"I'm sure the day will come," Horatio said. CSIs weren't easily disgusted, and Ryan had done, he believed, an admirable job of not letting his OCD get in the way of his duties.

"I want to be there when it does. With a camera."

"There's almost always one around," Horatio pointed out. "That was a good job, bringing in Lyall Douglas, Eric."

"It was mostly Calleigh."

"I understand that." He had heard the whole story, from both of them, and it matched up in all the details that both knew. He hadn't been happy about Douglas getting the drop on Eric, but Eric knew what he'd done wrong, and he was a man who learned quickly from his mistakes. "Still, you brought him in. We've got his fingerprints on the car's steering wheel and inside the trunk. We've got a weapon that will probably turn out to be the murder weapon. When we get back the DNA, we may even find out that he's the one who got Wendy pregnant."

"Right," Eric said. "But we probably have a better case if it turns out it was the other guy."

"Tony Aldicott. That's true. Jealousy can be a powerful motive. And juries get it."

"Well, Calleigh's going to interview Douglas. He likes to play the hard case, but I got a feeling when he sees what all we've got on him, he'll cave."

"Let's hope so, Eric," Horatio said.

Ryan went into Horatio's office wearing latex gloves and carrying a sheet of plastic and an evidence envelope. In the breast pocket of his lab coat he had a pair of forceps. He wasn't taking any chances.

Spreading the plastic sheet on the floor, he lifted Horatio's wire mesh wastebasket and dumped the contents onto it. Then, with the forceps, he rummaged through it. Miami-Dade County had been on a big kick about recycling, so there wasn't much paper in the trash—not much of anything, really; Horatio seemed from this evidence to be a pretty careful, thrifty guy. Ryan found a wrapper from an energy bar, the plastic wrap off a new printer cartridge, a couple of used paper cups, a pencil stub that wouldn't fit into a sharpener anymore, and the tissue H had sent him after. Still using the forceps, Ryan lifted the tissue, dropped it into the envelope, then set that on Horatio's desk and made a cone of the plastic sheet to dump the rest of the trash back into the basket.

He carried the envelope straight into the trace lab. Aaron Peters looked at him quizzically. "What's up, Ryan?"

"This," Ryan said, holding out the envelope.

Aaron looked into it. "It's a tissue."

"A used tissue," Ryan corrected. "The LT wants you to drop everything else and get to work on it."

"Looking for what?"

"I have no idea. Whatever you find."

"You want to wait?"

"I have some other stuff going on," Ryan said. "But maybe if it'll be quick."

"I guess that depends on what I find," Aaron said. "My guess would be mucus. But I'll jump on it right now if Horatio needs it in a hurry."

"That's what he told me."

"You want me to preserve some for DNA?"

"I think H knows who it's from," Ryan said. "But it wouldn't hurt."

Aaron dumped the tissue out of the envelope onto a sterile surface. There, he applied a swab to the mucus, which was still a little tacky on the tissue's surface, and dissolved it in a solution of water and methanol. A drop of this solvent went into a tube, which he inserted into an automated syringe, to shoot the stuff into the high-performance liquid chromatograph.

"This'll take a few minutes," he cautioned. "I've got to purify it in the liquid chromatograph. Then, since you've got no idea what we're looking for, I'm going to have to run mass spec."

"I know," Ryan said curtly. He didn't like being told what he was already fully aware of, and would rather do it himself than be lectured about it. Everyone had their own job to do at the crime lab, and just because he knew how to run HPLC and MS tests didn't mean he should push Aaron out of the way and take over. The dissolved mucus solution, called the analyte, would be forced through a tube of tiny round particles with a known chemical content, and the speed with which they eluded, or emerged from the tube's end, would separate them. From there the purified, separated samples would be run through a mass spectrometer, which involved converting the liquid to a gas through nanospray ionization, then using the mass spectrometer to generate a mass spectrum, which would show the mass "fingerprints" of the various compounds. The lab had a library of mass spectra to compare the sample's spectrum to, but if it turned out to be something truly uncommon, a mass spectrometrist would have to tell what the sample was by the fragments in the spectrum. "You're right, I don't have time to wait. All I know is that Horatio wanted it in a hurry. Page me when you're done."

"No problem," Aaron said. He was always willing to help, and Ryan felt bad for being short with him. He needed to work on patience. Civilians thought this stuff could be done in seconds—stick the questioned substance in a test tube, spin it around in a centrifuge, and the results would be spit from a printer by the time you could say "high-pressure liquid chromatography/mass spectrometry." Ryan knew that it took as long as it took, but when he wanted answers now instead of later, it was hard to allow the process time to work.

He had other things he could be doing, though. He took a portion of the used tissue in another sterile envelope, in case Horatio wanted Valera to run a DNA test, and left Aaron and his equipment behind.

*   *   *

"When do I get out of here?"

Calleigh sat down across the interview table from Lyall Douglas. He still wore the same clothes he had at his cabin, a blue T-shirt and a pair of jeans with the knees ripped out. He reeked of sour sweat, but his posture was casually defiant, his muscular arms crossed over his deep chest, and he studied Calleigh through brown eyes barely more than slits beneath folds of flesh. "I'm sorry," she replied. "Apparently you fail to understand the seriousness of this. You shot at a CSI today. Even if you weren't being charged with the murder of Wendy Greenfield, you wouldn't be going anywhere for a long time."

His drooping mustache twitched. "I don't know who that is."

"You don't know who Wendy Greenfield is?"

"That's right. Who is she?"

"She's the woman whose throat you sliced in her convertible. After you pretended to carjack her."

Douglas chuckled. "Sounds like you got this all worked out already. Too bad it's a fairy tale."

"It's no fairy tale, Mister Douglas," Calleigh said. "And we can prove every bit of it."

"How? You got witnesses?"

"Honestly? I don't like witnesses very much. Witnesses make mistakes. Evidence doesn't."

He put his hands flat on the table and leaned toward her. "I don't know how evidence can prove something that didn't happen."

"In this case, Mister Douglas, it will only prove what did happen."

"I already told you, I don't know this Wendy person."

Calleigh took a deep breath, making sure she didn't lose her composure. She had hoped that Douglas would cave easily. She didn't really need him to cave at all—the evidence they had amassed was telling enough, and she was sure a jury would comprehend it. But if he copped a plea, it would save the taxpayers the cost of a jury trial, and spare Sidney Greenfield some of the pain that would necessarily accompany one. Douglas had been read his Miranda rights, and so far had not insisted on a lawyer, so that was a good sign.

"And we can show that you do," she said. "We have prison logs showing that she visited you in jail. We have video showing you getting into her car. We have your fingerprints on that car, and on weapons found in the trunk of the car."

"That's not possible."

"It is possible. Beyond that, we have a Ford pickup truck registered to you that matches the wheelbase of the vehicle that was parked beside where you abandoned Wendy and her car. We have a hair found in your bed that I believe will turn out to be Wendy's. In your cabin, we found a red fiber. One hundred percent nylon, super-plush, Mitsubishi calls it—a perfect match to the carpeting in her car. Have you ever heard of Locard's Exchange Principle, Mister Douglas?"

"Is Locard a friend of this Wendy chick?"

"Doctor Edmond Locard is often called the father of forensics," Calleigh replied. "He was a French police scientist, and his principle states that any contact a person makes with any other person, place, or object includes the transference of physical materials. By touching Wendy, by having her over to your house, and certainly by killing her, you left behind traces of yourself and you picked up traces of her. We've already found enough to put you away for twenty-five to life. I would guess life, given how hard it'll be to find a jury in Florida that doesn't follow golf. Sidney Greenfield is a well-known man around here, and the murderer of his wife will not be looked upon kindly."

"Why would I do all this?" he demanded. His casual demeanor was gone now, his expression closed off, guarded.

"That's something you can answer better than me," Calleigh said. She was losing patience with the man. And she considered herself a very patient woman, so it took a lot to get to her. "But we also know that you both are acquainted with an inmate named Tony Aldicott, who was serving on a road-work detail not far from where you killed Wendy. We know that Wendy was pregnant. We found clothing in the trunk that we've ascertained would fit Tony, and we think you both planned to break

Tony out at the work site. You changed your mind, planted a car along the route, and walked back to the Quick Spree, which is why you were sweating so hard when you got there. Then you went ahead with the plan, except with your own little twist of pulling over en route and cutting Wendy's throat."

She paused for a breath, and to open a manila folder and take out a photograph. She slid it across the smooth tabletop. "You might recognize this," she said. "It's a knife we took from your cabin. It was used to kill Wendy Greenfield. It has blood on it that is being DNA tested right now." Unlike stab wounds, slicing or cutting wounds didn't reveal much about the specific weapon used, unfortunately, so matching the blade to the gash in her throat was unlikely. But the blood on the blade would tell the tale.

"Anybody could have put that knife in the cabin," he protested. His defense was weak, and he knew it; he offered it without enthusiasm.

"Looked to me like you guarded the place pretty closely," she said.

He tried on another smile, but it faded fast. "This looks bad, don't it?"

"It looks bad," she agreed.

"It was the bitch's own fault," he said. He could not have chosen a worse way to gain Calleigh's sympathy. "She shouldn't have got knocked up. Especially by Tony. Guy like that is supposed to be the goofy-ass best friend, not nail the chick, right?

Hell, if I hadn't of done it, Sidney probably would have when he found out."

Calleigh ignored the outburst and pushed a legal pad and a pen toward him, picking up the knife picture and putting it back in the folder. "You want to write out what happened? Tell it in your own words? Things might go easier on you if you do."

Douglas hesitated, then picked up the pen. "This could take a while," he said. "I don't write too fast."

"Take your time," Calleigh told him. *It's the one thing you have plenty of,* she thought. But she was a polite Southern lady, so she didn't say it.

27

HORATIO PARKED on the street in front of the Castaneda house, and he and Eric walked briskly to the front door. Horatio knocked, and a few seconds passed before Silvio's little sister, Faustina, opened it. She had on baggy black pants, a black T-shirt, and fuzzy socks—her standard uniform, it seemed.

"My papa's asleep," she said. "He been working nights, so you got to come back some other time."

"Actually, Faustina," Horatio said, "we came to see you."

"I got nothing to say to you," she said. "So looks like you wasted a trip."

"I don't think so."

She started to close the door. Horatio put his foot, salesmanlike, in its path. From behind her, Joe Castaneda's sleepy voice sounded. "Who is it, Faustina?"

"It's nothing," she answered.

"It's Horatio Caine from the crime lab, sir," Horatio called. Faustina shot him a glare that could have killed.

"Let 'em in, baby," Joe said. "I'll be right there, Officer, soon as I get some pants on."

"All right," Horatio said. He met Faustina's gaze with an inquiring expression. She relented and let go of the door. She turned and walked away, and Horatio had to catch her arm before she disappeared down the hallway to the back of the house. "Not yet," he said. "I still need to talk to you."

"I already told you," she said, trying on an abused pout. "Let me go."

"I'm sorry, Faustina, but I'm trying to find out who killed your brother. I would think you'd want to help with that."

"I don't know jack," she said. "If I did know, I'd deal with it myself. Or Los Danger Boys would."

"I know you believe that," Horatio said. "But in this case, it's much better to let the police handle it than your friends."

"They ain't my friends, they're my family. Silvio's too."

"Silvio is your family. So's your father. If you want to do right by them, you'll come into the living room for a minute."

Joe emerged from a bedroom. He had put on a clean white undershirt and a pair of khaki shorts, but he was barefoot and his hair was mussed and his eyes were thick with sleep. "What's going on?"

"I need some information from Faustina," Horatio explained.

"Help him out, baby."

"I don't trust no freakin' cops," Faustina protested.

Joe shot her an angry frown. "I said give him what he wants. For Silvio."

She spun out of Horatio's grip and plopped down into a chair, arms folded angrily over her chest. She stared at the far wall of the room.

"What are you looking for?" Joe asked.

"Actually, I'd like to know how tall Faustina is."

"What are you, about five feet?" Joe asked his daughter.

"Not even," she replied glumly. "Four ten."

"Four feet, ten inches." Horatio made a mental note of it. "If you don't mind, sir, I'd like to look in Faustina's room for a minute. And perhaps in Silvio's too."

"No!" Faustina barked. "See do they got a warrant, Papa!"

"I don't have a warrant, sir. I can get one, but I'd rather get this done quickly and quietly."

"This will help find out what happened to Silvio?"

"I wouldn't be here if I didn't believe that it would," Horatio assured him.

"Then you can look in her room all you want. We got nothing to hide."

"Papa—"

"Do you, Faustina? You have anything in there you don't want me to know about?"

"No, Papa. It's just—"

"I'm sorry to invade your privacy, Faustina," Horatio said. "It'll only take a few minutes, and then I think we'll have some answers."

"What do you mean?" Joe asked. "You don't think she had anything to do with it."

"I'll tell you after I've looked around a bit," Horatio said. "Mister Delko, please wait here with the family."

"I'll be right here, H."

Horatio didn't really think Faustina would run, but it didn't pay to take chances. With Eric hovering over her, she wouldn't get far if she tried.

He went into her room and opened her closet, ignoring a twin bed, a dresser with a mirror half-obscured by photos of her and her friends, hip-hop band stickers, and tattoo designs, and white-painted walls covered with more of the same.

The closet was shallow, and mostly full of black. Black shirts and jeans hung from a rod. He supposed the dresser would be the same—lots of black, with a few splashes of color that were probably gifts rather than items she had purchased herself. On the floor were a couple of pairs of shoes, including a pair of black sneakers, heavy Doc Martens boots, and one pair of dressier flats. Beside them was a white plastic laundry hamper. Horatio flipped up the lid and glanced inside to find what looked like several days' worth of dirty clothes.

Shutting it again, he left her room and crossed the hall to Silvio's.

Faustina's big brother had painted his walls midnight blue. Like the girl, he had some band posters tacked to the wall, but also a poster of the Miami Heat and a certificate showing that he had passed his high school equivalency test. His room, slightly larger, contained a desk (a glance showed that library books were overdue; Horatio decided to remind Joe Castaneda before he was hit with some annoying fines) and a dresser on which a wrestling trophy reared up over assorted bling and pocket change.

Silvio's closet looked much like Faustina's too, with more football jerseys and light-colored shirts than she had, but still a lot of black. He had a hamper that matched hers, probably bought at the same time at some discount store.

Something was missing, though. Horatio returned to the living room. "Faustina," he said, "you had a different pair of shoes when I was here before. Yellow and black checks, I believe."

Faustina didn't respond, just glared at her father when he spoke. "Oh, those are out on the back step," Joe said. "She got them muddy."

"Thank you, Mister Castaneda," Horatio said. "I'll take a look."

He went out through the kitchen and found the

sneakers just where the man had said they'd be. A dirty butter knife sat on the step beside them. When he turned them over, he saw that she, or someone, had begun to scrape mud from the tread of the right shoe, but had only made it about half-way, from the heel up. The left one hadn't been touched yet. He wondered if she'd been working on them when he and Eric came to the door.

Horatio carried them back into the living room. Faustina still sat where he had left her, hands tucked under her arms, defiance written all over her face. Joe lazed in another chair, clearly wishing he had been allowed to sleep. Eric stood between Faustina and the door with his kit in his hand.

"Eric, would you get out an evidence envelope, please?"

"You find something?" Eric asked. He put the kit down on the floor, opened it up, and withdrew a paper envelope.

"And a pair of tweezers," Horatio said.

Eric handed a pair over with the envelope. Horatio handed Eric the shoe, and Eric glanced at the sole.

"These are your shoes, aren't they?"

"Might be," Faustina said.

"Those are hers," Joe Castaneda said. "I got them for her on her last birthday."

"Papa!"

"Well, it's true. What about it?"

Horatio pointed to a blob stuck in the treads.

"This," he said, "is a butterfly larva." He plucked it out with the tweezers and held it up for the others to see. "I'll have to confirm it at the lab, but I believe we'll find that it's the larval stage of a viceroy butterfly."

"So I stepped on a damn butterfly," Faustina said. "So?"

"Not a butterfly, but its larva," Horatio corrected. "Not very different, except that butterflies can travel a lot farther than their larvae do."

"Still, it's just a freakin' bug, right? It against the law to kill one?"

"Not at all," Horatio said. "But the only native larval host plant for the viceroy butterfly is the Coastal Plain Willow tree. And we know there were some of those at the scene where your brother was shot."

"Are they rare trees?" Joe asked.

"Not terribly, no."

"So that don't prove nothing," Faustina said. "I might have stepped on it anywhere."

"Not anywhere," Horatio said. "They're not truly rare, but they're not everywhere, either. But you're right, by itself it doesn't prove anything."

"What you mean, by itself?"

"I notice you haven't washed your clothes in a few days," Horatio said. "I'm going to have to collect the clothes in your hamper, in addition to these shoes. My guess is that some of the clothes, and maybe the shoes, will test positive for gunshot residue. That, in addition to the larva in your tread, will put you at the scene of Silvio's shooting."

"I didn't kill my brother!" Faustina shouted. Her eyes brimmed with tears, and her petulance turned to grief.

"I know you didn't," Horatio said. "We know that the nonfatal bullet was fired by someone very small in stature, or else crouching at a very awkward, unlikely height. Someone who is four feet, ten inches tall would have been shooting from a natural stance. You didn't kill him, Faustina, but you did shoot him."

The tears broke free, began to flow. Joe Castaneda stared at his daughter, eyes agape with disbelief. "Faustina . . . did you?"

"That bastard Little Willy from the Kuban Kings dissed me," she said, fighting back sobs. "He tried to freakin' hit on me and then he blamed me when I didn't want to be with him. And Silvio didn't do shit about it. He's my big brother, he should have had my back, but he just stood there and let Little Willy talk that shit about me."

"I understand he threatened Little Willy," Horatio said.

"That was just talk. He didn't *do* nothing."

"That's no excuse to shoot him," Joe said.

"He got no excuse to stand there like an idiot while someone from another gang shows his sister disrespect! What kind of man does that? He don't stand up for his family, he ain't gonna stand up for anyone! I never meant to kill him, I just wanted to teach him a lesson. He can't step up when it's time, he'll never be a real gangster, that's all I wanted to show him."

"By shooting at him," Horatio said. "With what gun?"

"One of his nine-mils," Faustina said. "I threw it in the bay."

"That settles it," Horatio said. "The fatal bullet was the forty-five, not a nine. You hit him, but you didn't kill him."

She spun around to face her father. "See? I didn't kill Silvio!"

"But you were there when he died," Horatio added.

"Yeah." Her voice softened, and the sobs threatened to start up again. She swallowed one back. "I was. I was just aiming at him when he heard or saw someone else. He drew down on the other person. I freaked and my finger accidentally squeezed on the trigger and I saw him, like, jump, and then he fired a shot and the other person fired at him all at the same time."

"What did you do then, Faustina?"

"I ran like hell, what else?"

"And before you ran, did you see the other person? The one who did kill Silvio?"

"I got a glimpse of him when he fired, that's all. He was standing in some trees."

"What can you tell me about him?"

"He was a white guy. Older, like you."

"Did you notice his hair color? What he was wearing?"

"Short hair, I think. Dark, like brown or black."

"And his clothes?"

"Like a suit, I think. I can't remember for sure. I don't think a necktie, but maybe a white shirt and a dark jacket."

"Anything else you remember about him?"

"Nothing really. Just a regular white guy, bigger than you, maybe your same age."

"That's good, Faustina. Thank you."

"Will she go to jail?" Joe asked.

"That's not up to me," Horatio said. "But it's possible that she'll spend some time in a juvenile facility, yes."

"But she—"

"She shot her brother, Mister Castaneda," he said. "Not fatally, but it could have been fatal. The fact that someone else killed him, instead of her, was purely an accident. Then she tried to cover up the crime. I'm sorry, but a judge is going to have to decide what happens to Faustina."

28

"Too bad about the girl," Eric said when they were back in the Hummer. "And it's too bad she didn't get a better look at the other shooter."

"I think she got a good enough look," Horatio said. He pulled into the traffic lane and started back toward the lab.

"What do you mean?"

"Hang on." Horatio took out his phone and called Ryan's number. "Mister Wolfe," he said when Ryan answered. "Have you got anything for me?"

"My trash-diving expedition?" Ryan asked. "I think so, yeah."

"What?"

"Whoever used that tissue is suffering from allergies," Ryan said. "To a specific type of pollen."

"And that pollen is?"

"Peters says Coastal Plain Willow. It's highly allergenic."

"Indeed it is," Horatio said. "Especially to people who don't spend a lot of time around them. And it's in bloom right now, isn't it?"

"I think so."

"You saw some yesterday."

"I did?" Ryan paused. "Oh, at Bicentennial Park?"

"That's right."

"So this is related to that shooting?"

"I think it might be," Horatio said.

"Who used the tissue?"

"I'll fill you in when I know more. In the meantime, please get Valera started working up the DNA of the willow tree. I'd like to be able to match it to a specific individual plant. It wouldn't hurt if she ran the DNA of the person, too—I know who it is, but we'll need to be able to prove it in court."

"I'm on it," Ryan said. "By the way, Calleigh was looking for you a few minutes ago."

Horatio thanked Ryan, hung up, and called Calleigh.

"That nine-mil round the bomber fired at you," she said after greeting him, "that was recovered from the wall at the Ibanez house?"

"What about it?"

"I ran it through IBIS to see if the same weapon had been used in any other crimes."

"And?" IBIS, the Integrated Ballistic Imaging

System, converted images of fired bullets into mathematical algorithms, and compared those with others in its vast database at incredible speeds.

"And it has. A couple of nonfatal shooting incidents in and around Overtown, most likely gang-related. And . . ."

"And?" he said again.

"And it also matched the round Eric pried out of a tree at Bicentennial Park."

"The bullet that the victim fired, presumably at his killer?"

"That's the one. I think the bomber is using a gun he took from Silvio Castaneda after he killed him."

"That's what it sounds like to me," Horatio said.

"There's another 'and,' " Calleigh said.

"What's this one?"

"It's also a match for a bullet that just came in the door. From the body of that gardener downtown."

Which confirmed that the Baby Boomer had killed the gardener in order to steal his truck and equipment, thereby gaining access to the Ibanez home. "Thank you, Calleigh."

He put the phone away and filled Eric in.

"So wait a minute," Eric said when he was finished. "The bomber is the Baby Boomer, right?"

"Presumably."

"And the Baby Boomer killed Silvio?"

"That's what it looks like."

"But why? And does this mean you know who it is?"

"It does," Horatio said. The early evening traffic was thick, and he had to pay attention to it as well as to what he was saying. "I'll take the questions in order, if that's okay. As to the why, I think the Baby Boomer wants a fresh weapon when he hits a new town. He doesn't want to keep providing a trail back to his old haunts and his previous crimes, does he?"

"Probably not."

"So first he used the forty-five he brought to town, then probably ditched it once he had Silvio's nine-mil. For the duration of his stay in Miami, the nine—which could be connected to a local gang member, but not to him—would be his firearm of choice. Whenever he hits a new town, he probably looks for drug dealers or gang members he can take a weapon from, figuring that no one is going to look too closely into their murders, and also that any shootings he does will point back to the gang."

"Pretty smart," Eric said, sounding impressed.

"Not quite smart enough, though, is he?"

"I guess not, since you figured it out. What about the other part?"

"The who? That's easy, Eric. The Baby Boomer is Wendell Asher."

"The FBI agent?" He had gone from impressed to amazed.

"The same."

"But—"

"Asher has been sneezing and sniffling since I met him," Horatio said. "He's from Denver, which has an arid mountain climate. No Coastal Plain Willows there. But the night he landed—and remember, as an FBI agent, it wouldn't have been hard for him to find out where drug dealing was a fairly common practice in Miami—he went to Bicentennial Park and hid among some blooming trees. The allergens went to work almost immediately. When he was in my office, I let him use a tissue, and he conveniently threw it away in my wastebasket. Maxine will use electrophoresis and DNA fingerprinting to match the trace in his mucus to the trees in the park."

"But Asher has been chasing the Boomer for years."

"He says he has. All we really know is that he's been in the same cities the Boomer has struck in. He says he went there on the Boomer's trail, but I think it's the other way around. I'm sure his reports are detailed, precise, and almost entirely fictional. It's no wonder the Boomer hasn't been caught, if the lead investigator on the case is really the culprit."

"Wow," Eric said. "That's . . . that's incredible."

"We'll show Faustina a picture of Asher in a five-pack while she's in holding," Horatio said. They had waited at the house until a squad car showed up to take her in. "And once we have him in custody, she can pick him out of a lineup. I'm sure she'll cooperate if she thinks it'll help her get off more lightly."

"Probably, yeah," Eric said. "You know, it makes sense, now that I think about it. Asher is an explosives expert, right?"

"That's why he was assigned to the case in the first place," Horatio said. "Probably not a coincidence that he first struck close to Denver. Asher knew what he was doing, right from the start. He knew that he had the most expertise in the Denver field office, so he would be the likely choice to head the investigation."

"That's true," Eric said. "It's circumstantial, but—"

"A lot of it is circumstantial," Horatio interrupted. "Like the cotton fibers found at the shooting scene."

"From a pair of jeans, right?"

"Wrangler jeans," Horatio corrected. "Much more commonly worn out West than in Miami. I'll bet we'll find some in Asher's hotel room, though."

"Which will change that from circumstantial evidence to physical evidence."

"And physical evidence, Eric, is our specialty." Horatio took his phone out again and called Frank Tripp.

"Tripp," the detective answered.

"Frank, it's Horatio. I need you to bring in Wendell Asher."

"The Fed? What do you mean, bring him in?"

"Arrest him, Frank."

"You're not a guy who makes jokes like this, Horatio, so why don't you tell me what the hell's going on?"

"Certainly, Frank." Horatio ran down the evidence he had just sorted out in his own mind by discussing it with Eric.

"I don't know, Horatio," Frank said at the end of it. "It sounds compelling, but—"

"There could be someone else in danger right now, Frank. Just pick him up. We'll put him in a lineup for Faustina Castaneda. If she can't recognize him, then we can revisit it, but I'm convinced he's our guy."

"Okay, Horatio. I'll have him picked up. If you're wrong, there'll be hell to pay."

"I'll take full responsibility, Frank." Horatio knew he could ill afford to make more enemies at the Bureau, and he didn't want to jeopardize any of the federal funding that helped Miami have one of the most state-of-the-art crime labs in the country. But he didn't think he was wrong.

His phone rang a couple of minutes later. "Horatio Caine."

"Horatio," Frank's voice said, clearly disturbed. "I put out a be on the lookout for Asher, but I can't locate him anywhere and he's not answering his phone. He told me he was on his way to interview Emily Hurt, the judge who made the final determination on the Ibanez case, but I talked to a detective there who said Asher never showed up."

"Of course he didn't," Horatio said. "Because he's been playing us all along. The judge isn't the next target, is she? And neither is Alexx."

"I thought it made sense that Judge Hurt would be."

"Of course it did, Francis. But Asher is trickier than that. He's out there somewhere, planting his next device. And we've got to find him before he does."

29

FRANK MET HORATIO at the crime lab, and the two hunkered in Horatio's office with the *Miami Herald* and the records from the Ibanez court case. They combed through both, looking for any likely targets beyond the obvious ones. It was Frank who finally punched the newspaper with a thick finger. "I got it," he said.

"What, Frank?"

"Right here. Senator Sandra Davison is making a speech tonight at the Sandmoor House."

"Nice venue," Horatio said, picturing the trendy South Beach hotel. "She's the senator from Maryland?"

"That's right," Frank said. He put the paper down on Horatio's desk and pawed through the copies of court documents and news accounts of the trial. "But look here." He pushed a clipping toward Horatio. "She's also the senator who was the tie-breaking vote that kept the full Senate from debating the Ibanez case. She gave an impassioned speech about the family's right to privacy and Hector Ibanez's right to die with dignity, and it says she's more responsible than anyone else for sending the case back to the Florida Supreme Court."

"Which had already ruled in favor of Carmen Ibanez," Horatio remembered. "And the U.S. Supreme Court declined to hear the case. So unless Congress could change the law in time, that decision sealed Hector Ibanez's fate."

"That's how I read it."

"Why is she speaking in Miami?"

"Testing the waters'd be my guess. She keeps being mentioned as a dark horse presidential candidate. Hard to win the presidency without Florida, so she's probably down here raising money and tryin' to gauge her support. The article said it'll be her sixth trip to the state in the past six months, so if I was a betting man, I'd put my money on it."

"You're not a betting man, Frank?" Horatio asked.

"Not on politics. You can't trust those people to do anything that makes sense. At least in a horse race you know someone's gonna win."

Horatio steepled his fingers and rested his chin on them for a moment. "Her speech is at seven?"

"What it says here."

"And it's already after six. I think, Frank, that it would be a good idea to evacuate that hotel."

"Horatio, that's—"

"I know it's a tall order. And the hotel's owner or manager will complain loudly. But would we rather deal with some complaining or see a United States senator and possibly several hundred hotel guests get blown up?"

Frank studied Horatio closely. "You think this is going to be a big one."

"His biggest, I'd guess. We're not talking about a private home or a small clinic here, Frank. We're talking about a ballroom at a major hotel, and a United States senator. Asher is raising the stakes, and he'll have to back his raise with a big boom."

"You're right, Horatio," Frank said, nodding his agreement. "I'll make the call."

"You do that. I'll gather my team and we'll meet you over there. With a bomb squad and as many officers as you can spare. It's going to be a mess."

The scene was, as predicted, a mess.

Ocean Drive, the main street running along the Atlantic side of South Beach, saw heavy traffic at the best of times. Now, traffic was virtually at a standstill, because Ocean was partially blocked by emergency vehicles, police officers setting up a perimeter, and the hundreds and hundreds of people who had been forced out of the hotel—guests and those who had already arrived for Senator Davison's speech.

Horatio parked the Hummer on the beach a

quarter mile away, and Eric, driving a second one, did the same. They all gathered their equipment and jogged up the beach, then cut over toward the Sandmoor House. The hotel looked like some kind of alien spacecraft that had touched down, coated in coral, and painted pastel pink with green trim. *Not a lovely place*, Horatio thought, but it was devoutly modern inside and attracted its share of the beautiful people, even while maintaining its old Miami clientele. Somehow the combination drew unexpected events like the senator's speech.

The perimeter had been set at five hundred feet from the building. A command trailer had already been put into place in Lummus Park, on the narrow green strip just before the sand started, and Horatio headed there first. While the team waited outside, he identified himself to the uni at the door and went in. Taking in the people gathered around a small conference table at a glance, he introduced himself for those he didn't know. "I'm Lieutenant Horatio Caine of the Miami-Dade Crime Lab," he said.

A bespectacled woman with spiky black hair, wearing a silk pin-striped business suit with no blouse beneath it—or anything else that Horatio could determine—glared at him. "You're the Caine who's responsible for my hotel being empty?"

"If you're talking about the Sandmoor House, ma'am."

"I am. I'm Janice Garrison, the manager. And I

have a very significant event scheduled in twenty-five minutes."

"I'm aware of that, Ms. Garrison. I'm very sorry for the inconvenience. Did they tell you the reason for the evacuation?"

A police captain named Moe Trafford spoke up. "Of course we did, Horatio. I made very certain that Ms. Garrison understands the seriousness of the threat."

"It all sounds a little hypothetical to me," the hotel manager insisted. "We were just talking about it. Captain Trafford says this person normally attacks abortion providers, but now he's started attacking lawyers and judges. How does any of that translate to hotels?"

"It's not the hotel he's after, Ms. Garrison," Horatio replied. "It's the senator."

"We're not any happier about this than Janice is." The new speaker was a young man in a crisp gray suit. His tie had threads of silver in it, and his blue eyes were large and very sincere.

"And you are . . . ?"

"Peter Dalton, of Senator Davison's staff. She's got a major speech scheduled in just a few minutes. There's an audience of several hundred people out there who had their expensive fund-raising dinner interrupted. Since you kicked us out of the hotel, do you have any suggestions as to where we might want to hold it?"

"My suggestion would be to reschedule it for a

time when the senator's life isn't in danger," Horatio said. "Was the senator in the hotel earlier?"

"She has a suite there," Dalton replied. "She got in this afternoon, and would have spent the night after the speech. She's got a flight to Iowa in the morning."

"And where is she now?"

"We put her in a suite at another hotel, up the block," Dalton said. "For security reasons, we're not telling anyone where she is."

"That's probably for the best," Horatio said. "As long as you've got some officers there with her."

"She's in good hands," Captain Trafford assured him. Horatio trusted the captain's judgment. South Beach was his turf, and if he had responsibility for Senator Davison's safety, that was fine with Horatio.

He was about to respond when Frank Tripp banged through the door, looking like he wished he had never gotten out of bed this morning. "Still no sign of Asher," he reported. "He's driving a rental car with a GPS unit, which we found parked over on Collins, couple blocks down from here. It's empty, not so much as a gum wrapper that I could see. We tried to track the GPS in his mobile phone, but he's got it turned off. Probably ditched it anyway. I get the feeling he knows we're on to him."

"Which would make tonight his last stand," Horatio said. "And he'll want to go out with a bang. We'll clear the hotel as quickly as we can, but

I'm afraid there won't be any speeches made there tonight." He caught Jorge Ortiz's eye. "Are your people ready, Jorge?"

"We were born ready, Horatio."

At the moment, Horatio felt that entering a building containing a large explosive device might be easier than dealing with angry bureaucrats.

"Let's do it, then."

Ortiz grabbed his helmet from the floor beneath the table and stuck it on his head. As he rose, he tightened his chin strap. "Right behind you, brother."

The Sandmoor House had eighty rooms on nine floors. On the ground floor were the lobby, offices, a bellman's closet, a gift shop, and a café. Up a wide staircase were the meeting rooms and the ballroom where Senator Davison had been scheduled to speak. The ballroom had been decorated with red, white, and blue bunting—traditional, although not inspired. A raised dais held a few chairs and a podium, and behind it the flags of the United States, Florida, and Maryland had been arranged. The neatly ordered tables and chairs skewed, dinner half served, were indications of how quickly the room had emptied.

It would take a lot of hands to check the whole place, so Horatio and his team joined the bomb squad officers. Horatio carried a VaporTracer, a handheld ion mobility spectrometer that looked a little like a DustBuster. It, too, sucked in air, but much more slowly and in significantly smaller quantities. In this case, electrons interacted with the incoming molecules, turning them into positive or negative ions. Explosives formed negative ions, which were drawn through a drift chamber and toward a metal detector plate. The time it took specific ions to drift to the plate helped to identify their components, and a plot of ion current versus drift time created an IMS spectrum that could identify different substances.

To maximize the chance of finding traces of RDX, the base chemical of the C-4 that Asher used, the team employed different technologies, so that if one failed, another might succeed. Ryan and Calleigh's devices, handheld Raman spectrometers, used lasers to achieve the same result as the Vapor-Tracer. Eric had an electron capture detector with a gas chromatograph mounted on the front.

While the bomb squad officers spread out, some going upstairs to start checking the senator's suite and the guest rooms on the third floor, others remaining on the ground floor, the CSI team took the second floor, with its warren of meeting rooms and the big ballroom.

They moved slowly, carefully testing the air from step to step, particularly in places they couldn't see into well. Explosives released vapors, and anyone who had handled RDX would likely leave trace amounts of it on anything he touched.

Waving his device beneath the dais, Horatio got a positive reading for RDX. "I've got something here," he reported, flicking on his Maglite and pushing aside the bunting that draped the floor. With the light, he illuminated a wad of putty-colored material stuck to the bottom of the temporary stage. Copper wires coiled out of the putty to a small sealed box, no doubt a timer, attached beside it. Asher hadn't even bothered with a casing for this one, but there was enough C-4 there to blow anyone on the dais through the ceiling.

"A lot of it," he said, reaching for his phone to call Jorge Ortiz.

"I'm getting a reading here too," Calleigh said. She was scanning a doorway at the side of the room, which Horatio guessed led into a service hallway.

"We'd better—" he started, but Ortiz's voice on the phone interrupted him.

"Horatio, we've located three devices down here already," he said. "This guy wasn't taking any chances."

"No," Horatio agreed. "He wasn't. Jorge, we've got to get everyone out of this building. Now!"

30

HORATIO, CALLEIGH, ERIC, and Ryan raced down the wide carpeted steps, their crime scene kits banging against their legs, their flight made more awkward still by the explosives detectors they also carried. Nobody spoke—they all understood the gravity of the situation, and their mad dash was accompanied only by grunts of effort and the thunder of their footsteps.

On the ground floor, bomb squad officers were already making for the doors. Pounding footsteps echoed from open stairwell doors, as the officers who had started their search on the third floor descended.

Passing out of the hotel's climate-controlled interior, Horatio felt the familiar slap of Miami humidity. He kept going, across the cleared roadway and toward the beach, making sure only that his team ran ahead of him. They couldn't afford for anyone to stumble or trip. Horatio had been right about Asher's plan for tonight, but he had also been wrong. He wasn't just after the senator—he wanted to make a statement that would never be forgotten.

The first of the bombs exploded just as Horatio's feet hit sand. He dropped what he carried, reached out with both hands, and caught Calleigh and Ryan on the back and shoulder, pushing them forward. The three of them sprawled headlong to the ground, Eric close behind.

Horatio heard a series of tremendous booming sounds, felt shock waves sweep across him like ripples from stones thrown not quite simultaneously into a pond, then another wave of intense heat. Shadows strobed in the successive flashes of light. Glass and chunks of the corallike coating of the exterior walls pattered down around him like giant hailstones. "Everyone okay?" he shouted when the punishing rain slackened.

"I'm good," Calleigh said.

"Fine, H," Eric offered.

"Yeah," Ryan said. "I'm cool."

Horatio gained his feet and turned back to look at the building. Asher had timed his devices perfectly. He hadn't had the time or resources to completely destroy the hotel, and that had not been his intention. But he had done plenty of damage.

The bombs on the third floor—and possibly

higher, only a careful processing of the ruins would reveal that—had gone off slightly before the ones on the ground floor. Those in and around the second-floor ballroom were delayed another second or so. The result was that when the blasts below weakened the building's structural integrity, the upper floors were already beginning to cave toward the ground floor. If Sandra Davison had been on the second floor, she would have been caught in the middle, with just enough time for terror to set in, and then she and much of her audience would have been killed, either by the blast, by the weight of the floors above dropping down, or by the fall into the inferno waiting below.

Flames lapped out of the windows and thick black smoke roiled into the air. The crowd of onlookers had screamed at the explosions, and now that they were finished the noise level from their excited chatter seemed almost as loud as the blasts themselves. Firefighters rushed into action, uncoiling hoses and training the flow of water through doors and windows.

Apparently the perimeter had been sufficient to prevent most injuries. Horatio could see a few people who had been cut by flying glass or debris, and paramedics were already fanning through the crowd to treat them. None seemed seriously hurt, which he was pleased to note.

He wondered if Wendell Asher was in the crowd somewhere.

Probably not, he guessed. Asher was too smart for that; he would know that there would be too many eyes looking for him.

"Are you all right, Horatio?" Calleigh asked.

He hadn't stopped to consider. His ears still rang from his earlier encounter with Asher, but he didn't think there was any long-term damage from either. That luck couldn't hold indefinitely, though. He needed to find the rogue agent and put an end to his bombing career. "I'm fine, Calleigh, thanks. I'm just wondering where Asher is."

"He could be halfway to Orlando by now," she said.

"I don't think so. I don't think his ego would let him leave so soon. Bombers and arsonists like to see the results of their handiwork. And he knows we're on to him, but he'll also want to know who he killed, if anyone. If not—if he knows he missed the senator *and* us—he'll want to try again somehow."

She scanned the crowd, as he had done just moments before. "Do you think he's here?"

"He hasn't stayed on the loose this long by taking unnecessary chances, has he? But he's not far away. Holed up somewhere safe until he knows if he's finished here or not." He nodded his head toward the news vans beaming images into the sky. "Probably watching all this on TV."

"From a hotel room?"

"If I had to guess. But we can't discount the possibility that he's killed someone and is using their condo or house, either. He's certainly proven his willingness to kill for the sake of convenience."

"Like the gardener," Ryan said, joining the conversation.

"The gardener, and Silvio Castaneda, just so he could get a fresh gun. Who knows how many others over the years he has supposedly been chasing himself?"

"We've gotta find this guy," Ryan said.

"We will, Mister Wolfe. And we'll do it right now." He fished out his phone—thankfully not broken by his dive into the sand—and called Frank Tripp. "Frank, I think Asher is somewhere close by. A hotel room, a condo, someplace like that, watching all the commotion out a window or on TV. We need to fan out with sniffers, canine units, whatever we've got available. Asher handled a significant quantity of C-4 today, so he'll have residue on his hands and clothes."

"I'll get on it," Frank promised.

"Okay. We're on our way now too."

He closed the phone and looked at Calleigh, Ryan, and Eric. "All set?"

"Let's do it," Eric said. "I really want to nail this guy."

"That, sir," Horatio said, "makes two of us."

Dogs could be trained to sniff out nine different types of explosives, including RDX. They could maneuver almost anywhere, cover large swaths of territory, and follow a faint scent all the way to its source. As sophisticated as the handheld "sniffers" Horatio and his team used were, they would never be as efficient over large areas as trained canines. The only thing the dogs couldn't do was tell their handlers which type of explosive material they had scented. Right now, Horatio would happily work within that limitation.

The dogs, mostly German shepherds, muscular and alert, spread out with their handlers in tow, sniffing the air. They knew their task and set to it with apparent enthusiasm.

Horatio and his CSIs couldn't cover ground nearly as fast. Their mechanical devices needed time to test the air molecules, and although the machines worked quickly, they didn't match the speed of a dog's nose.

So while the CSIs were still testing the doorways of the buildings closest to the Sandmoor House, the dogs had already moved down the block. Horatio's phone rang and he answered immediately.

"Horatio, one of the dogs got a hit," Frank said. "Fair Coast."

"I can see it from here," Horatio said. "Thanks." He put the phone away and summoned the others. "Fair Coast! Now!"

They broke into a run, north up Ocean. They were beyond the sealed perimeter now, and pedestrians, as well as motorists trapped by snarled traffic, watched their progress, some shouting encouragement or curses.

The canine and his handler waited outside the Fair Coast, which had a fashionably cheesy tiki décor, with longboards set into concrete flanking the walkway and more at the low, flat steps leading into the lobby. Tiki torches burned on poles and suspended from the walls, masks grimaced all around, and palm fronds thatched everything.

"Caesar smells something here," the handler said when Horatio approached. "Detective Tripp said we should hang back and wait for you."

"That's right, Officer," Horatio answered. "Thank you."

"I've got RDX," Calleigh said, consulting her Raman spectrometer.

"All right, Calleigh." His gaze took in his CSI team as well as the canine unit. "I need all of you to get a new perimeter established around this hotel. Remember how much space was affected by the blast at the Sandmoor House, and give me more."

"You think he's got that much—" Eric began.

Horatio cut him off. "I don't know what he has on him, but I'm not taking any chances. The street's packed. You've got to move all those people, and right now."

"What about you?" Calleigh asked.

"I know Asher. And I know explosives. I'm going in."

"Shouldn't you wait for a tactical team?"

"There isn't time for that. Send them in, but I'm going now."

"Horatio—"

"Do it, Calleigh. Get me that perimeter. That's the best thing you can do."

She knew better than to argue with him. She and the others turned away, accompanying the uniformed officer and his dog, to do what Caine asked.

And Horatio, alone, went into the building.

31

"WHAT'S GOING ON, Officer?"

Three employees stood behind the check-in counter, a man and two women, all wearing Hawaiian shirts, khaki shorts, and name tags. The speaker was one of the women, African-American, tall and slender and lovely, with a shock of black hair trimmed short and standing straight up. A model, or a wannabe, Horatio guessed.

A dozen or so other people milled around the lobby.

"I need you to get everyone out of here," he said. "Outside, now. The police officers out there will show you where to go."

"Everyone?"

"The whole building," Horatio said flatly. "Use a fire alarm if you have to. But first, I'm looking for someone who probably came in during the last hour or so, carrying a suitcase or a duffel bag or something like that. He may have checked in earlier, but he just brought in another bag. He looks like an FBI agent."

"Like . . ."

"A big man. Dark suit, dark hair, nondescript face. You'd know if you saw him."

"There was someone like that," the other woman said. This one was blond, shorter, stout, and older than the other two, probably in her late forties. "You were on break, Jackie."

"Is he a hotel guest, ma'am?"

"Yes. He checked in day before yesterday, I think."

"And you saw him this evening?"

"Yes. Like you said, he had a big leather duffel bag over his shoulder."

"What room is he in, please?"

"Four-seventeen," she said.

"Does that room have a view of Ocean Boulevard?"

"Yes, it faces the ocean."

"Can you make me a key? Quickly?"

The one named Jackie handed him a key card. "Here's a master."

"Thank you," Horatio said. "Get everyone out, as fast as you can."

Horatio just hoped it could be done fast enough. Asher was upstairs. Since he could see the street from his room, he knew he was cornered.

And a cornered animal is the most dangerous kind.

He could wait for SWAT—they probably weren't far behind—but he was afraid that Asher would try to disrupt the evacuation of the hotel. At this point, knowing he was trapped, he might be willing to blow himself up along with everyone else. Motivated by a misguided sense of justice, he would know that a dramatic suicide could make a murderer into a martyr. That might have been his plan all along.

He'd been killing for too long. Horatio wasn't going to let him take any more lives.

A Klaxon started to blare throughout the hotel, and people began streaming out of the stairwell. When the fire alarm went off, the elevators locked up. Asher couldn't jump four flights, so if he tried to get out with the rest, it would be down the stairs.

Ignoring the frightened cries and questions of those racing down, Horatio drew his weapon, held up his badge, and started climbing against the tide, apologizing and excusing himself all the way. People rammed him with shoulders and bags, and some saw his gun and shrieked, but he took the hits and kept climbing, watching faces in case Asher tried to slip past.

By the time he reached the fourth floor, the stream had slowed to a trickle. Most of the people who were leaving had done so quickly, although

Horatio had no doubt that some had chosen to ignore the deafening Klaxon and stay in their rooms.

He held the stairwell door for a couple of young Asian tourists. "Please hurry," he said as they brushed past him. Behind them, the hallway was clear. Holding his weapon at the ready, he approached the door to room 417.

Asher could have gone against the flow too, up three more flights to the roof. Horatio didn't think he'd do that, though—he believed Asher was inside his room, preparing for the inevitable. An explosion on the roof would have little impact with most of its force dispersed into the air, and escaping from there, with police swarming toward the building, seemed unlikely.

He listened outside the door, ear pressed against it.

If Asher was in there, he couldn't tell.

Time to find out.

He slid the key card in the slot. When the light flashed green, he twisted the handle and shoved the door in. Asher hadn't set the dead bolt or the bar lock that could have kept Horatio out.

Inside the room, Asher sat, almost casually, in a chair beside an open sliding glass door that led onto a small balcony. From his vantage point he could see everything happening out on Ocean. Through the open door, Horatio heard sirens and shouted commands—the cops getting ready to storm the place. The smells of salt air and smoke wafted inside.

Asher held a nine-millimeter Colt 1911 in his hand, and he pointed it into an unzipped duffel bag near his feet. "That's far enough, Caine."

Horatio stopped just inside the room. "It's all over, Special Agent Asher. This building will be crawling with police in a minute."

"The more the merrier," Asher said. He sniffled. "That's what they say, right? If I'm going to go, I might as well take a lot of souls along with me."

Horatio could probably shoot Asher before the agent managed to detonate the contents of his bag. But he wanted the agent in a courtroom, and if there was a way to take Asher alive, he wanted to find it.

"That's not going to happen."

Asher cocked an eyebrow at him. "You're a good cop, Caine."

"Don't you forget it, my friend."

"You can still get out of here alive. I can wait until I see you outside."

"Not gonna happen."

"Why not?"

"We have some things to clear up first."

Close to Asher's chair, a water glass with ice cubes in it sweated on the hotel room desk. Without shifting his gun hand, Asher reached for the glass and downed the remaining water. The cubes clinked against the glass when he put it back. "Throat's a little dry," he said.

"I would imagine so."

"What is it we're clearing up?" Asher rubbed his red, chapped nose.

"You know the drill, Wendell. You've left me with a number of open case files. I need to close them."

"My trigger finger's getting tired, Caine. You want to know anything, you better start asking."

Horatio had been counting on that. "That's a bad sniffle, Wendell, but it's not a cold, is it? You killed Silvio Castaneda, in Bicentennial Park, didn't you?"

"Dope pusher? Sure."

"Why?" In any interrogation, it didn't hurt to start with questions to which you were already pretty sure of the answers.

"I needed a piece." Asher twitched the gun in his hand. "And cash. Dealers usually carry both."

"Someone else shot him at the same time."

"I know. They took off running when I shot him, though, so I went ahead and cleaned out his pockets."

"You left the drugs."

"What do I want with cocaine? Kid was a dealer, Caine, pushing dope in his own neighborhood. I did Miami a favor."

"That's one way to look at it," Horatio said. He edged farther into the room, slowly, a step every minute or two. Not enough to draw Asher's attention to the fact that he was closing the gap between them. "But it's not my way."

"Look, Caine, something you need to understand about me. I'm no whack job. I love my country. I worship the good Lord. These are the reasons I do what I do, nothing else. I know some people don't approve, but men of faith have always had to take extreme measures in His service, right? When I start working in a new place, I need some spending money." He kicked the duffel bag gently. "C-4's not cheap, you know? And I need a weapon not easily traced to me. I pick a drug dealer and it's win-win. I rid the streets of a useless predator, and I get the tools I need to continue my crusade."

"That's what this is to you?" Horatio asked. "A crusade?"

"You know a better word for it?"

"I can think of a few." Horatio didn't name them. He wanted to keep Asher calm as long as he could. Through the window, he heard whistles and running boots as the SWAT team closed in.

If the building was going to blow, this would be a good time, when almost no one remained inside. Soon, as he had threatened, it would be full of officers.

The Klaxon had finally stopped. Horatio's ears still rang, but inside the room it was quiet, just Asher's breathing and that incessant buzzing in his own head.

"You don't think much of me, Caine," Asher said flatly.

"No, Wendell, I don't."

"You're not a religious man?"

Horatio was a devout Catholic, but he didn't think that was any of the other man's business. "That has nothing to do with it."

"It has everything to do with it," Asher countered.

"No. I'm a law enforcement officer, not a judge and jury. The same goes for you. We have a system, don't we, Wendell, that we're sworn to uphold. You took that oath and you broke it. How can you square that with your faith?"

"Men of faith often have to—"

Horatio held up a hand, impatiently, using the motion to cover another couple of steps deeper into the room. "I've heard it, Wendell. It's a cop-out. Either you live by your promise or you don't. There's no gray area there."

"I've never killed anyone who didn't deserve killing, Caine."

"Maybe so, but then we're all sinners, aren't we? Even you."

"I know I'm a sinner. I try to repent through my actions."

"I believe," Horatio said, "that you're just making things worse for yourself."

"Think what you want."

"I do. And what I think now is that you're about to learn about judges and juries from an entirely different perspective. You're under arrest, Wendell Asher."

"You're forgetting something, Caine."

"What's that?"

"You're forgetting who holds the cards. You can shoot me, but not before I can get off a shot."

"That may be true."

"You know how much C-4 is in this bag? You want to be remembered as the dead CSI who lost a block of South Beach? I want a chopper to Cuba, Caine. This country is my home, but people like you have made it uninhabitable."

"You think they'll take you in Cuba?"

"I'll take my chances. Just get me a helicopter."

"I don't think so, Wendell."

Asher nudged the bag with his foot again. "You don't believe I have the C-4? You want to take a look?"

"I believe you," Horatio said.

Asher's face went cold. "Then make the call. I'm through talking to you. Make the call now, or I shoot."

"You're not leaving Miami, Wendell," Horatio said. "So I guess you'll have to shoot."

32

HORATIO HAD NEVER told Wendell Asher about his time on the Miami-Dade bomb squad. And like most FBI agents Horatio had met, Asher underestimated local law enforcement personnel. His threat to shoot the contents of the bag convinced Horatio that he didn't have a shock tube or any other immediate detonator, probably just more timers.

He could empty his whole magazine into a bag of C-4 without setting it off. He could throw matches at it. C-4 needed a small explosive charge to be detonated.

He caught Horatio's gaze and held it for long seconds, then his bleary, bloodshot eyes shifted toward the open window—trying to gauge how much time he had left before the room filled up with police officers, Horatio guessed. "I guess you got me," he said, beginning to raise his hands.

"Put down the weapon," Horatio ordered him.

Asher started to comply, then changed course and hurled the gun at Horatio.

Horatio batted it away, the steel of the rear sight slicing the side of his hand. In that instant Asher bolted from his chair, rushing him. Asher was as solid as a tank, and he slammed his shoulder into Horatio's midsection, driving him back into the wall. He caught Horatio's right wrist, holding it so that his gun pointed uselessly toward the door, and pressed his right forearm against Horatio's throat, legs spread too far for Horatio to reach with his own feet.

Asher was a couple of inches taller than Horatio, broad-shouldered, with muscles like corded iron. Horatio's left hand tugged at his right arm, but he couldn't budge it. With his larynx compressed, he couldn't draw air into his lungs. His vision darkened at the edges.

Horatio gave up trying to move the arm off his throat and instead closed his left hand into a fist with his thumb extended. Reaching around the agent's crushing arm and shoulder, he jabbed it at Asher's right eye. Asher jerked his head away. The thumb hit his cheek instead, and Asher responded by putting even more pressure on Horatio's neck.

The world was turning black faster now, as Horatio—already weakened and dizzy from the near miss at the Ibanez house—threatened to pass out. If he did, he knew, he'd never wake up again. Asher was a murderer through and through, and his "crusade" was just a justification for his crimes. He would, Horatio believed, be a killer even if he hadn't come up with that rationale. He wouldn't lose a moment's sleep over murdering Horatio.

Horatio figured he had one more chance to take out the bigger man before he blacked out for good. Asher kept his feet spread wide so Horatio couldn't stomp down on his tarsalia and break the bones of his foot, at the same time leaning in so close that Horatio couldn't get enough momentum to do damage to his testicles.

But maybe having those legs splayed out would be good for something.

Horatio drove his right knee into the agent's patella, hard, just above his right knee. Asher flinched from the blow, and Horatio followed by bringing his right foot back and slamming it into his opponent's left tibia. He heard the snap of bone beneath his shoe, and Asher let out a shriek of pain and dropped his arm. Horatio swung his left fist into the agent's cheek, knocking him to the floor.

Horatio leaned against the wall, sucking in a few deep breaths in succession. His throat burned, as raw as if he had swallowed acid, and he coughed a few times. But he kept his weapon pointed at Asher—who writhed in pain on the floor, tears filling his eyes, nose running—the whole time. Before the agent could recover, armored, helmeted SWAT officers filled the doorway, pointing their automatic rifles inside.

"You! Drop that weapon!" one shouted.

"One down, another one armed!" someone else reported into a radio. "We need a medic up here!"

Horatio tried to speak, couldn't, and instead drew back his jacket to show the badge and ID card on his belt.

"You're Lieutenant Caine?" the first one asked.

Horatio nodded, holstering his gun and touching his damaged throat. *Perfect*, he thought. *My ears are still ringing like church bells on Christmas, and now I can't talk either.*

"Is he . . . ?"

Horatio nodded again. "He's . . . under arrest," he managed to croak, barely at whisper level. "Get him medical . . . attention . . . and book . . . him."

A commotion at the doorway captured his attention, and he looked up to see Calleigh forcing her way through the SWAT team, followed by Eric and Ryan. "Horatio," she said, "are you all right?"

He nodded, touched his neck again.

"Did he hurt your throat?"

Horatio nodded. He was getting used to it.

"Do you need a paramedic?"

"This guy does," Eric said.

"Good," Ryan offered. "He deserves it."

Horatio nodded one more time. He would never enjoy violence, but there were times that it was warranted, and he didn't shy away from dealing it out when he had to.

This had been one occasion when he didn't feel the least bit sorry that it had been necessary.

"Come on, Horatio," Calleigh said, her blue eyes expressing her concern. "Let's get out of here." She started back through the officers, clearing a path for him.

"Right behind you," he croaked. He hoped no permanent damage had been done, because at the moment, his voice sounded distressingly like a rusty gate.

What made it okay was the truth contained in the old after-fight saying: *You think this is bad, you should have seen the other guy.*

Epilogue

"How's your throat?" Frank asked. Calleigh had brought Horatio back to the lab while Eric and Ryan processed the hotel room at the Fair Coast. The Sandmoor House was still too hot to go inside, but tomorrow that scene would consume the whole day, and maybe more. Frank had caught up with them at the lab.

Horatio swallowed. "I'll be fine," he said. His voice was coming back, but he was still hoarse, and he couldn't get much volume. He sounded like someone at the tail end of laryngitis.

"Hasn't been your best day, has it, Horatio?"

"No complaints, Frank. Any day we put away a bad guy is a good day."

"I had some detectives toss Asher's hotel room," Frank said. "The one we knew about, not that one at the Fair Coast. They found two pairs of Wrangler jeans in his stuff."

"Get them to the lab, so we can match the fibers from the Bicentennial Park scene."

"They're on the way now. It's gettin' late, Horatio, and you've been through the wringer. Why don't you go home? Think about takin' tomorrow off, too. This weekend I'm gonna throw some porterhouses on the grill and put some beers on ice, so if you want to come over . . ."

"Thanks, Frank."

Frank pushed the elevator's down button and the doors slid open. "I mean it, Horatio. I don't want to see you around here tomorrow."

He stepped into the car and disappeared.

Horatio would consider his advice, if his voice hadn't improved by morning. But he didn't think he'd take it. He rarely missed a day of work, and a couple of close calls wouldn't change that.

He was on his way to his office when Calleigh called his name. He turned and saw that Nina Cullen was with her, both emerging from Calleigh's gun lab.

"Calleigh told me what happened, Horatio," Nina said. "I'm glad you're okay."

"Thanks, Nina." He brought a hand to his throat again, as if to apologize for the rasp. "I'm good. How has your trip been?"

"Great, but too short. Calleigh's taking me back to the airport now. I'm on the last flight out."

"I wish I'd had more time to spend with you," Calleigh said. "It's been a crazy couple of days."

"That's okay, Calleigh. You are so awesome. Doing everything that you do here, all this important work, helping people, and still managing to have a life and a nice place to live—it's really been an inspiration."

"Well, thank you, Nina." Color flooded Calleigh's cheeks. "I'm glad you think that."

"Well, it's true. I don't think there's anything you can't do if you put your mind to it. And it's helped me make up my own mind."

"It has? In what way?"

She glanced at Horatio, then stuck her hands in her pockets, suddenly shy. "Well, it's not what Mom wants me to do, probably, but I figure if you're going to be my role model, and you can do anything, then I should be able to as well."

"So you're having the baby?" Calleigh's smile brightened the whole lab.

"Yeah, I think it's the right thing to do. I think I've got it worked out where I can take a semester off school, then go back and graduate. It'll slow me down a little, but I can handle that. And I know the trade-offs I'll have to make will be worth it in the long run."

"I'm sure they will, Nina," Horatio said. He'd had a hard time with family, himself—his mother murdered by his father, his wife Marisol killed right after their wedding, his brother Ray presumed dead and then having to go into hiding with Yelina and Ray Jr.—but in spite of all the troubles (*maybe* because *of them,* he thought), he still considered family the most important thing in life. The true pleasure of his job, beyond simply the application of science to police work in order to solve crimes, was the joy of bringing answers and order to families in the midst of their worst nightmares. "If anyone can pull it off, it'll be you."

Nina tugged her right hand free of her pocket and rubbed her belly, as if she could already feel the life growing inside. Calleigh watched her with evident admiration. "I'm glad you think so. Your opinion means a lot to me." She smiled at Calleigh. "Both of you."

Horatio couldn't help feeling a twinge of envy. He had hoped to have children of his own someday. He had been willing to put away that dream, to be with Marisol, unless her cancer stayed in remission and allowed her the full life they had both wanted for her. But maybe he would bring the dream out of its box again one day. One never knew what tomorrow might bring, after all.

"We'd better get to the airport," Calleigh said, pushing the elevator button. "Traffic shouldn't be too bad this time of the evening, but you never know for sure."

Horatio smiled at her inadvertent echoing of what he had just thought. "You never know, Calleigh." He and Nina came together and he held her tightly in his arms, squeezing her close. "You take care, Nina, all right? Be well, do what's best for the baby, and keep in touch."

"I will, Horatio."

He released her, and she started toward the elevator. The doors opened up and Calleigh stepped inside, moving from dark to light. Nina followed, beaming.

"And pictures," Horatio added. "I want pictures."

"I promise!"

"That's good." Maybe he would find another wife someday. Maybe children would call him Daddy after all, if not this year then next, or the one after that. He was in no particular hurry.

In the meantime, he had his crime lab family to look after.

Hands on his hips, head cocked toward his right shoulder, Horatio watched the elevator doors slide together. *Life goes on,* he thought. *In spite of all the terrible things people do to one another, there's always a new life on the way, new hope. A future.*

He offered a weary smile to the empty atrium, turned, and headed toward his office. Warm light glowed through the glass walls, a beacon against the night. When Horatio passed through the door, he felt like he had come home.

ABOUT THE AUTHOR

Jeff Mariotte has written more than thirty novels, including supernatural thriller *Missing White Girl* (as Jeffrey J. Mariotte), original horror epic *The Slab*, and Stoker Award–nominated teen-horror series *Witch Season*, as well as books set in the universes of *Las Vegas*, *Supernatural*, *Buffy the Vampire Slayer*, *Angel*, *Conan*, *30 Days of Night*, *Charmed*, *Star Trek*, and *Andromeda*. Two of his tie-in novels won a first-annual Scribe Award presented by the International Association of Media Tie-in Writers. He is also the author of many comic books, including the original Western/horror series *Desperadoes*, some of which have been nominated for Stoker and International Horror Guild Awards. With his wife, Maryelizabeth Hart, and partner, Terry Gilman, he co-owns Mysterious Galaxy, a bookstore specializing in science fiction, fantasy, mystery, and horror. He lives with his family and pets on the Flying M Ranch in the American southwest, a place filled with books, music, toys, and other products of American pop culture. More information than you would ever want to know about him is at www.jeffmariotte.com.

Play the Video Game
THE TRUTH IS YOURS TO DISCOVER

CSI:
Crime Scene Investigation™
HARD EVIDENCE

Featuring the voice and likenesses of the entire CSI cast

AVAILABLE NOW
at video game retailers everywhere.

www.csivideogames.com

Blood and Gore
Sexual Themes
Violence

CSIHE-4